MW00596657

THREE MILES OF EDEN

SEAN PATRICK SMITH

Three Miles of Eden

ISBN: 978-1-7350089-0-5

Cover design by Jessica Bell
Cover images: akokoke, cherylvb, Wirestock
Interior design by Amie McCracken

For Pamela Baumann who read every chapter of this novel as it was being written.

For Joe: I still have conversations with you every day. I hope you are seeing this.

1

I'd decided there was nothing creepier than the ringing phone of a deceased individual. It meant someone didn't know.

Also, considering that this particular deceased individual was floating face-down in a lake, I found it pretty amazing that the phone was ringing at all. Some of those Otter Boxes are remarkable. It's an "Earth, Wind & Fire" ringtone—not what I would have expected from a white, suburbanite slob. But I digress. There's a dead person in the lake.

I really should have organized my iPod songs into appropriate setlists. The reason being I found myself skipping through multiple songs that were ill-equipped to inspire me through my morning run. These segues of silence enabled me to catch the familiar strains of "Earth, Wind & Fire" and thus see a dead person.

The body was caught in the current of the drain near the dam. It meandered toward the drain until the poor bastard's head bounced off the steel grate a few times. And then I felt nauseated. The body jerked and then drifted back out into the lake, and that's when I saw it—a pontoon boat with a retractable forest green awning and an Evinrude engine. The right arm of the body was sticking straight out. The guy was tethered to the boat.

I'm not a cop or a soldier or an emergency room physician. So, although I'd seen a dead guy before, it was only one, and it wasn't within yards of my house. After a bit of lightheadedness, I had a revelation: I knew the boat. The board shorts, the bloated, white torso with a skunk trail of graying back hair…Christ, it was Rob, and Rob was dead.

Jesus Christ.

Tightness. Inexplicable tightness gripped my chest.

I can't breathe.

My head felt stuck in an aggressive 360-degree panorama. I dropped to one knee.

Orient yourself. Settle.

When everything stopped spinning, my eyes landed again on Rob. I realized that he wasn't Rob any longer. He didn't even look real. He looked vacated, an empty shell that used to house my friend.

And there was nothing I could do about it.

2
The Worst of Times

My name is Ray McCarthy, and before I relate to you the events of that summer, I have to be up front: I was a bit of a drunk. I wasn't an all-day plastered, fall-down type of drunk. But I was a can't-wait-for-the-clock-to-strike-noon drunk. No way was I going to drink before noon. That's for drunks. It was the only way, in the beginning, that I could manage the void.

The irony of this situation is that my wife was an addict, and I hated her for it. I was just a casual, social drinker—a glass of Champagne when one of my articles or books was published, a few cocktails at a celebratory event was the norm. That changed a month before the abovementioned summer.

It was my fault. The night before it happened she had driven high on Vicodin with my daughter. It was the latest lowlight in her rapid devolvement into prescription painkillers. I gave her an ultimatum: involuntary committal to a treatment facility or divorce with supervised visitation of our daughter.

Addicts are liars. They're liars because they are ashamed of their addiction and because they must protect that addiction at all cost. They get creative, crafty, and thorough in this pursuit. You'd think in this digital era of Amber alerts and social media, it'd be quite difficult to just dis-the-hell-appear, but she emptied the cash from the one account to which she still had access, and she successfully went off the grid with my little girl.

My little one was only five years old, very smart, but only five. I could not expect too much help on that front. Deputy Rhyne said it was just a matter of time. The money would run out. A mistake would be made.

There was a bright spot two weeks later when an errant selfie of my daughter popped up in my Facebook messages. My wife still had her tablet, and apparently, Ava was playing with it. An hour later I noticed that my wife finally deleted the account, but I was already in the local SBI office. Their techs traced the IP address to a library in Georgia. Cops canvassed the area, but there was nothing.

Every night I went to bed with that picture in my head. She wears a distracted smile, and unkempt blonde curls halo her face. Every morning I woke to the image of her puckering to kiss me goodbye on the steps of her daycare—the last time I held her. I should have held on longer. That afternoon I went to pick her up and discovered the wife had gotten there already. At that point, I was alarmed only by the wife's possible condition upon pick-up. By 7 p.m. I was worried that they were dead in a ditch. At 9 p.m. the Amber Alert was issued.

Then for more than a month I just waited for 12 p.m. to arrive, and the clock ticked loudly.

The dam of Sequoia Lake was cordoned off for the next twenty-four hours. Oddly enough, this was not the first dead guy to be found floating in here. The community of Seven Lakes North Carolina originated as a retirement place back in the late 1970s. It evolved to more of a family type atmosphere in the '80s and '90s. There had been the occasional swimmer who succumbed to the occasional heart attack. I was certain that that was what happened to my old friend Rob Erwin.

It was in the '80s when I met Rob. We were both transplants from the metropolitan North who took full advantage of the freedom and amenities of a rural gated community. We fished, and biked, and built forts in the woods with our buddy Arden Miller. Arden was a native of nearby West End, and he helped us understand the southern accents and colloquialisms. He also translated our northern accents and colloquialisms for our classmates at West End Middle.

Arden…Jesus, there was a name from the past. Where he ended up, no one knew. I think he might have invented the concept of "off the grid."

A man in pleated pants and collared shirt approached me, waving me under the tape and inviting me to approach him. The sheriff's deputy guarding the tape turned to me.

"The detective wants to speak with you."

"Thanks," I said, and then further advised, "I called the wife. She will be here soon. She will not be OK. Just a heads up."

Rob's wife Candace was emotional to begin with. Today she would be a basket case. There'd be no indication of the fact that her marriage to Rob was in the shitter. Rob and I both made poor spousal selections. We both thought younger women would mean less emotional baggage. We were wrong. Our lives have always been an eerie parallel to one another.

I met the detective mid-dam. A mid-morning sun broke through some of the overcast skies and spotlighted us as he introduced himself.

"Detective Howard Spruill. I understand that you found him."

"I did. He's a friend of mine. Robert Erwin, age forty-four. Lives—lived—on 144 Firetree Lane."

Spruill looked up from his notepad and regarded me anew.

"I'm sorry. You're very matter-of-fact. Have you done this before?"

"Yes...No. When I recognized him, I almost threw up. I've just written scenarios like this before."

"You're the writer looking for his daughter."

It hurt. It hurt to have someone refer to her but not by name—like she was a case instead of a person, or I'm just overly sensitive. Spruill looked to be in only his early thirties, but he carried himself like a weary law enforcement veteran. He was methodical and difficult even to phase emotionally, and that was because his main task was the drug problem that pervaded our surrounding rural area. Spruill dealt mostly with traffickers, but with drugs comes death, and so he was adept at dealing with that too. Anyway, all I could do was nod in the affirmative. Spruill sensed a change in me and thus went back to business.

"Tell me everything. His life, his wife, his job, his friends, his hobbies..."

"His life is good, not great. Candace is a self-involved drama queen and a whore. You'll know her when she arrives. Other than that, she's charismatic and pleasant to be around. Robert is an architect. In fact, he designed most of the houses built around here in the last eight or nine years. He's a transplant like me. His friends? Me. Hobbies? Fishing, his lawn, and old movies. He has one daughter. Then, there's his mother."

***

Rita Erwin wiped her brow and studied her handy work. Every summer she made it a point to touch up the navy-blue shutters of her cottage—a little bit of Massachusetts on the shore of a southern lake.

She remained at a complete loss as to why her son gave up a partnership in a prestigious architecture firm to design cubby holes in the South and marry someone she was sure had been conceived by two cousins on a dirty sofa during a barbecue.

Rita viewed Candace with a seething disdain that only a New Englander could simultaneously nurture and keep under wrap. Most times her stoicism was such that you wondered whether or not she was human. Only after Rita spent extended periods of time with Candace did a subtle snarkiness emerge as well as a visible crack in the armor. A facial tick developed beneath her left eye, and this usually happened when Candace would rant about President Obama's falsified birth certificate. It looked as if her superego exhausted, Rita's raw id was literally trying to jump out of her skin and devour the stupid bitch.

Candace was the cherry on this shit-filled sundae that is North Carolina. Seven Lakes is a pretty enough place when the summer humidity was not draining the life out of you. There are plenty of transplants with whom to commiserate, but North Carolina isn't Massachusetts and Raleigh isn't Boston. The pension and benefits Ed bequeathed to her, however, went a hell of a lot further down here. In the meantime, she had her circle of friends and her responsibilities to the furniture business.

What would Colonel Ed have thought of all this? He would have loved it…most of it anyway. The years Rita and Ed lived in Seven Lakes while Ed rode out the last of his military career at Bragg were his favorites, Rob's too. Ed would have played every golf course, fished every lake, drank Mint Juleps on the porch of the Carolina Hotel in Pinehurst, and Rob would have been right beside him, and right beside Rob would have been Raymond. What a triumvirate of bull-shitters that would have been. Rita would have liked to have seen it…heard it. Certainly, Ed would have casually assessed both of Rob and Ray's significant others and the smart money would have been on neither Rob nor Raymond walking down the aisle with their respective tramps.

Raymond the writer.

How in God's name was she going to mediate that situation? Ray would either turn the debacle with his wife and child into a book, or he'd drink himself to death.

Rita heard footsteps swishing through grass and turned to find none other than Ray himself descending the lawn.

3
The Detective

I was wrong. It was not "Earth, Wind & Fire." It was just the singer, Phil Bailey, duetting with Phil Collins. "Easy Lover." That was the song serving as Rob's ringtone when I found him in the water. Rob was a sucker for Phil Collins or anything Genesis. It's amazing what your mind will tumble to when it's desperately searching for anything on which to grab hold and designate as "resolved."

I shit you not, the moment I came up with that song title, I heard Candace at the end of the dam howling like a banshee.

"That's the wife," I offered to Detective Spruill as a conversation ender. We both stared off into the lake.

"I'm going to need to speak with her too, the sooner the better."

"My advice would be to meet us at Rob's house in an hour. You'll have to let this performance run its course because it's gonna regardless of what you say or do."

Spruill nodded, and then he turned to me.

"I watched closely as they pulled Mr. Erwin out of the lake. He has a gash on his head. He has bruises on his forearms and his torso. The torso bruises could be from bumping into things as he drifted about the lake, but not the forearms, especially the one tethered to the boat. Your friend right-handed?"

"Yes," I said. "I'm not following you."

"Defensive wounds. Your friend was in a hell of an altercation, and he held his own. That is my first impression."

"Someone killed him?" I don't know why this was a revelation. Rob sure as hell didn't tie himself to his boat so as to face ski around the lake. It just seemed such a foreign idea that anyone—I mean anyone—would want to harm him.

"Let's see what the medical examiner comes back with. I do need you to expound on that wife being a whore comment."

That stopped me cold. Jesus. In a moment I was going to have to comfort Candace, and now I'm going to have to go into that with the knowledge that she's a suspect.

"Detective Spruill, Candace is ten years younger than my friend and smoking hot. I have no doubt that her marriage to Rob was partly a security thing. She also adored him, needed him. He leveled her out. Yes, she ran around on him with pretty boys. If I were you, I'd climb that tree and see if there's a view to behold, but I'm pretty sure you'll find nothing of consequence."

Spruill nodded again. I turned to cross the dam back toward Candace, and then a thought occurred to me, and I turned to the detective.

"Hey, Rob and I had a habit of bouncing from one martial arts class to another. It was probably an early mid-life crisis thing—jiu-jitsu class, kickboxing, etc. The latest was a combat hapkido class with some retired military types in Southern Pines. Rob didn't look like much, but he took to those classes like a duck to water. Something about individual movements blending into complete maneuvers catered to his studious nature.

Spruill cocked his head "You want me to look at the guys in the class?"

"I think you should look for a guy with defensive wounds of his own, and maybe you should look for more than one guy."

As I walked away, I thought about the day when, only three weeks into class, Rob was doing demonstrations for the rest of the group with our two instructors. The older instructor was going at half speed. The younger one was most certainly not, and Rob put him to the mat. It was unbelievable. I had never seen him move that fast in my life. I tried to compartmentalize this thought as I approached the sobbing stick figure clinging to the police tape at the end of the dam.

When I was within ten feet of her, she frantically beckoned me with outstretched arms and then held on to me as if she were drowning. The sobs quickly dissolved into rapid-fire anxiety.

"Ray, oh my god, Ray. "

The embrace was like a death grip, but at least she wasn't howling. Her delivery continued into my left ear.

"What are we gonna do Ray? It can't be him. It can't be. He's our whole world. I haven't even seen him this morning. So, I was calling. I thought he went fishing. Jesus, oh, Jesus Christ."

"Candace…" I held her at arm's length and looked her in the eye. "It's him, Candace. He's gone. I don't know what happened, but he's gone. We will process this tonight and in the coming days, but right now we have responsibilities. You must tell Jenna. You must tell Rita. We have to speak to the police in an hour. Right now, I need you to focus on what Rob was doing yesterday, and especially last night."

As Candace visibly trembled before me, my internal composure faltered, especially when I heard the word "gone." That's where Rob was now, gone. We would not get beers later at the Lakehouse Bar and Grill. We would not go on that trip out west this summer. Something just dropped out of me at that moment, leaving an anxious, empty feeling in my gut. I guess it showed.

"Ray? Ray? Are you all right? Say you're all right. Rita is the only one home now. I can't tell her by myself."

"Yes…Sorry. I'm tired. OK, where's your car?"

"Parked by your house. Come on."

The lingering debate in the community was why a woman of means like Rita Erwin would live under the same roof as the daughter-in-law she flat out despised. The answer was two-fold: Rob wanted it that way, and Rita didn't technically live under the same roof as Candace. Rob had a section of his fairway-looking back lawn leveled off via retaining walls in two places. He didn't like how the grass just tumbled unobtrusively toward the lake. In one section was a rose garden. In the other was a grey, two-bedroom, cedar shake cottage, the likes of which you'd find on Cape Cod. Though charming and not utterly incongruous with the craftsman–style main house, it looked a little out of place. Rob had built it himself, and he built it to please. The man loved his mama.

Rita wore a scarf in her hair and a white polo shirt tucked smartly into a pair of pressed khaki pants—her standard chore outfit. A paint can was open and not a drop had been spilled.

She was touching up the blue shutters of her cottage.

Candace had lagged only a step or two behind me until we reached the backyard. Then she stopped cold, unable to proceed. This pause I expected. I continued down the hill without a word. Rita had the brush in hand and appeared to have paused mid-stroke, lost in thought.

Though I didn't think I make a sound, she turned to face me, her hand shielding the sun from her eyes.

"Hello, dear. To what do I owe the pleasure of your spontaneous company?"

"Hello, Ms. Rita. Can I step into your cottage with you for a moment?" Her expression was what I'd call quizzical yet bemused like she was about to receive illicit information of great worth.

"Of course we can," she said with a smile. She quickly sealed the paint can and atop it laid the brush. She received me with a companionable hug and a kiss on the cheek as if we had not crossed paths in a month, but that might have been sympathy. At that moment I was the only one with a crisis (now multiple crises). That was going to change.

"Tell me, dear. Tell me that she's leaving him." Rita said as she swept in the door and pulled the scarf from her hair. "Or he's leaving her; I don't care. I'm sure either way he'll give her the house, and I'll have to move. I don't have to tell you that I'm exceptionally fine with that."

I took a seat on the edge of a Moes sectional sofa with stainless steel fixtures. The whole place was furnished in a distinguished 1960s retro look. It felt as if Don Draper, or perhaps Colonel Ed should be pouring himself a scotch in the corner of the great room. Except for Ed's Vietnam tour late in the decade—which he rode out right beside his buddy from Korea, Colonel Jim, the '60s were a good time for the young Erwin couple.

I was counting on Rita's war bride resiliency to get her through this moment.

"Rita. I have news, and it is not good. Rob is gone." Rita spun around, looking hurt.

"You mean he just ran off and left us? I can't imagine he—"

"No Rita. They found him in the lake. He died either last night or early this morning."

The color drained out of Rita as if she were becoming a photo negative of herself. She stared as if she were watching an 8mm film of her son's entire life in a span of seconds. Finally, she slumped into a wingback chair that faced the sofa. This was the first stage of resiliency, resignation to the truth. Quietly she spoke.

"Was it a heart attack? Was he swimming?"

"I don't know. He was on…He was with the boat. They found him and the boat."

"Where's Jenna?"

"At the high school. I'll drive you."

"No. I will tell her myself. Where's Candace?"

"At the top of the back yard." Rita got out of her chair and peered through the blinds.

"Coward. I'll address her later. Right now, I need more details. Then I will drive to Pinecrest and pull Jenna from class before she hears from someone else. On the way home, I'll stop in Buck Adam's office and tell him to begin getting Rob's affairs in order. Buck's people can contact Rob's office."

Commencing a tactical plan to deal with logistics of a disaster was Rita's way of delaying the emotions of a disaster. That and anger—anger that her boy was gone, anger that her only grandchild was going to be crushed. Anger that the only person she had left besides Jenna was Candace. Candace was going to take a passive-aggressive beating these next few days. My dilemma at the moment was how to deliver the details of the situation, because I was going to have to give her the details of the situation, and all of them, because Spruill was going to be on the premises in forty-five minutes.

"Rita, we have to stay here. In less than an hour a detective is going to have to speak to you and Candace. Like it or not, you and Candace are going to have to weather this together for at least a while."

Rita nodded and returned to her chair. "Why a detective and not a sheriff's deputy?"

"Suspicious circumstances are surrounding Rob's death. He was bruised up pretty bad, like he had been in a fight. They found him in the water."

Rita's hand covered her mouth. Then she took a breath.

"I thought you said they found him with the boat?"

"They did. He was tied to the boat."

Rita Erwin passed out cold in the wingback chair.

4
Visits

Rita was out for roughly two minutes, and when she awoke she was neither embarrassed nor pragmatic. She was just there and nodding yes to everything I said, including the part where I said I was going to retrieve Candace so the two of them could be interviewed by Spruill together. I fixed her up with a drink on the back deck of her cottage, poured one for Candace too, and went back up the yard to acquire the other Mrs. Erwin.

I ushered Candace out to the deck with Scotch in hand. She put it down, and she and Rita embraced before taking their respective Adirondack chairs, too hurt to hate and too stunned to speak. Good enough.

"Ladies, I'm going to wait for a Detective Spruill in the driveway so I can lead him down here. Then I'm going to run home for a while. I'll call the main house in an hour and see how you want to handle Jenna. Right now, concentrate on what you can remember and on answering the detective's questions."

They both smiled. Rita said "Thank you," and then the two of them held hands as they sat.

Spruill was already in the driveway when I got there.

"What's the lay of the land?" he asked as he pulled his considerable lank from the cruiser. I estimated him to be a smidge over six feet tall.

"For two people who don't like each other, they are companionable in their grief."

"That's normal," said Spruill, "and that will change."

"I told his mom all the details I know. When I got to the part about him being found in the water and tied to the boat, she fainted."

Spruill nodded like this too was normal.

"I appreciate you getting that out of the way. I'll take it from here. Here's my card. You and I will be speaking quite a bit."

I took his card and gave him mine.

"Walk around the right side of the main house. Go down the yard to the cottage. Walk right on through the open front door to the back deck. They're expecting you."

Spruill proceeded without another word. It was at this moment I realized I was a mile and a half from my house without transportation. Luckily, I was still dressed for running. I broke into a light jog and attempted to order my mind.

With less than a half mile to go, I turned from Firetree Lane on to Cherokee. For the last mile I'd been running at a pretty good clip, as if putting distance between me and this day that was not yet over. It seemed to work. The tangle of foliage that ran down the left side of Cherokee was laced with honeysuckle, and its sweet smell put me at ease. A wind-shaped oak tree arced high over the road to grasp branches with its neighbors on the other side. The resulting canopy gave Cherokee a covered bridge effect.

The moment of calm was short-lived. As I turned left to descend the hill of Shadywood, I spotted the sheriff's cruiser parked in the cul-de-sac.

Dead in a ditch. Dead in a ditch. They're dead in a ditch.

Easy, Ray. This could be about Rob.

It wasn't. I knew it wasn't. I didn't know whether to run, walk, or stay right where I was. I took a tentative step forward, and then another.

Deputy Rick Rhyne was well-acquainted with Seven Lakes. He had spent twenty-six years patrolling the neighboring Foxfire community. He gave me an affable wave to let me know that his visit was about nothing of consequence, and so my pace picked up.

"Hello Ray. I was just in the area." He smiled apologetically, knowing that I always assumed the worst—not to mention that he probably saw me stop dead in my tracks. At fifty-eight years old and with hair that was more salt than pepper, Rick had a way of quickly putting you at ease. A visit from him was more like a visit from your favorite uncle. Incidentally, he had the most perfect mustache I'd ever seen.

"I heard about your friend Rob. I'm sorry. You're having a tough few months here I know."

"Yes. Thank you. Rob was a good guy."

"Ray, I'll be honest, I don't have any new info on your daughter, but I'm here in that regard. I want to ask you a few questions about the wife."

We always referred to her as "The Wife." Most people knew that I had no desire to speak her name because I was at another level of angry. When this was over, she was going to either rehab or jail, and probably jail. My marriage was over, and when I was finally able to make that official, my wife's name would then become "Ava's Mother."

"OK, shoot."

"Your doctor is Michele Clarke, right?"

"Yup. For the both of us. I haven't seen her in a while."

"Yes, and neither has your wife. So, we were wondering where your wife got her pain meds."

"That's a good question. Michele would not prescribe that stuff in a million years for the minor aches and pains for which we saw her. Of course, you know I always scoured the house for pills. When I did occasionally find them, they were hidden in a bottle marked for something else, like in an old prescription bottle of Amoxicillin, or in a bottle of Advil PM."

"That's what I thought," said Rhyne. "Did she ever see another doctor?"

"I don't think so, but…"

"I don't think so either, but she got them from somewhere. There are a couple of physicians in the area that we're watching, but I don't think your wife got her pills from them. Doctors get kickbacks from drug companies to prescribe some of their premier meds, and some doctors get greedy. The problem is, we keep track of the people who repeatedly visit these two doctors of concern, and your wife never turned up on either list."

"So, you think you have a bigger problem here."

Rhyne sighed and leaned on the front fender of the cruiser.

"Ray, eighty percent of the world's pain meds are consumed by the people of the United States, a country that hosts only about five percent of the world's population. I read that somewhere in an article by Sanjay

Gupta. Opioid abuse is a huge problem, and our little neck of the woods is no exception. I'd say meth and opioids rival each other as our two biggest problems here in Moore County. Pills are in the lead currently. Oh yes, and don't forget that heroin is making a comeback."

"Jesus."

"Ray, you've got a lot on your plate right now, emotionally speaking. Why don't you occupy your mind and do some research on this for me? Poke around the house, talk to friends, see if you can find something."

"OK."

"And Ray, why don't you go see Clarke? You might also want to talk to a therapist. Your recycle bin is looking pretty full. That stuff is not gonna help. In fact, it could make things worse."

Initially I could answer with only a grimace. Then finally I said, "I'll see what I can find out. Thanks Rick."

Rhyne settled in his cruiser and rolled down the window.

"I'll check on you soon. Get some sleep if you can."

You have no idea Rick. If I didn't drink, I wouldn't sleep. It's only a matter of time each night before I see Ava.

The first thing I resolved to do was switch to Scotch. It's more potent, will do the job quicker, and it will significantly reduce the contents of my tell-tale recycle bin. Problem solved. Next, I made a list of things I needed to accomplish within the next twenty-four hours. It was a pretty messed up list: buy Scotch, research opioids, and write Rob's eulogy.

An hour later I checked on the Erwin house. Candace had gone to the high school to collect Jenna. The principal already had her out of class and in the office. Apparently, Jenna received the news stoically, hugged her mother, and then quietly went back to class. She may be a dead-ringer for her mom physically, but there was a lot of Rita on the inside.

At around 7 p.m., I brought them some Chinese take-out. Rita received me at the door, said Candace was drinking steadily, and that Jenna had arrived home, changed, and then taken off on a mountain bike without so much as a word. I told her that was normal, that everybody has their way of processing these things.

"Or not processing them," said Rita, referring to Candace's whiskey transfusion out on the deck. Obviously, Rita had recovered herself and was assuming command of the crisis.

I arrived home to find a pair of long legs propped up on the railing of my front porch.

Jenna.

She was slouched in one of my rocking chairs with her hands folded neatly in her lap. She stared right through me. I stepped up on the porch, kissed her on the forehead, and took the rocker next to her.

"Uncle Ray, how did this happen?"

"I don't know honey, but I'm gonna find out."

"I know. I knew you would." A single tear ran from her right eye. She didn't seem to notice. "I wish Ava was here. She gives good hugs."

"Yeah."

Suddenly Jenna's facial features came to life and she turned to me.

"I'm sorry. I shouldn't have said that."

"It's OK Jenna. It's not your fault she's not here. You want something to eat?"

"Does this mess have something to do with Mom cheating on my dad?"

Whoa. I should have known she knew, but I was not prepared to address this so soon.

"Jenna, listen to me. Your mom has issues no doubt, but you know what? Your dad and I talked a lot about this. They were not going to get a divorce. Your dad believed your mom loved him, and I think he was right. Regardless of the bad decisions she's made, she would not let anything bad happen to your dad. She would not be able to live with herself if she were in any way responsible for hurting him."

Jenna sat up, but she had resumed that stoic, blank stare.

"She knew cheating on him would hurt him, and she sure as hell did that."

Touché. Damn it, Rob. I'm going to have to valiantly defend the wife I was trying to convince you to divorce.

"Yes, but she tried to hide it. If she didn't care a thing about your dad's feelings, she would not have bothered hiding anything."

Jenna stood up. She's as tall as I was, and with her short bob of blonde tresses and sharply-defined jaw, she looked like a pissed-off version of Taylor Swift.

"If she cared about him at all she wouldn't have been cheating on him. She was hiding it because she would have nothing if she left him."

Well, I was not going to explain to a teenager (even a bright one) the community property laws of North Carolina. Candace would not have left the marriage empty-handed. My only option was the truth.

"Your mother is an insecure woman with an insatiable need to feel pretty and desirable. That's why she cheats. Also, she knew your dad did not want a divorce, knew it just as well as I did. I tried like hell to convince your dad to pull the trigger on a divorce. He wouldn't do it." Jenna quietly sat back in the rocking chair, both eyes now leaking.

"Then what happened Ray?"

"I don't know honey, a robbery maybe. We're pretty safe here in Seven Lakes, but we're not immune to crime. Remember when someone stole all my tools out of the shed? Cars have been broken into in the past few months. A few years ago, someone in West End got shot. It happens. It just doesn't happen much here."

"What are we gonna do?"

"We get through these next few days. Then we snoop around and see what we can see."

5
Slippage

The sky was an impossible blue, the sand a blinding white. I emerged from a stand of palm trees into the humid air of the Caribbean in early summer. She's a few feet from the shoreline in a toddler tankini adorned with sailor hats, digging a hole. She's having one of those conversations with herself too. Apparently, Captain Barnacles and the Octonauts were overseeing the excavation. The beach was not even a quarter-mile long. It's deserted, breeze-swept. Finally, she saw me, that joyous amazement of hers breaking across her face. She got up and ran.

"Daddy! I've been waiting for you. You took so long. Oh my goodness! Look at the water Daddy. It looks like blue Mr. Clean!"

I held her while she continued to talk. I was lost in the familiar smells of baby skin and locks of blond hair. She had a vise grip around my neck, and that's still not tight enough.

"Did you finish your work Daddy? Are we on bah-catian now?"

I realized at that moment that I was in the Providenciales of Turks and Caicos on Sunset Beach near Pelican Point. This was the deserted stretch of beach I ran every morning while on my honeymoon, long before there was an Ava.

"Yes, honey. We're on vacation."

She slid down my torso, grabbed my hand, and led me toward the water.

"Daddy I'm so glad you're here. It took forever, and I missed you. I have important bidness going on over here."

She plopped down beside her hole. There was an assortment of small sand tools, a plastic bucket.

"What are we building honey?"

"Daddy we need a place for that." She pointed a few feet away to the water's edge where Rob's bloated, vacant corpse lolled in the gentle waves.

I sprung forward in the wooden rocker on my front porch, my feet slipping off the railing and crashing to the concrete. The pins and needles of my sleeping feet raced up my ankles unbearably. A half-empty glass of Scotch shattered. My head throbbed, and my face was hot. Dawn was breaking across the North Carolina sky.

I leaned over the railing and vomited on the roses. Then I sat on the front stoop and cried…quietly and profusely.

The best way to clear one's head, physically and emotionally, is to exercise, and so I adorned myself in the Adidas, dry-wick garb of my hardcore running days. At some point during the 3.3-mile sojourn, I would write my best friend's eulogy and begin to process this mess.

The first 150 yards of this run was straight uphill out of the cul-de-sac, which sucked, especially when you're hungover. The good news was that Cherokee Trail was another 100-yard stretch of level, shaded recovery before I got to the lake and started keeping time.

As I turned right onto Firetree and began to cross the dam, I caught sight of the overflow drain where I had found Rob, and I continued to stare. I couldn't avoid staring at it. My gut hollowed out. I was afraid of it.

Finally, I passed the drain, and my eyes let go of it and noticed the sky. It was an ethereal bruising of peach and purple and looked more like a sunset than a morning sunrise. Blood was coursing through my body faster now, and my headache began to fade, but my vision not so much. The end of the dam was somewhat out of focus and dominated by a shimmer—the kind caused by heat radiating off the summer pavement. At 6 a.m., though, there wasn't much heat to be found.

My steps felt lighter, and my pace quickened. At the end of the dam, there was a slight downgrade—almost like a ramp. I descended it like I was shot out of a gun. For a moment I felt weightless, like I had just plummeted several feet in a rollercoaster. The shimmer dissipated and I continued to haul ass down the road.

I rounded the bend and came upon Pete and Barbara Murphy's place and wondered how they were doing. They were from New York and were the only people my folks and I knew when we first landed in Seven Lakes. They were also one of the few couples I knew from those days still kickin' around.

Next were the Fausts—Mary and Fred, except Mary left Fred at some point in the late '90s. I remember when I found the grumpy old bastard out front maniacally painting over Mary's name on the yard sign.

Well, I'll be damned.

Mary must have returned because there was a brand-new sign with her name on it. Way to go Fred. Didn't think you had it in you.

I prepared for the hill, the one that snaked up beside the house with the lean-to roof and the gorgeous view of the lake. It's not a long hill, but it's steep as hell and longer than I wanted it to be. I amped up the pace. I wanted to be a quarter of the way up that hill before my old legs realized they were on it.

What the hell happened?

I cut my pace. One of my favorite houses to ogle was gone. Instead, there was a cleared lot squared off with foundation markers. There was no manicured sod meandering toward a beautifully stained dock, no giant picture windows reflecting the morning sun; everything was just gone.

Who does that? I know undeveloped lots on the lake are scarce, but who the hell eradicates a house like that to build one from scratch? And when had this happened? I knew I ran past here sometime in the last few days.

I plodded up the hill. Though I hadn't felt this good in years, some of the steam had left my engine. I didn't need any more changes. It might be stupid to feel heartsick over a house, but that's what I was. Of course, it was more than just the house. There was a reason I came back to live here, to build a life on the foundation of the best one I knew. Now not just some of the faces, but even some of the landmarks were disappearing.

I ran on. A familiar tune came out of my inner jukebox. It finally dawned on me that I had forgotten the iPod.

The road behind was rocky. But now you're feeling cocky! You look at me and you see your past. Is that the reason why you're runnin' so fast? And she said...

Suddenly the tune got a lot louder, and I realized that it was on the radio of an oncoming car. I drifted to the road's shoulder.

Ain't nothin' gonna break my stride. Nobody's gonna slow me down, oh no. I got to keep on moving.

It was an ancient Buick Regal circa '83 or '84 with a two-tone paint job—brown below the door line and tan above. I hadn't seen one in years, and I certainly had not seen one in that kind of condition. My mom had one. The long chassis, angularly cropped on the ends, the curve of the trunk making it look like it had a tiny spoiler. The sight of it took me to a happy place. The old folks around here sure did hold on to their cars, and boy did they keep 'em shiny.

Ain't nothin' gonna break my stride. I'm running and I won't touch ground. Oh no, I got to keep on moving.

I passed the Bartlett's house and saw that Dave had had someone take his hedges down about three feet. It was there that I decided on the first line of Rob's eulogy, and that I would always speak of him in the present tense: "I've known Rob since we were eleven years old, and he is my best friend."

Then everything in my life changed.

I had only completed a mile and a half, but the sun had shot to a higher point in the sky. It looked as if it were 11 a.m., which was ridiculous. I heard the sound of tires on the road and the flutter of a small engine. I turned to see a blue golf cart about to even up with me.

"Hello, young fella. Movin' pretty fast today I see."

Art Dykeman was within arm's reach of me robustly piloting his Yamaha in gray slacks and a green golf shirt. His hair was a fading reddish brown struggling to keep at bay the grayish white rapidly encroaching from the sides. The last time I had seen him, his hair was stark white and he had long given up going to get his mail via golf cart.

Also, I had attended his funeral in February of 2014.

I matched Art's pace for several strides while this sunk in. Then he merely raised his hand, said "Adios," and hung a left on Cottage Grove Lane where he disappeared from view.

I stopped cold and walked across Firetree to where Cottage Grove began. There was no Art. There had to be 200 or more yards of clear sightline down the hill. I should have still been able to see him, but he was gone.

Well, this confirms your hallucinatory nervous breakdown Ray, congratulations.

I was not ready to accept this rationale. He was too real. I could smell Art's cologne. I took another step down the hill and found that I couldn't. I took a few steps back and broke into a jog back down the hill and again collided with nothing. This time the collision sent me ass-first to the pavement. Cottage Grove Lane shimmered before me.

"Jesus Christ, what the hell is happening?"

Like the way ripples in a lake slowly quiet while the stone sinks to the bottom, so did the shimmer. As the shimmer relaxed, Cottage Grove looked more like a glass storefront that is equally transparent and reflective. What emerged was the figure of a blonde, adolescent boy in tube socks and Velcro-secured Nikes sitting on the pavement. He was oddly familiar.

I stood up, and so did the boy. I approached the reflection, and so did the boy. I raised my hand to shield my eyes from the sun...

Dear god, it's me.

I was staring at my twelve-year-old self in the summer of 1984. My bladder let loose; luckily there wasn't much in the tank. I looked in the reflection and saw the boy's leg was wet. Finally, I looked down at my own feet to find that they were three sizes smaller and clad in tube socks and Nikes. I wasn't just looking at my twelve-year-old self. I was my twelve-year-old self.

I did a rapid reassessment of my run: the Fausts still being together, the Buick Regal, the song...

Your favorite house wasn't demolished. It had yet to be completed.

"And Art Dykeman is alive and well." I said out loud while staring at myself. Fear shot through me.

Was I trapped here?

It was the fear that allowed me to gather myself. Fear of being trapped and not seeing Ava again. I had more than a mile and a half of run left, and I began to cover it quickly.

The terrain of Seven Lakes has not changed too much since the '80s, and so there weren't too many surprises on the way home—just a pristine Pontiac Fiero blasting out Duran Duran. Naturally, I felt lighter and faster because I was lighter and faster. It was at about this age that I went to the AAU National Track and Field Championships, and it was hard to keep from looking down at my little legs to see how fast they were moving.

I passed the community pool and heard the clamor of children yelling and splashing, the warble of the diving boards as kid after kid attempted to make a splash that would reach the lifeguard in her perch. I had a feeling that if I tried to climb the driveway to the pool that I'd be shut out just as I had been on Cottage Grove. The question was would that happen when I tried to turn on Cherokee and go home?

Finally, the edge of the dam came into view, and I saw the shimmer. My pace slowed. The anxiety was crippling. Down the hill to the intersection of Firetree and Cherokee, fifty yards—nausea—twenty yards—weightlessness. I turned on to Cherokee and felt like I was suddenly carrying a bag of rocks on my back and assumed, hoped, I was settling into my 175-pound frame.

I looked down to see that I was again wearing Adidas running shoes and dry-wick leggings. I also confirmed that I had indeed pissed myself a little. The sun was again on the horizon and beginning to climb. It was 6:30 a.m.

I walked the length of Cherokee. Now that the fear of being trapped had abated, fascination returned.

How had this occurred? Could I do it again?

Then epiphany…

Rob Erwin was alive and well in that time.

I didn't know what I could possibly alter thirty-plus years in the past to keep me from burying my friend in a matter of days, but it was sure worth a shot. Maybe I could even leave myself a clue as to when my wife would take off with Ava. Or, perhaps, I could make everything a lot worse.

No. It couldn't be worse. I would run. I would run, and somehow, I would save my friend.

***

The first thing I did when I got home was make a new list of priorities, and it was an even more messed up list than the last one: verify that this happened, slip the time continuum again, go in with an agenda and find my deceased friend.

I couldn't decide if the first item on the agenda was the most or least difficult. I did decide that I would most definitely not drink. I briefly considered getting a psychological evaluation at Daymark Recovery Services.

The list was god at that moment. It was the only thing anchoring my racing mind. What were the rules to this? How had I triggered it? There was absolutely no explaining what had just happened, and there was no concrete way to verify it other than doing it again, and with more blood than Scotch flowing through me next time.

However, there was Anne Dykeman.

Anne. I met Art and Anne in 2001. I didn't know them when I was a kid even though I lived just a few houses away. I snatched up the phone and pulled up her contact.

And just what are you gonna ask her, Bubba?

Too late, the phone was ringing.

"Hello?"

"Hey Mrs. D. It's Ray."

"Oh Ray, How's that baby girl of yours?"

"Just fine." I hope. "At that age where she'll soon start bossing me around."

She laughed out loud.

"Well, it never stops. She'll be doing that for the rest of your life. What's on your mind?"

"I wondered if you had a picture of Art in his red golf cart back, say, in the 1980s?"

"Certainly I do somewhere."

"Do you still have the golf cart?"

"Why? You in the market? Ha, no, I sold that one to a fellow down the street. It was our second one, and those suckers are not cheap, especially the batteries. What's this about Ray?"

"Oh, I was just…wait. Second one? What color was the first one?"

"Blue, and it was gas. More expensive to buy, but the upkeep is minimal, should have held on to that one. We did stick with the Yamaha brand though."

It was blue. The flutter of the motor…

"Ray?"

That feeling of plummeting down a roller coaster descent invaded me again.

"I was just going to have Art make a cameo in a short story I'm thinking about setting in that time."

"That's intriguing. You'll send me a copy?"

"Ah, of course. One more question: What color was Art's hair originally?"

"He had dark hair. He was a dark redhead originally but was already turning gray when we moved here. I'll send you a picture on Facebook in a few minutes. Keep me posted on the story."

"Will do. Thanks Mrs. D."

I scrambled into the bedroom to retrieve my laptop. I was still logged into Facebook from last night when I had been answering the endless condolence messages and postings about Rob. It was only a few moments before Anne's message popped up.

I took a breath and opened it.

There staring at me was the Art Dykeman I had seen this morning, this time posing with his blue Yamaha on an overcast day and wearing jeans and a blue sweatshirt. If I had a wingback chair, I might have fallen back into it and passed out cold just like Rita.

6
Extraordinary Loyalties

Colonel Jim Dorn's indoctrination to the Philippines was marching through Manila with the First Cavalry during World War II, and he fell in love with it much the same way Ed did North Carolina. He got out of that war without a scratch, emerged from Korea with minor dings, and then he and Ed damn near got their heads blown off at La Drang.

Jim met Ed in Korea shortly after the First Cav got their ass handed to them at Unsan. He was nursing a head wound, smoking a cigar, and losing patience with an intelligence officer while trying to teach him some rudimentary Chinese in that Boston accent of his. Jim liked Ed immediately, and the two became casual acquaintances who shared the occasional cigar.

It was next to that shitty little river in Vietnam, though, that Ed and Jim became lifelong friends. It was a hell of a way to kick off a war, and he and Ed promised themselves that if they got out of that one, it would be their last one. There were other lives to be had.

Ed made the rank of colonel before the end of Vietnam. Jim did much later, but the two of them were so inseparable and well regarded by their subordinates, most simply referred to them as "The Colonels."

It was shortly after La Drang that they orchestrated their first leave together. They took a pass on China Beach and went straight to Manila. The fact that he would forever have a hitch in his step—and later set off every metal detector with which he crossed paths—resonated with Jim. It fostered a lust for life that became evident in Manila.

Though he and Ed hit every bar together, Ed would turn in at midnight and write letters to Rita. Jim would run the brothels until dawn and then spend the next day recovering. It was Ed who would arrange for transport to the surrounding islands, tasting the local produce, and learning the native customs. It was Ed who found the property Jim was standing on at this very moment.

Jim returned to the Philippines numerous times in the '70s, discovering the natives' extraordinary talent for making furniture, especially the rattan that seemed to occupy every sunroom in the American Southeast. He began making inroads with some of the corrupt officials of the Marcos administration where loyalty was purchased at a very reasonable price.

However, it wasn't until the 1980s, when Ed was riding out the last of his military career in North Carolina, that Jim really set up shop in Cebu. Jim returned to the states only to visit Ed, or to attend funerals. There were many funerals, especially for the Vietnam vets, and it was always cancer. He and Ed would go to these unfortunate military reunions together. They'd watch the fellas get drunk, bitch about the self-indulgent books their former commanders wrote, share stories, and cry. Jim and Ed would then retreat to Seven Lakes and spend time with Rita and Rob.

When the Philippine government transitioned, Jim transitioned with it. Corazon Aquino commenced an initiative in the '90s to redistribute farmland to the natives, but it didn't phase Jim.

He treated the locals well. They already lived on his land rent free, and he paid them to work it. When other landowners panicked and looked to sell, Jim bought. Those landowners would later kick themselves when Aquino relented and demanded that the landowners offer stock options instead, but it was too late. That's when the rumor began that Jim was having an affair with Aquino. The truth was, Jim just did the administration a favor by keeping tabs on some of the illicit groups threatening to orchestrate a coupe. It was easy. Most of them were acquaintances of his from the Marcos days. The rest were lingering communists who couldn't possibly organize an appreciable threat. The pay was good, and he liked Aquino. She was a good person and a badass. Jim had dinner with the family numerous times. He taught the kids to play baseball. He even campaigned for Benigno III's presidency in 2009. It was these relationships that kept people out of his business. As much as he liked Benigno, though, the truth was that in 2009, Jim simply needed a new project to occupy his mind because that was the year he returned to the States to bury Ed.

He had delivered Ed's eulogy at a huge Catholic Mass in Boston. Rob had already moved back to North Carolina, and Rita had resolved to follow him down there. Jim had prepared a job offer for Rita to be his furniture liaison in the Southeast. She too would need to occupy herself with something, and the way she spent money, she might also need the additional income.

Now, sitting on a hillside overlooking his furniture plant that, on paper, was owned by his Filipino partner, Jim steeled himself to again listen to Rita's voicemail. He would have to return to the States and bury another Erwin, the one he had come to think of as a son.

Jim played the message. He then stood and began walking in a direction opposite his plant, straight up the foothills. He saw Ed in 1966, drunk in Manila, dancing with himself while singing "Til I Waltz Again With You." He saw Rob in 1974 balancing on Ed's knee while Rita wiggled shoes on to his feet. He saw Ed proudly standing on the first tee of Pinehurst No. 2 in 1986, cigar in hand, sun gleaming off his rapidly balding head—Jim reached up and absently ran a hand through his snow-white crew cut. He saw Rob and Ray proudly displaying fish they had just pulled out of Lake Echo. He saw Rob graduating from Massart. He saw Ed smiling and pretending to smoke his unlit cigar in the oncology ward of Massachusetts General.

The moistness in Jim's eyes began to spill on to his cheeks as he crested the last ridge. He looked down into the colorful hectares of land below secured by razor wire and unseen, armed personnel. Life is indeed unpredictable, Jim thought. Squeeze from it what you can while you can.

7
The First Goodbye

"Rob, move your ass. Whatever it is we get has to be pre-marinated so we can just toss them on the grill. We're losing daylight, and you know Ava gets nervous if we linger on the boat too long after dark."

"Relax, Ray. We cruise on the lake first, cook when we get in. Has Ava gotten over that damn movie yet?"

"Nope."

It was April. Yellow pollen gathered at the shores of the lakes like the fringe on a skirt. Ava had learned that Disney would release the sequel to *Finding Nemo* by the end of summer, and so she was watching *Finding Nemo* on what seemed like an endless loop. She particularly liked Nemo's buddy, Dory, a Pacific Blue Tang fish with a memory problem and a repetitive inspirational song.

"Just keep swimming. Just keep swimming. Just keep swimming, Daddy!"

Ava got nervous on the water as evening settled in. She would go to the bow of Rob's boat and begin singing the Dory song to let us know it was time to head back to the safety of land.

Rob and I bailed out of my truck and hurried across the grocery store parking lot when the unmistakable thunder of Metallica came from over our shoulders. We turned to find a pick-up similar to mine shuddering to a halt. In a spot a row forward from where Rob and I had parked. From it emerged the silver-maned Father Baumann complete with clerical collar.

Rob and I exchanged a bemused look, shrugged our shoulders, and approached our priest. Rob and I were Catholics. Rob and I were shitty Catholics, meaning we were raised Catholic, and as adults we only darkened the door of our church for funerals and on holidays.

"Master of Puppets. One of my favorites, Father," I said.

Baumann grinned as he strode toward us and extended his hand in a firm shake to me and then Rob.

"Ray. Rob. How are you gentlemen? On the lake today?"

"Headed there next, Father." said Rob. "You keep listening to the metal at that volume and you might not be able to hear your parishioners in a few years."

"Ray, how is Ava?"

"Waiting breathlessly for the next Disney animated feature. How are things out in the country?"

"Loud. No noise or ordinance out on Route 73."

Rob and I laughed.

"It's a long way from Brooklyn, but I like it. It's a nice change of pace," said Baumann.

For the most part, Father Baumann was like every priest I'd known: genteel, scholarly, and exceedingly kind and patient. Rob and I always wondered how he had been sent to our small burg, and like gossiping old biddies, we baselessly theorized it had something to do with an attractive female parishioner because Baumann was not an ugly individual and attendance at Sacred Heart Church in Pinehurst had been way up.

"Gentlemen, I don't want to keep you. Will I see you Sunday?"

"Chances are slim. Forgive me Father…" said Rob.

***

Father Bauman officiated (if that is the right word) Rob's memorial to a packed house at Sacred Heart.

Baumann's liturgy reflected the good Father as a man. In many ways he was traditional to the core. He even shuttled the clergy to Rita's house to commence paying respect to the deceased. The old guard of Pinehurst Catholics appreciated this. It may be why they overlooked his braided gray hair and embraced his marginally salacious humor.

"Rob always ended our conversations by delivering a tongue-in-cheek apology for being an unforgivable heathen and a lapsed Catholic. It didn't matter if I caught up with him at a grocery store or the post office."

The faithful laughed at that, and not just politely.

"There was ceremony to go with these lines, a deepened voice and a profound bow, begging my pardon."

I knew this routine well, and I knew Rob ripped most of it straight from *The Highlander* starring Christopher Lambert and Sean Connery. I looked to Jenna immediately. Both she and Rita sat side-by-side in manufactured stoicism the entire service, but this anecdote broke her. Jenna always watched that movie with us, and she always gave us hell for Sean Connery playing an Egyptian in a film focused on a Scotsman.

"True, Rob's church attendance was suspect, his knowledge of scripture incomplete, but I tell you that I am certain I have never met a man who—perhaps unbeknownst to him—"

The faithful tittered again in unison

"...lead a more blessedly decent and Catholic life. He balanced temperance with fortitude, and he was prudent and just. Today Heaven cries out for the way such a man has been taken from us. Let us pray."

"God our Father,

"Your power brings us to birth,

"Your providence guides our lives,

"and by Your command we return to dust.

"Lord, those who die still live in Your presence,

"their lives change but do not end.

"I pray in hope for my family,

"relatives and friends,

"and for all the dead known to You alone.

"In company with Christ,

"Who died and now lives,

"may they rejoice in Your kingdom,

"where all our tears are wiped away.

"Unite us together again in one family,

"to sing Your praise forever and ever.

"Amen."

Where Baumann diverted from tradition was letting a layman like me deliver a eulogy at the conclusion of his service—that and holding an entire Catholic Mass with an empty casket. Rob would be spending a few more days with the medical examiner. Rita, Jenna, Candace, and I would lay him to rest in the Seven Lakes Cemetery when the time came.

Father let me know I was up by sharing with the congregation the story of how Rob and I "learned of his peculiar musical tastes in the grocery store parking lot."

I took to the lectern and surveyed the crowd. It fanned out in a pie shape under cathedral ceilings. The stained-glass windows dappled colored light on the people sitting at the end of the pews. I saw welcome sights—my mother in the third row, Colonel Jim positioned directly behind Rita with a hand on her shoulder. He was sullen, square-jawed, and still sporting a Stallone-like physique in his late '70s. I noticed Detective Spruill standing under a window that depicted Jesus catching a beat-down by some Roman soldiers. All of them were here to say goodbye to a man whose voice was still freshly captured in my phone mailbox and whose fishing pole was still rattling around in the back of my truck.

Spruill nodded at me as if permitting me to begin.

"I've known Rob since we were eleven years old, and he is my best friend.

"He is certainly my oldest friend. He may very well be my only friend. But with such a friend, I really don't need anyone else. We both moved to Seven Lakes within months of each other. We returned North within a year of one another, and we promptly came back to Seven Lakes as adults. To city-dwellers like us, this area—with its lawns, its lakes, its golf courses, its horses and rambling forests—is amazing. It certainly beat New York and Boston in the summertime where the best a kid could do was maybe open a fire hydrant. Its security gives rise to a spectacular amount of freedom, and Rob and I, along with our buddy Arden, spent long afternoons fishing, riding the horse trails on our bikes, and building forts in the woods with materials liberated from construction sites."

The subdued laughter from the crowd temporarily halted the sniffles and muffled sobs that had begun, and I was grateful. Whatever levity was left in me, I needed it as much as everyone here, perhaps more so.

"Rob and I are almost as inseparable as Ed, Rob's dad, and Colonel

Jim. We've been each other's confidants for over thirty years. Every move we've ever made—personally, professionally, or otherwise—had to have the input of us both. Moving back to the big city didn't stop us. How many teenage boys remained in touch with their far-away pals before phone and Facebook? Not many. Rob's the only reason a diehard Yankee like me would take a Greyhound bus and endure a Fenway double-header surrounded by the enemy."

The congregation laughed—a short burst. It felt good talking about my friend.

"When I couldn't find the exact swing-set that I wanted for my daughter's third birthday, Rob built one out of cedar…didn't even tell me. I just came home and it was there in my backyard. He'd been building it in his garage for three weeks while he listened to me complain about the lousy craftsmanship of today's toys."

It was at this point I noticed Spruill's attention on something in the back of the church, and that something was Eugene, Rob's construction foreman, standing uncomfortably behind the last row of pews, his hand massaging the back of his massive neck. He stared toward the front of the church, but not at me—his attention was trained on someone else—and so I continued to stare at him.

"My daughter has always been Rob's daughter too, and I'll always be Jenna's Uncle Ray, and that's how we'll get through this. Together. God doesn't control every random act that happens on this earth, but I do believe he sets circumstances in motion that restore balance, or that at least shed light. If we listen, if we follow, we might very well be able to reassemble ourselves and move forward. That is my hope. So, I will listen for my friend, because in thirty-two years he has never not spoken to me, and I don't expect him to remain silent now."

Be it appropriate or not, applause followed. I descended from the pulpit and walked down the center aisle. Rita dabbed at her eyes. Beside her Candace sobbed. Colonel Jim nodded at me with red-rimmed eyes. I stared at Eugene all the way down the aisle, and then I walked right out of the church.

The mass concluded and the faithful spilled from the church steps to the Sacred Heart lawns and sidewalks to politely commiserate. I slid off the open tailgate of my truck to fulfill my portion of this protocol. As I approached the entrance of the church, Baumann noticed me and began excusing himself from a conversation with a wheelchair-bound retiree who looked as if her memorial service was not too far in the offing.

He approached with a genuine smile and his hand extended toward mine. I offered a weak smile in return as his other hand clamped down on my shoulder.

"I don't think I've ever heard a eulogy applauded Ray. You have a gift."

"Thanks. That service was not the epic saga that I remember most Catholic Masses to be."

"Well, you know in a retirement community like this, the longer the service, the more you run the risk of a parishioner meeting the almighty in person during it. And that's not particularly good for business."

I shook my head and stifled a laugh. I resolved right then and there to get to know Father Baumann better at some point.

"Good stories, Father, and a fine liturgy. No wonder your parishioners like you so much."

"Ray, I know being a good writer involves being a good researcher, and that's what I think you should do in this situation—from a distance. I'm not fool enough to think you'll stay out of this completely, but I don't want you too involved. I have a bad feeling about this situation, and I'm concerned."

And he was. I could see it on his face. It was like I had a sign on my head that read *hell-bent on screwing things up*.

"Don't worry, Father. I've got my hands full with my other situation."

"We'll find Ava, Ray. Deputy Rhyne is correct. The money will run out. Besides, you're not the only one who can snoop. I'm going to pay you a visit later this week and explain to you an idea I have."

I was stunned. Apparently, I'd generated enough concern for people to coordinate with each other.

"You get around, Father."

"Not really. Deputy Rhyne and I play golf together. But I do have a responsibility to my parishioners who are neck-deep in struggle, and that is you, regardless of how well you are holding up."

"Young Ray has always been made of steel. He'll be fine, Father."

Colonel Jim approached with Rita on one arm and Candace on the other. He broke from them and hugged me, holding the back of my neck with his callused right hand. Then he retreated to arm's length and patted me on the cheek.

"Colonel."

"Coming by the house later?"

"Yes."

"Good. I have something for you."

Baumann went to Rita and spoke softly in her ear as his hands enveloped hers. He kissed her on the forehead and then turned to Candace, repeating the same routine. Both women began to cry.

"If you'll excuse me gentleman, I must see to the rest of my duties. Colonel, please find me before you leave."

We nodded to Baumann, and then he was off.

"That is an interesting fellow," said Jim.

"He is. I don't think they make 'em like that anymore…if they ever did. What do you have for me Colonel? A patio set?"

Jim smiled and threw an arm around my shoulder. We began to take a few steps toward the parking lot.

"No, smartass. It's something Rob wanted you to have. We haven't looked at the will. However, in Rob's safe deposit box was a letter to Jenna entitled 'just in case.' In it he asks her to retrieve random things from his office and make sure they get to certain folks. I didn't think Jenna would be up for that, so I handled it. While doing so, I stumbled upon this…collection."

"Got it." Of course, Rob thought Jenna would be in charge of these decisions. He did not imagine his mother would outlive him. I wondered if Jenna was, in fact, the executor of the will, and if so, where did Candace fit in? I didn't overthink the emergency letter. Rob liked to be prepared for everything, and sometimes random concerns and ideas just came to him. It was easier to write them down and stick them in a box.

"It's good to see you. Gonna spend some time stateside?"

"Only a couple of days. Then I'll come back before the end of the summer."

I turned to look at what was left of the Erwin family. Rita was receiving the condolences of friends with a polite smile and watery eyes. A few feet away, Jenna was doing the same. Candace was drained pale and staring catatonically off into the distance. It was the same look she would have on her face when they arrested her. I approached my truck and briefly stared at the fishing pole lying in the bed. I fired up the engine and plugged the phone in, making sure to first select *Queen's Greatest Hits* on the music app.

I put the truck in gear and drove away with the kind of anxiety that only hope can inspire.

8
Revenant Voice

The headgear for sparring sessions is insufferable. It never fits right over my big ears, and it irritates the shit out of me. Also irritating the shit out of me is the fact that I've been hit like thirty-seven times. Rob is that fast. He's moving in for another combination. Not this time, my friend.

Rob has a tell. He cocks his head to the right before he is going to throw a left-handed jab. When he does I throw a left hook and tattoo his cheek solidly. Now I move in for my combination but pause. Rob has a thousand-yard stare going on, and I realize he's out on his feet.

"Oh, shit Rob, sorry."

A moment later and Rob shakes it off.

"God damn, Ray."

I grab his elbow and lead him over to the corner for some water.

"You have concrete in your head and rocks in your gloves," he says.

"Dude, you telegraph that combination. I just got lucky."

"Maybe, but I've hit you a hundred times, and not only are you still bright-eyed and bushy-tailed, but then you come up with a thunder-punch like that? It's like sparring with Rocky Balboa."

"Well." I laugh. "I guess that makes you Apollo Creed, which makes sense 'cause you're better and faster than I am. But even if Apollo Creed was Caucasian, you'd still be the most Caucasian Apollo Creed ever.

He laughs.

"You are an asshole, and you are buying the beer."

I awoke in my daughter's room where I had slept in the bed left unmade for a month. I was huddled up with her plush, *Frozen*-themed throw blanket. The rich smell of baby enveloped me and put a hole in my heart. She'd be missing this. It was her go-to sleeping blanket, forgotten by Mom in the rush of escape.

I stumbled out and found my way to the hall bathroom. I fumbled through my wife's medicine cabinet looking for Aleve or Motrin or something. I found Advil and dumped pills into my hand—double checking to make sure I wasn't downing some stashed Vicodin.

Ava's Terrycloth swim cover-up hung like a ghost on the doorknob. I pictured myself wrapping her up in it as she ran to me out of the surf. I left the bathroom.

Last night's memorial reception had begun as a subdued affair where the casual acquaintances of the community were received by Rita, Candace, and Jenna with a mixture of tears and smiles.

Colonel Jim retreated with his Scotch back to Rob's cedar-paneled office and stared at the lake.

When the food was eaten and all that was left was only the old friends and relatives from Boston and the military, the real drinking commenced. Candace and Jenna retired to the back deck. Rita had run out of steam and retreated to her cottage. I found Jim still in the office holding court with what remained of his and Ed's First Cavalry.

"Ray!" A portly former gunnery sergeant harrumphed his way across the room with an extended hand. I could not remember his name for the life of me. "My wife just downloaded one of your books on to her Kindle. Congratulations. When's the next one?"

I looked up to see Jim mouthing the name James to me.

"How are you James? Thank the missus for me. I'm not sure when the next one is. I've got a lot going on."

"Of course you do. This is all heartbreaking. If there is any way any of us can help, let me know."

"I will. I appreciate that."

Jim rose from Rob's leather desk chair.

"Gentleman, I have to spend a few private moments with Ray to sort out some of Rob's business. It won't take long. I suggest we adjourn to the gazebo by the lake where there is an additional supply of Bushmills. That will allow those tired ladies an opportunity to retake the house and get some sleep."

All four gentlemen either shook my hand or patted me on the shoulders as they filed out of the room. They would stop at the deck and offer more kind words to Candace and Jenna, and then the booze and the salty reminiscences would recommence by the lake and run until dawn. Regardless of their elderly status, each man would then scale the grassy hill without issue and flawlessly drive back to their respective rented cottages.

Jim reached beneath Rob's desk and produced a briefcase. He quickly placed it on the desk and snapped it open. From it he withdrew a bottle of Aberfeldy 21, and then turned to reach for a pair of glasses.

"You keep Scotch in a briefcase?" I asked.

"Nope," said Jim. "Rob did. I gave this bottle to him a few years ago. He had yet to open it."

He handed me a glass and offered a rather matter-of-fact toast.

"To Ed and his boy—my most favorite people formerly of this earth. Their family is the only family I've ever had. At least they are together."

I sipped. A warm, caramel-oak flavor settled over me.

"To you Ray. You're my family too, and I have a proposition for you once you've had a look at your 'inheritance.'" With that he yanked open a bottom drawer and pulled from it a length of dirty PVC pipe clumsily duct taped at both ends.

I was too hung up on the word "proposition" to register the significance of a dirty, white tube. Then it hit me.

"The time capsule." I whispered.

"Is that what that is?" The hint of a smile crept into the corner of Jim's mouth.

The pipe was dirt-encrusted. Still etched into the plastic via Arden's hunting knife was the following:

Open 2004

I gathered it up in my hands and held it with a kind of reverence. I noticed that one end had been opened and then resealed. I looked up at Jim.

"I didn't open it. Rob did. I think he designed a renovation to the house where you guys buried this thing."

My god. My favorite house that looked out on to Lake Sequoia, that's where we buried it, right inside the door of the crawl space. I had to smile at the image of Rob—at the very least in his thirties—digging around the crawl space of a house that was not his. How the hell had he slipped away and pulled this off?

"When did he do this?"

Jim resettled in the leather chair behind the desk.

"I'm not sure, but it was not in 2004, neither of you guys had moved back here yet."

I pulled off the tape and immediately found a letter that did not look like it had been part of the original package. In it was the voice of my friend.

Ray –

I found this on May 15, 2016 in that house you like so much. We extended a deck and then enclosed it to make a Carolina Room. I guess you too had forgotten what we buried there. Well, I didn't!

Actually, I did. It wasn't until I was looking where the ducts lead in the crawl space that it dawned on me. And it was still there! My goal was to reveal this sucker to you on a special occasion, whether it was a birthday or some sort of anniversary.

I decided to wait until all this craziness settles down with these wives of ours. I just wanted it to be me and you and Jenna and Ava, sitting on the deck, happy and content and settled, because really, you guys are all I need. If you're reading this, then that time has come.

Have a look-see. There are some surprises. Enjoy your trip through time, Highlander. Glad you made it to The Gathering with your head intact!

Pals for life,

Rob

Tears began audibly hitting the paper before I could fold it up. It wasn't lost on me that Rob sounded as if he intended to end his marriage, but I was just too sad to care about that at the moment

"Ray, I'd like to take at least one thing off your shoulders. I want to hire a private investigator to see if we can track down Ava. Then I want your permission to quietly buy off your wife, getting her to dissolve your marriage without issue. Then she can take her pile of money and go dope herself up somewhere that is not here."

"Thanks, Colonel, but I'll handle my divorce. I think I'll take you up on that private investigator, though."

Jim nodded.

"Good, because I'm already working on it. I'm going to join the boys and give you some time with Rob."

Jim paused in the doorway, and it felt as if he were composing himself.

"And Ray, you were a good reporter, good at finding things. Do you think you can find the people that did this?"

I was surprised to find my head nodding in the affirmative.

"When you do…if you're sure. Contact me. I'm going to give you a new telephone number to reach me." With that, Jim slipped out of the room.

It did not require much intelligence to intuit that whomever I found would have a long, slow accident far away from here, and I thoroughly did not care. I turned the time capsule over and out tumbled Luke Skywalker in his X-Wing fighter pilot gear. This had been mine, and I had forgotten where it went. The rules of the time capsule were coming back to me. We each had to part with something that meant a lot to us. Right after Luke came one of Rob's favorite fishing lures, and then one of Arden's many knives, probably the one he used to etch the capsules main directive.

There were three tickets to see Ghostbusters in a theater that was now a car dealership. Next were the letters—we each were supposed to write down what we saw ourselves doing in twenty years, as well as any other prognostications we deemed appropriate.

Rob and Arden both said I would be an Olympic athlete. I said Rob would be one of those Bass tournament fishing champions. Rob and I both thought Arden would live in the wild like Grizzly Adams. Either that or he'd be an assassin—for all I knew, he could very well be some kind of military spook.

I said there would be another Star Wars movie—nailed that one, kind of.

Rob said that I'd marry Olivia Allen—nope.

Arden was the one that said if I did not become an athlete, I'd write stories for a living.

Finally, there was a Polaroid picture of the three of us, arms around each other, fresh out of the Seven Lakes pool with our six-dollar haircuts plastered in odd directions, Rob and I roughly the same height, Arden lanky and two inches taller than us. We are grinning like fools, half tanned, half sunburned.

I reassembled the time capsule and quietly walked from the office and right out of the front door of the house. Jim would understand, so would Candace and Jenna. Memorials are for the living, a time to commiserate and reconnect with loved ones far away. At some point, though, you had to return home alone to process and to commune with the dead, hoping they heard you.

"I love it
when a plan
comes together."

—Colonel John "Hannibal" Smith,
The A-Team

9
The Gathering

It may be weird to shower before a run, but it allows for two things: for a man of my age to loosen up, and for a stressed individual to process and itemize. What had my attention was the time capsule, specifically the movie tickets in the time capsule. Ghostbusters was released in the summer of 1984, and the capsule was supposed to be opened in 2004, twenty years later. Twenty years seems like a nice, round number that adolescents would select. So, yes, that capsule was buried by the end of the summer of '84.

Judging by the way I had appeared, the way Art Dykeman had appeared, and the heat I had felt, my time slippage may very well have been to that summer or just before it. That was something I most definitely had to pin down.

I toweled off and slipped on a random pair of shorts and dry-weave T-shirt. It didn't matter what I had on because in less than half a mile it would be something else. I tumbled out the door and tried to contain the pace. On the dam, I avoided looking at the drain and focused on the haze in the distance. At the end would be that permeable membrane to another era.

As I approached, I could see my reflection. I was still my forty-four-year-old self, but that would change. I could already feel the weightlessness, the nausea. My feet got faster. I tipped my head forward and rushed into a place where all things were still possible.

I immediately felt a wash of humidity and heat that had not been there before. I had tipped out the door at 6:30 a.m. It was not 6:30 a.m.

in this place. Over my left shoulder, I heard the whiney, emotive voice of Morrissey coming from a transistor radio.

I was looking for a job, and then I found a job

And heaven knows I'm miserable now…

I turned to see a teenage girl with considerable hair sunning herself by Lake Sequoia. I pressed on. I knew where I would find them. I noticed the sun was higher in the sky. It looked more to be either 11 a.m. or 12 p.m. Slowly the lakefront house came into view. Though my last trip through this anomaly was only days ago, I could see that there was now a foundation and framing in place. Time moved faster here. As I passed the house, I stared at the entrance to the crawl space. Was that capsule already there? Should I stop and see? I didn't want to yet. I was afraid that I would be locked out of that space much the same way I had been bounced out of Cottage Grove when I tried to follow Mr. Dykeman.

I passed the Bartlett's house and rounded the bend to what was mostly a rolling straightaway to the beginnings of the Lake Echo dam. I slowed a bit, almost subconsciously, and I became anxious about what I could and should accomplish in the next two miles. I noticed the Velcro strap on my right shoe had popped loose. I stopped and bent down, and then I heard a familiar voice off to my right.

"Raymond, get in there and straighten your room. I've been on you about that for two days now."

Holy shit. My mom.

She wore white running shorts and a gray Duke T-shirt. Her feathered, Sue-Ellen Ewing hair blew back off her shoulders as she was walked forcibly forward by a large golden retriever on a leash. She was striding across a crabgrass lawn, our lawn.

How could I forget that, for a time, we lived right on Firetree Lane? With mouth agape, I studied the gray, wood-paneled, ranch house with the one-car garage turned into a den. The cornering road was Sandspur Lane. Yes, this was the place.

"Honey, are you feeling all right? Is it really that healthy to go running in the middle of a summer day? I thought you did this in the evening?"

Buck, my best furry pal growing up, head-butted my thigh hello.

"I…yes, normally I do. I'm not really running; I'm just gonna jog down to Echo and see if I can find Rob and Arden."

I bent down and held Buck's face in my hands for the first time in decades. My eyes welled up a bit.

"Well that's fine, dear, but just go in and put your clothes away and make your bed. The Marouns will be over later. Just because it's summer doesn't mean we have to live like heathens."

"Ah…OK…"

What the hell was I going to do if I attempted to walk into this yard and some invisible force tossed me back into the street?

I patted Buck on the head and took one tentative step into the yard, then two. I jogged across the lawn and made it to the porch. I turned to see Mom continue walking Buck down Firetree toward Cottage Grove. I opened the screen door and stepped in.

It was even smaller than I remembered. The living room, dining room, and kitchen all sort of blended. There was a sliding glass door by the dining room that led to a screened-in porch. To my right was a short hallway leading to the bedrooms. I took a breath and prepared to run into my little brother. I poked my head into his room to find only bunk-beds neatly made up, and his multitude of Legos poured back into their plastic tubs. A He-Man action figure rode triumphantly astride a large Tonka truck.

The door to my room was closed and covered with a large poster—the 1984 Duke Basketball team stared at me from the moon, declaring that they had *The Right Stuff.* Jay Bilas stood with large, folded arms and all of his hair, daring me to contradict this sentiment.

Inside it was how I remembered. Track and field ribbons adorned the wall. A black and white television stood at the foot of the small bed. I wandered over and straightened the sheet and comforter. I gathered T-shirts off the floor, and then I saw my towering bookshelf with no books. On it instead was an Imperial Starship with a pod where Darth Vader could sit in peace and take off his helmet. There was the Millennium Falcon, a Tie-Fighter, and an X-Wing Fighter. I opened the canopy and found Luke in his pilot gear.

That's two questions answered. I could walk onto some properties—probably only the ones that bordered Firetree—and the time capsule was yet to be completed and buried.

I folded and placed my T-shirts in the third drawer of my dresser and started to make my way out of the room. There was a calendar on the wall next to the door. It was most certainly the month of June 1984. As far as what day, I was less-than-dutiful in crossing off the days as they came and went. I guessed it was the middle of the month, which meant June of 1984 was progressing at least a few days faster than June of 2016. The third week of June was circled, and the word *Qualifying* was scrawled between the Thursday and Friday boxes. I knew immediately which meet this was—my first qualifying race for nationals, where I qualified but got beat. I was boxed in by multiple runners while the leader galloped away. I finished third. I uncapped the pen hanging off the calendar and wrote myself a note:

Grab the lead or stay in lane two.

I jogged off the lawn and back on to Firetree. I was less than a half mile from the bend that became Echo Dam. When I made that turn, I saw a figure standing on the other side of the guardrail, on the edge of the rocky bank of Lake Echo. To the left of the road tumbled a steep, grassy grade to Lake Sequoia. The figure cast a line into the lake. I knew who it was merely by the way he moved.

As he came into closer view, I could see the camouflage pants that he wore regardless of how hot it was. A dirty V-neck shirt and boots completed the ensemble. His head was topped with a mesh baseball cap that advertised some trucking company.

When I was within steps of him, Arden Miller turned to me and spoke.

"Damn Ray. Don't you ever stop runnin'?" Both of us broke out into a smile.

"How'd you know it was me?" I asked.

"I can tell it's you just by the way your foot falls on the asphalt."

"How the hell do you do that?"

Arden's smile broadened. Those big horse teeth of his, healthy and naturally straight, shone. It was so good to see him.

"Who knows? If a pile of brush is rustling, I can name the critter movin' around in it. It's just what I do. Besides, how many races of yours have me and Rob been to? You're almost always way out in the lead. I just got used to what your feet sounded like all by themselves."

Arden suddenly turned his attention out toward the lake. A moment later something grabbed my shoulders and whispered in my ear.

"Boo."

It felt like I leaped three feet in the air before I spun around.

"Dude, are you OK?"

A twelve-year-old Rob Erwin stood before me, sandy-haired, tanned, and full of life. I was speechless.

"Man, note to self: Do not sneak up on Ray. I think he just had a stroke." Rob smiled as he ambled over the guardrail with his pole and tackle box. He wore a blue shirt with the Superman insignia; it just barely covered his slight belly-chub that never seemed to go away. His spindly legs were on display via a pair of white, Umbro shorts.

"Arden," Rob asked. "Did you see that rerun last night of the *A-Team* finale?"

"I don't watch reruns. Besides, no one ever gets shot on the *A-Team.*"

"Well, somebody got shot last night. Somebody tried to shoot Hannibal but got Murdock instead. And because Decker was still chasin' 'em, the A-Team had to go on the run and try to pull the bullet out themselves."

Arden turned to Rob with wide eyes.

"They get caught?"

"Yup. We missed that episode while working on that stupid book report for Ms. Sylvia."

"Oh, yeah. That girl's diary is the most depressing thing I've ever read. How long did we study World War II anyway?"

"Wait until you have to read *Night,*" I interjected.

"He speaks!" said Rob.

"What's *Night*?

"It's a book. More Nazis."

Arden shook his head.

"I'll take a pass. Onto more important matters: when are we going to see *Ghostbusters*?"

I stared at Rob, whose attention was now directed at tying his lure. Now that I was on the spot, it was hard to conceive of anything other than holding it together. My biggest concern was not saying anything weird, not saying anything that suggested there was a forty-something man in this twelve-year-old frame, an adult that knew that the *A-Team* ran for only four seasons, that there were four additional *Star Wars* movies, and that *Ghostbusters* would be remade with virtually an all-female cast.

My other concern was that if I remembered everything happening here in this anomaly, so did my twelve-year-old counterpart. Random thoughts had begun invading my consciousness: How many miles I was supposed to run that day; my brother bursting into laughter that morning and blowing *Boo Berry* cereal all over the table; the social studies test coming up next week. I was pretty sure I was sharing young Ray's body and consciousness, not commandeering it. In a way this was good. He would retain all the details of my interactions with Rob and Arden and be able to resume his own timeline without skipping a beat. I just had to make sure that my adult mind and mouth did not paint him into some corner.

Arden spoke up.

"Hey, we haven't seen *The Temple of Doom* yet, and it's been out for a month."

"We can see both!" exclaimed Rob. "And hey, my dad and I saw *The Natural* last weekend, and there was a preview of a robot movie coming out in the fall."

"What's that about?" asked Arden.

"It stars the guy who won the Mr. Olympia title like eight times. He's a robot that goes back in time to kill somebody who's gonna be important to the future."

"That sounds pretty cool."

"It sounds rated R," I added. "We'd have to sneak in to see it...like we did *First Blood*, and you know how that worked out."

"Yeah, but we look older now," said Arden.

I had to laugh. We barely looked our actual age. I remembered we did try to sneak in to see *The Terminator*, and we got tossed out of that one as well. We'd see it on VHS more than a year later. I couldn't suggest when to go see *Ghostbusters* because I didn't even know what day it was. Not that it mattered too much in the summer. I was privy to some of young Ray's goings-on, but not all of them. With my luck, I'd suggest a day where he was committed to some track meet all the way in Raleigh.

"Let's go see *Ghostbusters* tomorrow," said Rob. "We'll go early and blow some money in the arcade. Then we'll go to the pool."

"Sounds good to me," said Arden. "Ray?"

"Yeah," I answered. I just had to trust that this was how it was supposed to play out. We always snuck Arden into the Seven Lakes pool by saying he was my brother, and it worked. Not only did Arden and I look nothing alike, but my brother was usually in the pool whenever we showed up. How I wished I could revisit the pool and play shark in the deep end, or play foursquare on the patio during the adult swim. But time moved differently here, and trying to gauge when to enter this anomaly so as to arrive when we were all headed to the pool would only give me a migraine.

Arden reeled in his lure and meandered farther down the shoreline. Rob settled down on a particularly large rock, content to just let his lure bob in the waves. I took a seat next to him and tried not to stare at his profile.

"Ray, that robot movie gave me an idea. I think we could travel through time."

My jaw dropped. My mind raced to how we might have perhaps manufactured this time slip ourselves.

"What exactly do you mean?"

"I mean there's a way to come back and visit this point in time from the future. Do you know what a time capsule is?"

I was both relieved and disappointed at the same time. For a moment I thought there might be something more to this slip in time, something that would give me more control. "Yeah, I do. You bury stuff from this time period, and you dig it up years later to see what life was like back then."

"Exactly. I think we should do something like that—you, me, and Arden. Then we come back when we're old men and dig it up, like in the year 2000."

So that's how it happened. Rob saw the preview of *The Terminator*. The 2000s seemed like a magical, far-off time to us back then, a time when cars would be able to fly and light sabers became a reality.

"How about 2004? That would be an even twenty years."

"Perfect," said Rob. "We'll have to use something that won't rot in the ground. I was thinking a big piece of PVC pipe."

"OK, what'll we put in it?"

"I'll have to think about that some more. We should definitely write letters to our future selves. That would be cool. What you think we'll be doing in 2004?"

Here is where I had to be careful.

"Well, we'll be thirty-two years old. We'll be out of college, have jobs…"

"You'll be a runner still," said Rob.

Arden, who'd apparently been listening, came back up the shoreline.

"Bullshit," he said. "You can't run forever. How do you make a living doin' that? Besides you ever read one of Ray's stories? That's what he'll be doing. That's where the money is. My momma goes through a book a month. There's this one guy she reads all the time, Stephen King. I'm pretty sure that guy is doin' all right for himself."

Rob looked directly at me.

"What do you think I'll be doing?"

"Oh, you'll either fish in those Bass tournaments, or you'll build stuff."

Rob seemed to consider this for a moment.

"You're probably right. You'll be married. Think I'll be married?"

"I think we'll be having too much fun to be married yet."

"No way I'll be married," said Arden. "My folks fight all the time. I don't need all that."

"Girls don't really like me. I won't be married," Rob said.

This was an admission to which I didn't know how to respond. Rob had always been insecure about girls, and he carried it with him right into adulthood. It's probably why he fell head over heels when someone as beautiful as Candace took an interest in him.

"Girls like you plenty. Trust me; you'll see. Just be careful whom you pick."

Though I doubted it highly, part of me hoped that I hadn't just given advice that erased my Goddaughter Jenna right out of existence. Much as I didn't want to leave, I knew the productiveness of this moment was waning. I could only cause trouble now if I lingered.

"Well, that settles it," I said. "We will all write letters and predict what we'll be doing in the future. Then in twenty years we can dig it up and read how wrong we were while we fish. "

"Or how right we were," said Rob. "I think we should put some other stuff in too."

"Great. What about *Ghostbusters*?" asked Arden.

"One o'clock show. My dad will take us."

"I love the Colonel!" said Arden.

With that, I got up and squeezed Rob on the shoulder.

"I gotta split. See you guys tomorrow."

I jogged away, looking over my shoulder to see both guys waving farewell and recasting their lines. I would not run tomorrow. If young Ray were going to the movies, then he would not be available for me to inhabit—if it worked that way. I crested a hill on Firetree and decided to test this theory again. I took a left on Overlook Drive and was promptly bounced to the asphalt where I sat watching my reflection wobble back into frame. That answered that.

I gathered myself and continued on Firetree to connect with the Longleaf dam. A few teenagers waded on the shoreline of the small lake that bordered the grassy hill rising to the pool. I could see kids on the diving board. As I got closer, I should have been able to hear the din of boys and girls in full summer, but I heard nothing.

II approached Cherokee Trail and felt weight settle back on to my frame. The lightheadedness cleared as I stepped on to Cherokee and out of the anomaly. I walked, silently. I turned on Shadywood to descend into the cul-de-sac and stopped. An F-150 pickup sat in my driveway.

Baumann.

***

Father Baumann could see Ray paused at the top of the cul-de-sac.

That poor man had to be on the brink of a nervous breakdown, he thought. Baumann was sure Ray would assume his priest was simply keeping an eye on a parishioner's emotional health, but that was not the case. If Tom could not find Ray's little girl, no one could. Tom would do it because he felt he owed Father, but the truth was that Tom was retired, bored, and good at heart.

He had tested the idea of helping Ray on Colonel Jim only to find that Jim was dead set on intervening in Ray's situation.

"Tom sounds like exactly the kind of individual I need," Jim had replied. It was a response that revealed quite a bit about the Colonel. He was accustomed to running the show, and he was accustomed to getting results in a variety of ways. The response also suggested that Father had perhaps not delivered an accurate image of Tom, at least not the Tom he knew now. It did not matter. Jim had quickly agreed to reimburse all of Tom's expenses, and he suggested a fee for services rendered pending results. That would be unnecessary. Tom would be offended by an offer of payment. He'd accept reimbursement of expenses.

For the first time in weeks, Baumann had something to offer Ray besides condolences and platitudes. He had a plan, one that might restore a man running very low on faith.

10
Tom

Tom Cianci retired to a six-acre trotter farm in Goshen, New York. This had always been the plan. It was cinematic horse shit that a man could not retire from city business and exist peaceably. The first five or six years had been great, and then the arthritis had advanced. He had to hire more people. After that, the farm damn near ran itself. He just collected training and boarding fees and signed checks.

Infinitely more tech savvy then most people his age, he had kept in touch with young Father Baumann via email. Young? Baumann was in his fifties at this point, which made him…never mind. Old is what it made him, old but not useless. Baumann knew that, and Baumann liked to help. The subject line of his last message was "missing child." That had gotten Tom's attention.

Tom tracked down plenty of missing people in his younger days, but most of those people had abducted themselves. It didn't matter though. A parent running off with her kid made the same mistakes as the average lowlife. This lady had already made mistakes, social media of course. In a digital world, everything has a trail. Tom had made a living of possessing the most accurate information in a timely manner. It was why he was still breathing and operating a horse farm. It was how he had met Baumann.

There had been a receiving problem from the Red Rose Restaurant in Brooklyn. Tom went to inquire. The manager simply received shipments in addition to his weekly deliveries of fish and meat, and he was reimbursed for this trouble. The problem had been two-fold: a shipment was lifted, and the manager was relieved of his reimbursement in exchange for remaining healthy. This had all been done to get the attention of Tom's boss.

For the next week, Tom rode a bicycle to the Red Rose dressed in apron and dirty trousers. With his sleeves rolled up, he entered the kitchen through the rear entrance and began scrubbing pots. The shipments had already been redirected to an establishment in Red Hook, but protecting the Red Rose was both good business and the right thing. Also, you could not let messages go unanswered.

Sunday evening, the reliever of the shipment, and a large friend, arrived in a car that had been parked near the restaurant every night. They'd been watching, and they'd gotten impatient. Tom stumbled into the manager's office with a pot, complaining in Italian that the water had been shut off and what he was holding was all the water there was. The gentlemen in question were sitting comfortably in front of the manager's desk. Tom promptly dropped the scalding water in the enforcer's lap and then blackjacked the muscle to the ground. He escorted the enforcer to the delivery truck at gunpoint. The cook dragged the muscle. Two additional associates used the delivery truck to transport the interlopers to Tom's boss.

Tom peddled his bike down Union Street to a Catholic Church he visited each day to make sure the window he'd unlocked was still, in fact, unlocked. However, he knew the evening Mass had let out only thirty minutes before, and so the chances were high that he would still be able to walk right in. He'd stashed some clothes under the seat in a confessional. He would ditch the bike, hop the train on the corner of Fourth Avenue, and be gone.

The church was open. His clothes were missing.

Sitting in the first pew was a teenage altar boy holding Tom's neatly folded suit in his lap. Tom approached him. The boy looked over his shoulder and spoke.

"I found these yesterday, but I left them where they were until tonight. I didn't tell Father McNamara. If they were for Mass, you missed it. "

"They weren't for Mass." There was no point in lying. The kid was sharp.

"I didn't think so. This suit is much nicer than the ones I see on the parishioners. Follow me, and I'll show you a room where you can change. The train is right around the corner, but I bet you know that."

After a moment, the boy spoke again.

"One question: How were you going to get in if I hadn't still been here?"

Tom showed the boy the unlocked window, and he gave him the bicycle after assuring the lad that it wasn't stolen. He continued to visit the church. It was the last place people would look for him. It was right about the time Tom became the boss that he had to start addressing the boy as "Father."

He'd find Father Baumann's missing sheep. He'd seen what drugs could do. The drugs always ended up being in charge, and that meant the little girl was in danger. That was not acceptable. Colonel Jim Dorn—that's still how the man introduced himself—sounded every bit the military individual, but he also sounded like some of the bosses with whom Tom had had to deal. Tom knew the sound of a man who operated outside the lines. Hell, he was pretty sure Jim Dorn didn't concern himself with lines.

11
The Solace of Business

Rita Erwin was done crying. Well, she wasn't, but she resolved to stop crying for a while, mostly because Candace was doing enough blubbering for the both of them. As she saw it, there were two choices: self-medicate with dry martinis while sorting through her son's memorabilia, or get a doctor-prescribed anti-depressant and go back to work. If the call she missed this morning was any indication, the self-medication route was a dead-end.

Jim had suggested the latter, and she had conceded. Having to take Effexor each morning was going to be a daily blow to her New England pride and resiliency, but it was what had to be. She could coordinate her son's final arrangements, assist with estate issues, deal with the attorney, and keep Rob's current construction projects on track to completion because those were impersonal tasks. She could not go through Rob's things. Christ, Ed's closet had remained untouched for two years, smelling of tweed, turf, and aftershave, and she had been prepared for Ed's end, had made a reasonable peace with it.

She would never make peace with this. A parent can't outlive their child. When Rob was born, he filled any remaining holes Rita still had in her heart, and he did so for Ed as well. Life with your true love is a life well spent, but there is no replacing someone whom you instantly and unconditionally love at first sight, and who loves you back the same way. Rob loved his mom, loved her exactly the same his whole life.

His whole life.

A little more than four decades on the planet was not a life, and for it to end as it had…

What Rob filled her heart with could not be replaced, not even with the love she felt for Jenna.

Rita was resigned to the fact that she would drift through the rest of her days like a wraith. Though she was ingrained with an iron-clad work ethic that would organize and fill her days, emotionally she'd be vacant until she saw her boy again.

Jenna meanwhile consumed herself with preparing for Duke. The acceptance letters to Duke, North Carolina State and Massachusetts College of Art and Design had arrived during the weeks of April. Jenna decided to pass on her dad's alma mater, vowing to do what neither Rob nor Ray ever had the option to do: live in North Carolina her whole life. Ray had thrown a ridiculous party at the Seven Lakes Country Club, going so far has to have someone in a Blue Devil mascot costume escort Jenna into the building.

So, while Candace made her daily trip to the liquor store for a bottle of courage under fire, Rita resumed her duties as a wholesaler for Abian Industries of the Philippines.

She had begun her day by perusing the digital packing list to verify both the contents and the worth of each item. She also confirmed that "Made in the Philippines" was stamped on every item, which was the law.

The email from Manny Reyes, Jim's plant manager, and majority company owner, described a forty-foot shipping container that held lamps, lamp bases, umbrella bases, fossil stone table tops, and a large amount of aluminum patio furniture with a total value of $15,000.

The next step was to email Wyatt, her customs broker, to pay the import duty and to arrange for inland transport.

Wyatt Halsey had been an Air America pilot who got drunk one night with Ed in Manila. The next day, still drunk, he flew Ed and Jim to the Island of Cebu in his Pilatus PC-6 Porter, which had stalled twice in mid-air. Back then, Cebu was an untamed no man's land whose only claim to fame was that the native inhabitants killed Magellan. Ed had simply wanted to see something wild and natural that wasn't exploding. Jim just indulged Ed's day trips when they were on leave together. Now Cebu was the command center of Abian Industries.

Rita was on the other side of Scotland County, traveling down Route

74 and headed for Southport. Jim had always mandated that she meet the transport truck at the interchange of Route 74 and Route 211 near Lake Waccamaw and escort it back to Route 73 near Ellerbe.

This rule had initially seemed odd to her, but then she had begun staging the furniture in her warehouse for the owners of the mom-and-pop furniture companies throughout North Carolina. They had come, the same ones every time, paying for their wares from their tablets by electronically transferring funds to the assigned accounts. They blinked not an eye at the price, which was more than three times what the items were listed as being worth. The shipping list was correct. If the value had not been accurate, that container would have sat with customs on Jim's storage dime until inspectors tore it apart to see why it was so inordinately valuable.

Jim's shipments were never held up.

The buyers had to know what the items were worth, but they ate the mark-up with a smile and then loaded the pieces onto their trucks and left. Rita didn't ask questions. She raked in close to $135,000 in compensation, which meant Jim did just over a million dollars' worth of business. It was extraordinary. At this rate, she would put Jenna through Duke without her having to borrow a dime from the Feds. That reminded her. She would have to drive Jenna to Duke in September, the ceremonial departure to college. She picked up her phone.

"Siri, call Ray McCarthy."

***

I continued to sit on my porch long after Baumann had climbed back into his truck and departed. I wasn't sure that anything more bizarre could be packed into a single day, but again I was wrong. I'm wrong a lot.

My family was originally from Brooklyn, and so the Cianci name was familiar. It wasn't a good or bad kind of familiar; it was just shady. It made me see Baumann in a new light. I was most certainly going to Google the shit out of both Father Baumann and Tom Cianci later that evening. In the meantime, I was glad to have a Cianci on my side and apparently on the job.

What I wanted to do at that moment was open my laptop and have a look at the social media doings of one Eugene Sawyer, who had been on my mind since the memorial. Eugene was an enormous square-jawed southerner who had been Rob's right-hand man on the job site. As the construction foreman, he'd kept everyone on schedule, never hired half-ass subcontractors, and was generally well-liked among his crew.

Eugene thought Rob was the most talented man he'd ever seen. Rob designed craftsman- style buildings which avoided fads that would eventually seem dated, and he balanced cost- effectiveness with sturdiness and class. Not only that, Rob would occasionally show up on site and help frame, just because he liked being out in the sun.

What I couldn't get over though, was how uncomfortable Eugene looked in the church, and how he had been staring in the same particular direction the entire time.

Eugene's Facebook page revealed an extreme allegiance to the University of North Carolina football team, as well as a fondness for hunting and wakeboarding. His pictures from a boat outing on Badin Lake suggested an affection for hanging out with good 'ole boys and beautiful young ladies. That wasn't surprising. The pictures also showed off his professional wrestler-like physique.

His friends list was uneventful. Rob never messed with Facebook, so he wasn't on there. Candace was, but Candace was on mine and everybody else's friends list, so was Jenna. I pondered this a bit. The memorial had been on a Saturday. Eugene could very well have drowned his sorrows the night before and been hungover at the service. That and I was sure stuffing his pectorals into that ill-fitting suit had not been the most comfortable thing he'd ever experienced. Eugene did not have a strict security setting for his page, so I perused his timeline. There was a comment left two days before from a Chad Nelson.

"Dude, sorry about your boss. Been looking for you for a few days now. Answer your phone or come by the restaurant tonight."

So, Eugene was MIA. I'd been to Eugene's house in West End at least once. I was pretty sure I could find it again.

My phone suddenly lit up with an unlisted number. There was a brief internal debate about letting it go to voicemail, but curiosity got the better of me. The voice on the other end was old and gruff, but familiar.

"Is this Mr. Ray McCarthy of North Carolina?"

There was a whole lot of Brooklyn in that voice.

"Hello, Mr. Cianci."

"I gather you've had a conversation with the Father." His accent elongated the a and dropped the r.

"Yes sir. What is it you do Mr. Cianci?"

"I'm retired."

Retired from what?

"I'll get right to it young man. I am headed down I-95 toward Savannah at the moment. I'm going to have a look at the browser histories of the PCs in that library. I know your wife has a tablet, but it was your daughter who was playing on it at the time, so I think Mrs. McCarthy was probably on a PC. You write books, Mr. McCarthy. Your wife a reader?"

"No, not really."

"Then what is she doing in a library? She not even read your books?"

"No."

"If I were you, I would adjust my marital arrangement when this is over, Ray. May I call you Ray?"

No shit, Tom.

"Certainly."

"I am going to text you an email address when I hang up. I need you to send me pictures of the wife and your daughter. I need the make and model of her car, and I need pictures, phone numbers, and addresses for her family. Where do most of her family live?"

"Nebraska."

"That might be too obvious and too far to drive with a toddler, and she is going to have to stay in the car. The minute she tried to board a plane, the jig would be up. Unless…how much money did she get out of your account?"

"About ten grand."

"That's not a whole lot. Chartering a plane would take half her money and most private companies she'd have access to don't go that far. How bad is her habit?"

"Bad and getting worse I would imagine."

"Then she is going to run out of money pretty quick."

Ten grand was a whole lot to me, but I guess when you're buying a place to stay every night plus gas, food, and a steady supply of drugs. Christ, Ava was probably in the car when she was buying drugs.

"I know what you're thinking, Ray. I'll find her, and I'll find her quick. She's been on the road almost a month. That is perfect. She's going to be cash poor, and she's going start leaving a trail. I don't need much."

I did not feel better. My hands were shaking.

"My wife is smart and judicious with money Mr. Cianci. She will stretch that ten grand to the limit."

"Noted. Then she's smart enough to seek out under-the-table employment, the kind where the kid can be with her while she does it. That will limit her opportunities. And Ray, don't be entirely surprised if she comes back to you. She may run out of options and hope that a month without your family put the idea of rehab out of your mind."

I'd considered this.

"What would you do if that happened Mr. Cianci?"

"I wouldn't send her to rehab. Send me that information. I'll be in touch."

No, I didn't imagine he would, but I didn't want to imagine what Tom Cianci viewed as an alternative either.

My phone lit up again. This time it was Rita.

"Hello, Ms. Rita. What are you up to today?"

"Furniture dear. I am driving to the shore. I realized how fast September was going to get here and I had a question for you. Actually, I have two requests of you."

Rita sounded much more like herself. Clearly, she was throwing herself back into work for the time being.

"OK, shoot."

"First, I want you to come with us when we bring Jenna to Duke. We'll need your truck, and Jenna—we—need you there with us. We want you there with us."

"Of course. I planned on being there."

"Wonderful. That's settled. Secondly, I'm going to need you to get Candace out of jail."

My adrenaline dumped. All I could think was what might have happened and whether or not it had anything to do with Rob.

"What? How?"

"Well, I don't know for sure," said Rita, "but I have two missed calls from the Carthage detention center on my phone, and I have not seen Candace or her car since I turned in last night. You might want to check your phone."

"I don't have a voicemail from her."

"I didn't have one either, dear, but I have two missed calls from the wee hours of the morning, and the woman stays intoxicated. Certainly, she would have called you first. Perhaps you were intoxicated too."

Rob, your mom is a bitch.

"I don't blame either of you if you were, but I have a business to run here. Please liberate the harlot and call me when you know what happened."

"Will do."

Rita had a point. Candace was a mess when last I saw her, and if this had anything to do with Rob, there would have been a voicemail, and it would have come from Detective Spruill. I checked my phone…no missed calls. I didn't bother calling the detention center. I just got in the truck and headed to Carthage.

***

Rick Rhyne met me at the door of the detention center.

"Yeah, she's here. We found her passed out in her car near the dam of Lake Auman in Seven Lakes West. When she woke, she said she had wanted to watch the sunset. It was 5:30 a.m."

"Maybe she meant sunrise," I suggested.

"Maybe she was still drunk out of her mind," Rhyne countered.

"Well, that's how she was when last I saw her."

"We're not going to charge her. She's been through enough, but we did want to scare the life out of her."

"I'll play along and try to set her straight. Thanks, Rick."

I waited in my truck. Candace stumbled out the door looking like Courtney Love after a night on the strip—eye make-up mottled and running, hair in severe disarray. She settled in the passenger side and slammed the door.

"Don't judge me, Ray. You've been lodged in a bottle for a month." She finished this statement with an exasperated sigh of stale, whiskey-tainted morning breath.

"You're welcome. Should our first stop this morning be the VanCamp law firm?"

"They did not issue me a citation, and besides, it's Sunday. Where's Rita?"

"On her way to the beach."

"Bitch," Candace said with another sigh.

"Candace, can I ask you a question?"

She looked at me like she anticipated some wicked smart-assery to come next. "Nope, not yet honey. Give me a moment."

"Why did you call Rita?"

She stared out the windshield and seemed to deflate.

"Because we seemed to be on the same page as of late. It was nice. I thought she might actually understand and hold her tongue for at least a while. I expected there would be a lecture this morning, and then maybe a drive, some lunch, some talking."

I nodded.

"You're wondering why I didn't call you. The truth is Ray, I figured that you would be either passed out or incapable of driving."

You figured right, but that's not going to inspire me to be any less vicious with this next line of questioning.

"One more question."

Candace turned her careless gaze back out the windshield.

"What?"

"Are you still banging Eugene Sawyer?"

Her mouth dropped open as she slowly turned to me while retreating closer to the passenger-side door. I could see the wheels turning, her computer rebooting and running through the available countermeasures like the Terminator—Response: defensive anger with accusations of an equally personal nature.

"What the hell, Ray? Are you out of your mind? Have you killed your last remaining brain cells with your daily dose of Bushmills—yes, I know you switched to the hard stuff—I just buried my husband…"

The truck came to a screeching, smoking halt in the middle of Dowd Road.

"Shut your damn mouth. Shut it!" It was as if something had taken control of my body— a pent-up rage virus that finally found an open window. Candace visibly shrunk before me.

"We didn't bury anything Candace! Rob is still lying on a medical examiner's slab, beat to death! Everyone knows you slept around. Everyone! I am simply asking if you also mounted Eugene. Don't you realize that all of your affairs are now suspects? And you what? You want to look at me aghast like I've offended your dignity as a lady? Answer the question!"

"Yes," she said in little more than a whisper.

I continued to yell, but I put the truck back in gear and continued down the road.

"Yes, what? 'Yes' you mounted him or 'yes' you're still mounting him?"

"It's over. It's been over."

"Who ended it?"

"I did. He was falling in love with me, but I loved Rob."

I began to speak like a normal human again, but the virus was still very much there.

Candace gently wept in her little corner of the truck.

"Yeah. It showed. You know, I used to tell Rob that you loved him. I told that to Jenna too. I told that to Spruill as well. I explained your extra-curricular activities as an insatiable need to feel young and pretty. Do you know Rob was about to leave you?"

She looked up at me, not shocked, but wounded and leaking.

"Wh-what? How do you know that? How could you know that?"

"He left me a letter. In it, he described a day when all the craziness ended, a day when he and Jenna and me and Ava could all sit on the porch and enjoy each other's company without any wives. What does that tell you?"

"That could mean anything—a father-daughter day, something."

"No Candace. It meant that he had reached his limit. It meant that the hurt finally outweighed the love."

Candace said nothing for the rest of the trip. There were no more tears. She merely stared out at the passing tobacco fields. When I pulled into the driveway, she exited without a word and jogged to the front door.

12
Watch and Learn

One half of Route 73 exited West End in an easterly direction, away from the deceased Stanley Furniture Plant. Not even a mile from the stop light, on the left, was a field of tired-looking, extremely-used cars, trucks, and public service vehicles that were "reconditioned and ready for their second life." Sitting among them was Detective Howard Spruill in his unmarked police cruiser, his gaze trained on Eugene Sawyer's home across the street.

Howard just didn't like Eugene's look during the memorial service. He was uncomfortable—a different kind of uncomfortable, a distressed kind of comfortable as if something in the church was actively causing him anxiety. Then there was that fixed stare of his. It wasn't right.

Howard thought the likelihood of Eugene being involved in Rob Erwin's death was slim. Rob handled all the complicated aspects of the construction business. Eugene simply handled the site logistics and the actual construction. He made a damn fine living at it. The intervening factor, though, Mrs. Erwin. Eugene Sawyer was a good-looking young man, and Howard could imagine that Candace was difficult to resist. If an affair had happened, well then that complicated things, and Howard's job was to sort out every possibility. He was bored. He was tired, but he needed a win. The county's opioid problem was still a problem. Now, of all things, heroin was making a comeback. Spruill's office had little in the way of investigative leads. Thus, he sat in his cruiser car staring across Route 73 at the porch of an admirably-remodeled 1950s-era home. He wasn't bored for long, and that was because Ray McCarthy was a pain in the ass who didn't listen. Howard got out of his nondescript Dodge quickly.

***

The plan was to go home and send Tom Cianci all the info he needed. Then I had to appease my publisher by constructing an outline of the book I had promised. Those folks were aware of Ava's disappearance, and so they had cut me some slack. They published a collection of my short works under the condition that I deliver a novel inside the following year. They were getting nervous.

What had I done instead? Well, I wanted to get in Eugene Sawyer's face before anyone else. I wanted to look into his eyes and see for myself what had happened between him and Candace. I wanted to do it before Candace succumbed to anxiety and coached him with a script. So, at this moment, I was striding across Eugene's lawn toward his plank-board front porch. The door was open, and I didn't knock.

Eugene was an unkempt hulk sitting at his kitchen table dissecting a carburetor for a late '70s Camaro, the one sitting in his barn going on three years now. Beside him was a Mason jar of what turned out to be Mountain Dew and rum. He looked up in surprise, and then resignation quickly set in as he turned his attention back to the carburetor.

"Hello, Mr. Ray."

"You don't look too surprised to see me."

"I haven't been answering my phone. I figured sooner or later someone would come calling. Didn't expect it to be you though."

"Are you OK Eugene?"

"No."

"Employment worries?"

He looked at me like I was insane and then resumed control over his facial features.

"No, Mr. Ray," He exhaled. "Someone will buy Rob's business when Ms. Rita gets tired of runnin' it herself, and it runs like clockwork. I expect whoever does buy it will keep everyone in place for just that reason. I was Rob's friend; though I'm not sure I deserved to be."

"Is this about Candace?"

Eugene looked up from his carburetor again, and his face fell. He didn't look scared, or anxious, or even resigned. He just looked sad and a little ashamed.

"I guess I shouldn't be surprised that you know about that. Did Rob know?"

"Eugene, Rob knew about Candace's affairs, but I don't think he knew you were one of them. I won't lie to you; it would have hurt his heart. Still, though, I wouldn't get too down on yourself about that in particular. Candace's genitalia is like the Bermuda Triangle. People get abducted into it and are rarely seen again. I do have to ask you some more serious questions."

Eugene winced and then nodded his head in the affirmative.

"Who broke off the affair between you two?"

"I did. I couldn't take the guilt anymore."

And I actually believe you big man. You look like shit.

"Were you in love with Candace?"

Eugene seemed to consider this for a moment.

"I think there was a chance of that, yeah, but that only made me feel worse. So, I told Candace that I was going to come clean to Rob. She did not like that idea, but she told me to do whatever I thought was right. Then she told me to go to hell even though I told her I'd take all the blame."

Rob knew whom to blame, Eugene.

"Did you go see him?"

"I did, but I never got to tell him a thing. And then the next day he was dead."

"Wait! What? You went to see him the night before he died?"

"Jenna let me in and led me down to the lake. Rob was fiddling with the boat. We shot the bull about boats, fishing, football, nonsense like that. He could tell I was nervous, and so he finally asked what was really on my mind. I got up off the boat and walked about the little dock while Rob tied a lure on to one of his fishing poles. He let me work my way up to it, but I never got it out. I got as far as 'I need to talk to you about Candace…'"

"And then what?" I was on the edge of my seat.

"Then I saw the look on Rob's face. He looked confused and concerned, but he wasn't looking at me. He was looking over my shoulder."

"And?"

"And then lights out. Nothing. I turned to see what the hell he was looking at, and somebody clocked me over the back of my skull somethin' fierce."

"Excuse me gentleman, but I figured it was time to stop eavesdropping and to start being a part of the conversation."

Eugene and I both flinched like adolescent boys caught with a Playboy magazine. We looked in disbelief at Detective Howard Spruill.

"Jesus, Spruill. You just scared the life out of us; how very Scooby Doo. What are you doing here?"

Spruill surveyed us with his hands on his hips as if he were about to commence a lecture.

"The bigger question is what the hell you think you're doing here Ray? Hold your response. I'd much rather hear Mr. Sawyer's narrative."

Fear descended on Eugene. No doubt that this was the conversation he'd been attempting to avoid, permanently.

"There's nothing much more to tell," stammered Eugene. "I was out. I woke up. The house was dark and the boat was gone. I figured Candace came home, saw what was happening and cracked me over the head. Then she and Rob had it out, or made up, on the boat and were giving me a chance to leave."

"What time was that?" asked Spruill.

"The clock in the truck said 10 p.m. I had gotten there while there was still a good deal of light in the sky, about 8:30 I guess. Rob and I bullshitted for most of an hour before I worked up the courage to say why I was there."

"Then I can tell you it wasn't Candace," said Spruill. "Her cell phone pings put her in Southern Pines until midnight. Her cell records say she called the office of Art Blue in Carthage twice: once at 9 p.m. and again at 9:46 p.m.

"Leaving a message for the county's most notorious divorce attorney because of what she feared would come next," I chimed in, "and probably did so rambling drunk."

"She did," said Spruill. "I've listened to the message. Mr. Sawyer, put some shoes on. You're coming with me to give a formal statement. You will cooperate in every way imaginable in the hope of skirting an obstruction charge. Are we clear?"

"Yes, sir."

Eugene stood up, nodded at us, and then strode out of the room, scrambling to tuck in his shirt as he went. I turned to Spruill.

"I believe him."

"I don't care, Ray. You can research whatever you want, but you will stay away from my potential suspects and/or witnesses. You will screw this up regardless of how smart you think you are. There is a reason I don't write books, and there is a reason you don't wear a badge. Are you and I clear?"

"Yes."

"Good. I believe him too. The medical examiner's report is complete. Rob died of blunt force trauma—his skull is broken. Also, his ribs are broken and his left lung is collapsed. His knee cap is broken and so was his left forearm. He was dead before he entered the water. The time of death matches up pretty well with what Mr. Sawyer just said. Is Eugene big enough to do that kind of damage? Probably, and that's one reason I believe him."

I stood silent for a moment. I was too caught up in the list of injuries. My harmless, wonderful friend had been absolutely dismantled from head to toe, and it sounded as if dumping him in the water was only insult to injury. When finally I tried to speak, my voice cracked, and I had to clear my throat.

"I…I don't understand what you said…that you believe him because he's huge." Spruill nodded as if he expected this question.

"It's because a weapon was used, something resembling a police baton. Eugene would not need a weapon to beat on someone, and he would not need friends. The bruises on Rob's solar plexus and his lower back are from strikes; so are the ones on his face, feet, and hands of different sizes. Rob faced multiple opponents and did so for more than a few minutes. That's probably why they finally cracked him over the head a few times with the baton; he wouldn't go down. I'm going to guess that said baton is also what was used to take out Eugene."

"They thought he'd be alone," I said as if I were quietly talking to myself. "Rob spotted them, so they were committed to following through. They took out the behemoth before he complicated everything."

"I sure as hell would have," continued Spruill. "Plus, Eugene just said

Rob's daughter led him down to the lake. I doubt he would have allowed anyone to see him if his intentions were to harm your friend."

"Do you think Candace sent a small army of assholes to convince Rob to either rethink divorce or maybe write a large check?"

"That's really what I want Eugene to help me sort out. I've spoken to Jenna. She's the one who confirmed that Eugene paid the house a visit, but that's about all she was able to do thanks to the concert she was listening to on her tablet. Anything you want to tell me, Ray?"

"Yes. I would never have believed it, but I think Rob might have been considering divorce over a month ago. His Uncle Jim gave me a letter. Last month Rob found some stuff we had as kids, and he was holding it for a special occasion. The letter mentions a time when he and I could sit down and enjoy life without wives."

"Is Uncle Jim the older man with the crew cut who escorted Rob's mom through the memorial?"

"Yes. He's more of a family friend, but Rob and I both call him 'Uncle.'"

"Scan the letter to me. If you want to help, Ray. Come up with a list of names—guys Candace had an affair with and their friends. Look into old acquaintances from her childhood. She grew up here right?"

"She did, in Robbins."

"Good. Let's see if there's a group of yahoos that would do damn near anything for their good-looking friend. I'll cross-reference your list with what I get out of Eugene."

Eugene stepped tentatively back into our presence, and Spruill escorted him to the unmarked cruiser I locked up the house for Eugene. There wasn't much more dysfunction I could take or that I could cram into one day. It was time to decompress.

Then the dreams would come. The dreams always came, and they hurt.

13
On the Road Again

Ava McCarthy sat dozing in her car seat. It was hot. She wanted to go back to the cabin where sometimes the air conditioning worked. It was almost dark, and it was bath time, but they were driving. Mommy's back hurt, and she was looking for her medicine.

Last night they had slept in the car. Mommy was tired and was just going to rest her eyes, but then it was morning. Ava had wet her car seat because she wasn't wearing a nighttime pull-up. She could never wake herself up to go to the potty. Even if she could, she would never get out of the car at night. Hopefully, Mommy would make it back to the cabin tonight, and maybe they could cook.

Littering the seat was every plush toy character from *The Secret Life of Pets*. That's what came with Happy Meals. Ava was tired of chicken nuggets and frenchy fries. Tired, and she missed her daddy.

She didn't understand why they were on bah-cation without him. She didn't understand why bah-cation had gone on for so long, or why they did not talk to Daddy on the Facetime. That's what they always did when he was away. There had been no hugs, no squeezies, no ugga-muggas, nothing. Maybe Daddy was lost and couldn't find them? Maybe Daddy needed help.

Ava let herself drift into sleep. There she could see Daddy. She would call him and show him the way.

Please come, Daddy…Mommy needs help…Ava needs help…please come….

***

We were playing hide and seek, and it was the worst game of hide and seek ever. Ava counted with her eyes open, watching where I tried to run off to hide. When she hid, she called out or tried to whistle to lure me to the spot. She loved to be found. This time she had asked me to count extra-long, and the result was that she made a magnificent shelter to hide in by tucking one end of a blanket into the dresser drawer and the other end between the mattresses of the bed. Inside she had barricaded herself with the obscene number of decorative pillows that adorned the master bedroom.

I entered the room, and she giggled.

"I hear you."

Instead of running to her, I entered the master bath and looked in the tub, and then the closet. I opened bathroom drawers and cabinets.

"I know you are here, lady!"

The giggling got louder. Apparently, I was taking too long, because the next thing I heard was...

"Please come, Daddy."

I ran into the bedroom and burrowed my head under the tent and through the pillows. There she was, blonde and disheveled as usual, and giggling madly.

"Ah-ha! I have found you, monkey."

Ava cupped my face in her hands and looked me in the eye. She put her forehead to mine.

"Daddy. Don't wait too long to get me."

***

Tom Cianci negotiated the last stretch of Henry street and came to a stop in front of the Carnegie Library in Savannah, Georgia. He studied the short flight of steep steps to an entrance flanked on either side by wall-mounted, bulbous lanterns and found the Prairie-style architecture incongruous with the rest of Savannah.

"This looks like a police station and is named after a deli," said Tom aloud to no one.

He quickly pulled up his research on his phone. He was definitely in the right place. Opened in the early 1900s by a handful of African-American men using their personal collections of books, the staircase Tom was looking at was the main entrance to Carnegie and led to the second floor—which is where he needed to go.

Tom approached the front desk to find a pleasantly-attractive woman in her thirties managing it.

"Hello, Ms.…ah…"

"Abeni," she said, "Abeni Wallace. To whom am I speaking?"

Tom placed a hand on his chest and bowed slightly forward.

"I am Thomas Cianci, Ms. Wallace, Tom if you will. I need some assistance. Do you remember a woman with a little girl, both Caucasian and both blonde? The little girl had a tablet. Not long after their visit, the police showed up."

"Oh, yes, but we've all been interviewed by officers already."

"I know," said Tom. "I know everything the police know, and that information led to nothing but a brick wall."

"Who are you?" asked Abeni.

"I'm what you'd call a private investigator hired by the family. Morgan is the mom's name. The little one is…"

"Ava," said Abeni. "She introduced herself. Mom did not look pleased."

"That's correct."

"She led me all over the library wanting to look at stuff. It was a quiet afternoon so I indulged her. Her mother was all over the place."

"Was she on a computer?"

"Yes."

"Do you remember which one? And how far do the browser histories go back?"

"Oh, we don't save the browser histories. Plus, they were here weeks ago. Even if the histories were saved, it would be like searching through a pile of trash for a diamond."

"Did she use a terminal that searches the catalog?"

"Yes, sir. But that doesn't save a search history either."

"Ms. Wallace, I'm hoping you can show me what parts of the library they visited—not everywhere Ava dragged you, but the places where you encountered Mom."

"Yes, it was only two places. Is Ava okay?"

Tom had no qualms with sharing information with someone who was sharing with him. Also, it never hurt to intrigue a source so that they were invested in the story.

"For now, she is. Mom is holding it together. For how much longer, no one knows. Mom's got a problem, and she's trying to fix it herself rather than use professional help. I wanna find her and take her home before the cops do."

Abeni nodded slowly. "Come with me," she said.

Tom followed the young lady to the children's section.

"This is where I found her first. She had pulled some books for Ava and sat her down at a table. Then Mom went back over this direction. She was doing a lot of hard looking and seemed to know her way around the library. Ava said they were on vacation, though, and so I thought it was unusual where I saw Mom next."

Abeni stopped five aisles down from the children's area in what looked to be a reference section.

"It makes sense to me Ms. Wallace."

"Not to me. You could pull up a lot of this on your phone."

"Not unless you want to be found," said Tom. "She got rid of her smartphone for the same reason she stayed off your computer. Only place she messed up is letting the kid on that tablet. Ava stumbled on to the internet just by opening Mom's messenger application. Phones ping off towers—the nearest one—and the location is recorded. Probably Morgan was digitally paranoid about leaving a trail on your computers too, or she thought the temptation to check social media would be too great."

Tom looked over the shelves: *Fifty States Fifty Ideas*, *National Geographic Road Atlas 2015*, *National Geographic Road Atlas RV and Camping Edition*. Tom looked to the upper shelf and saw all the Fodor's travel guides: *Alabama*, *Belize*, *Colorado*, *England*, *Essential France*…

"Ms. Wallace?" asked Tom. "You guys are this close to Disney and don't have a travel guide for Florida?"

"Let me go search the catalogue."

She returned a few moments later, her brow furrowed.

"We have a Fodor travel guide for Florida, or we are supposed to. It's not checked out."

"Morgan could not check it out because she is not a local resident," said Tom. "Let's just make sure it's not tucked in the wrong place. These books get checked out much?"

"No. The Florida one has not been checked out for over a year."

"You see many people looking at these shelves?"

"No, and the ones I do see here are much older."

"That's because us old folks made our money and wanna travel, dear," Tom smiled. "Thanks for your help Ms. Wallace."

Tom patted her on the shoulder and made his way to the exit. He fired up his Lincoln and used the Bluetooth to call Ray.

***

The phone rang obnoxiously loud. It was loud because it was tucked directly under my ear in the little gap between the pillow and the bed. I managed to sleep in my own bed, but I had done it in my clothes. I picked up the phone. It was 10 a.m.

"Hello, Ray."

Brooklyn was on the line.

"Hello, Tom. Are you on the move?"

"Yes, young man, I am, and thank you for sending the info I requested so quickly. I am at the Carnegie Library. "

I wondered what Tom Cianci could have possibly found that the authorities missed, but I also had a feeling that Tom did not get this far into old age without being one step ahead of everyone else, even when everyone else had a head start.

"I saw what I expected to see."

"What was that?"

"A concentrated search for cheap places to lay low. Morgan was studying atlases and walked off with a travel guide for Florida. I'm going to focus on trailer parks and campgrounds. Trailers and cabins rent cheap, and they have kitchens of course. Your wife will think that is more cost-effective at first, and people on the run gradually step down their accommodations. She will end up in a campground if this goes on much longer. Trailer parks and campgrounds usually have some menial labor opportunities as well."

"Do you think my daughter is safe?" There was a long pause.

"I think it depends on how advanced your wife's addiction has gotten. Your wife appears to be an educated and pragmatic woman, even though she left you on impulse. If she did not care about your daughter, she would not have taken her, so she will make her safety a priority. However, don't forget about the impulse part of this story. That impulse was one of fear and desperation, and that impulse only gets worse as the money runs out and as the monkey on her back gets bigger."

"The monkey will eventually be the priority." I said.

"That's how it's gonna go, but it will take some time. In a few days, I'll be only a step or two behind her. In fact, I might be able to do better than that. What is your wife into pop-culture-wise? And what are Ava's favorite cartoons and Disney characters?"

"What's this about Tom?"

"Aliases, my boy, aliases."

People say hope is a wonderful thing, but I would counter that. I would argue that hope is a dangerous thing. Hope is like a pedestal, and when things fall apart, the crash to the ground is infinitely harder. I couldn't help it though. I needed to believe in Tom. I did believe in Tom, and so I put all of my emotional eggs in his basket.

"I'll be waiting for your call," I said.

"Do more than that. Figure out how you want to handle the pick-up. You'll have to do it unless you want me to tip off the authorities so they can rush in. They'll have to be called anyway, but it might be better if Ms. Ava could run right to Daddy."

Daddy. Don't wait too long to get me.

"I'll be there."

"Good man. Talk to you soon."

14
Take a Look at Me Now

My runs had always started between 6 and 6:30 a.m. I was uncertain what would happen at 10:20 a.m., and I wondered if my window of slippage was confined to the early morning. By the time I hung up with Tom, got dressed, and shuffle-jogged out of the cul-de-sac, it was almost 11 a.m. My pace quickened across the dam. I saw the shimmer; the weightlessness ensued; and then I blasted into a bygone era at a blistering pace.

I was anxious after crossing the Lake Echo dam. It looked to be closer to 3 p.m. in 1984—the hottest part of the day, and I had not seen a soul. I scaled the hill where Firetree Lane intersects Overlook Drive. Overlook horseshoes around and intersects Firetree twice. About 100 yards from the second intersection sat Rob's 1984 home. The wooded lot next to it was where he would build his dream house in 2010. He had a nice view of tiny Sequoia Island and its faux lighthouse. As I passed the first intersection, I looked into Overlook and saw my reflection, a Blue Devil basketball jersey and silver running shorts. It was when I descended to the Longleaf dam that I glimpsed them. Arden and Rob side-by-side with towels slung over their shoulders.

The pool. They're going to the pool.

I guess I was going to find out if I could join in. There quite simply was no reason not to try. Who knew how long this anomaly would last, and what would it matter if I was bounced to the asphalt in front of my friends? I could hear the tail end of Rob and Arden's conversation as I approached, and of course, Arden knew I was there.

"I don't know. I called him. Maybe he's there already," said Rob.

"Or maybe he's galloping up behind us as usual," said Arden. He turned and walked backward to offer me that toothy, knowing grin. Rob looked over his shoulder and lit up.

"There you are! I've been looking for you all day. Dad cut a piece of PVC pipe for the capsule, and I've capped one end. I already put the *Ghostbusters* tickets in. Now we each have to put in something personal, and then we write our letters. Man, wasn't that movie awesome?"

"It's right here, Ray. It's looking at me," Arden recited and then cackled with delight.

Rob chimed in next.

"Ray, when someone asks you if you're a god, you say 'yes'!"

Then I couldn't help myself from letting loose my own favorite *Ghostbusters* quote.

"We came. We saw. We kicked its ass!"

We all burst into laughter on that one. All at once I had an overwhelming desire to stay here, to never leave the summer of 1984, and to see how time progressed. I would do it all over again with the knowledge of what was to come.

We began scaling the short, hilly driveway to the pool. I took a few tentative steps and winced…nothing happened. I just kept walking. There was a short tunnel of hallway that funneled us to the pool. I braced myself again to be bounced out, and then I heard the shriek of the whistle as the cacophony of raucous children enveloped us.

"Adult swim is over! Perfect timing," said Rob. "Dude, where's your towel?"

"I don't need one," I said as I signed Arden in as my brother in front of a disinterested lifeguard with permed hair and a mouthful of Bubblicious gum. "It's a hundred degrees outside."

"Yupper," said Arden. "We'll have to play Four Square in our sneakers if we want to keep the skin on our feet."

We stepped quickly toward two unoccupied lounge chairs with striped, faded cushions and began peeling off our shirts. A radio was playing, and the familiar voice of Phil Collins drifted toward us.

How can I just let you walk away?

Just let you leave without a trace?

When I stand here taking every breath with you, ooh…ooh

You're the only one who really knew me at all….

"I love this song," said Rob.

"Good night!" exclaimed Arden with disgust. "You are such a woman. How can you listen to this sappy crap? "

"I don't know. I kind of like it," I said.

Arden gaped at me.

"You? The guy who listens to Rush? You're kidding me. Both of you need to come over to my house and listen to Iron Maiden before you grow lady parts. We'll shoot the compound bow at the fake deer in the backyard. That'll fix you. Oh, and speaking of lady parts…"

Arden gestured over my shoulder. I turned and found myself speechless.

She was at least two or three inches taller than me—and maybe a year older. She was one beautiful, slender line up to her sharp chin and her dark, slicked-back hair that fell to her shoulders. No one should be that pretty at age thirteen. She broke into a smile as she approached me. I just stared into her green eyes, expressionless, because composed, forty-something Ray had departed, and there was nothing left but an adolescent boy, helpless and enamored. Olivia. Olivia Allen was the first girl I ever fell for, and the image of her advancing toward me in that swimsuit had held a place of reverence in my mind for thirty-two years.

So take a look at me now

Well there's just an empty space

And there's nothing left here to remind me

Just the memory of your face…

Arden's voice brought me back,

"Come in Ray. Over? I think we've lost him, Rob."

Then Rob was by my side whispering something that I had always said to him.

"It's just a girl, Ray," he smiled, "Just a little girl."

Olivia stood before me and planted her hands on her hips.

"How did you do in your track meet, Ray?"

"It's uh…There was no race today. I think qualifying is next week."

"Oh, then maybe we could catch a movie. I think *Ghostbusters* is playing."

"We saw—"

Rob interrupted me.

"Arden and I saw it. Ray is dying to see it. Hard to get up with him on the weekends in the summer—too many races, but I think he is free this evening, and I think my dad has to go into Southern Pines for a while. He could give you guys a lift."

Olivia enveloped her arm with mine and whispered in my ear. "I'd really like that. I think we should go."

Then she stood up straight and looked at Rob.

"I don't even have to ask my mom. As soon as I tell her I'll be with Ray and Colonel Ed, she'll be totally cool with whatever we do. Do you think your dad will be OK with that Rob?"

"Oh, yeah. Definitely. Like I said, he's goin' down there anyway to hang out at the Kiwanis Club for a while...plenty of time to see a movie."

"I guess we're seeing *Ghostbusters*," I said with a tight grin.

I did not remember seeing *Ghostbusters* twice. In fact, I didn't remember ever going on what amounted to a real date with Olivia. It seemed I was changing things without consciously trying to do so. This inspired both optimism and fear. I could end up changing things I did not want to change.

Is your life so stellar now? Would a total change be so bad?

I had a stellar daughter, and I wanted to see her again. I most certainly did not want to inadvertently erase her from existence, regardless of how slim that chance was.

"It'll be fun. You buy the tickets, and I will get the popcorn and the soda. Deal?"

"Deal." I found myself saying. There's a seven o'clock show—"

I heard an eruption of water as someone hoisted themselves out of the pool near to us. What followed was the slap of wet feet on cement approaching us and an obnoxious voice I knew all too well.

"What are you little turds up to today? Action figures? Building another fort in the woods?"

Scott Windham was the good-looking son of a doctor who lived on Lake Sequoia. His dad thought we were all buddies in spite of Scott being three years older than us. Truth be told, he was, and probably still is, a colossal, spoiled prick.

"No Scotty." Olivia took control. She always ran interference for us when it came to Scott, and she had a beautiful way of talking down to him that made you wonder who was older than whom. "Ray and I are going to see Ghostbusters. You will have to play all by yourself."

"It's Scott, and I thought you guys went to see *Ghostbusters* yesterday?"

Prick. My anger was rising, and I had to remind myself not to let my forty-four-year-old mouth write a check my current body could not cash. However, Arden decided to do it for me.

"Me and Rob saw it. It was awesome. You know as well as I do that Ray always has some race to go to in the summer. He's got real shit to do. You got time on your hands to ride your goofy Moped and bust down forts built by kids minding their own business."

Scott watched Arden warily. Arden was so tall it was hard to tell the age difference. And if Arden let loose his inner redneck, Scott knew there was a chance that Arden might very well whoop his pretty-boy ass. So, Scott slapped the shit out of me instead.

"What the hell?" exclaimed Arden.

I collapsed in a heap to the ground. It was a downward, open-handed strike that caught me flush on the cheekbone. Had it been a closed fist, I would have been unconscious. Rob struggled to hold Arden back. Olivia knelt beside me and held her hand to the side of my face. Dazed and confused as I was, I still felt all tingly being that close to her. It was quite amazing.

"You're a coward," yelled Arden.

"There's a price for everything fellas. You can't just run your mouths. I'll just slap the shithead closest to me."

A whistle shrieked.

"Language!" yelled a diminutive, feisty lifeguard as she rapidly descended her perch and marched toward us. She stepped right up to Scott and reached up to jab him in the chest with her finger.

"Scott, you're out of here for a week. I don't care who your daddy is."

"Hey, this guy got in my face."

As the cobwebs cleared, I stood up and realized he was pointing at me.

"Ray wasn't even looking in his direction," said Rob with a degree of urgency. "Ray wasn't even talking to him. Scott just slapped him for no reason."

"That's true," said Olivia.

She had entwined her arm with mine again, and I decided that I wasn't going to let young Ray go on a date with a completely bruised ego. I slipped my arm out from under hers and squared my shoulders to face Scott's smirking countenance. Then I drove my right shin straight up into his wet crotch, a direct hit.

"Ohhhh!" yelled Arden and Rob in unison.

"Those are some strong legs, Scotty," continued Arden. "That had to hurt. That hurt me just watchin' it."

It was Scott's turn to crumple to the concrete, and when he looked up at me, he offered a tight grimace of pain, but his eyes said there would be repercussions, awful repercussions. Olivia stuttered a few steps backward and put her hand over her mouth. I couldn't tell if she was horrified or stifling a grin.

"All of you stop. Ray, stand back. Scott, you deserved that and then some. You get out of here now."

A pair of Scott's pals jogged over to pick him up. One was a prissy-looking prep, the other wore a mullet and looked like an extra in the Patrick Swayze movie, *Roadhouse*. The trio stumbled away awkwardly, and I shifted my attention back to Olivia. It turned out that it was a grin she was stifling.

"Aren't you full of surprises?"

Arden and Rob brayed laughter.

"I think we need to celebrate this moment with a game of shark in the deep end," said Rob.

"Agreed," said Arden.

"Yes, I think so," said Olivia, holding her hand out for me to take it, and I did.

It had been decades since I played shark—essentially a game of tag. There was no other way I wanted to spend the afternoon. I trailed a step or two behind Olivia, my right hand in her left as we made our way behind the lifeguard stand. I did not register the significance of the shimmer or our reflection until it was too late.

I bounced off of nothing and was thrown to the ground. Olivia passed through a shimmer with Arden and Rob. No one seemed to notice what had happened, but then Olivia returned looking concerned.

"Ray! Ray, are you OK? What happened?"

"I think I hurt my ankle on Scott's balls. It just gave out. I should probably get some ice on it. It'll be OK."

Arden and Rob rushed back into view.

"What happened?" Rob asked.

"He hurt his ankle when he kicked Scott."

"That's not good," deadpanned Arden.

"Don't worry. I'll just go home and put ice on it."

"How are you going to do that?" asked Rob. "You're like two miles from home."

"Ah, Mom is home. I'll give her a call from the lifeguard office. It's not hurt badly." I stood up and looked at Olivia. "I'm still going to the movies."

She smiled.

"Let me help you to the office."

"No. No, I'm fine. Go play. You're the fastest swimmer. The game will suck without you."

"That's right," said Arden, "Walk it off like a man. He'll be fine. Come on."

Rob hesitated. I nodded and made a shooing gesture with my right hand. He and Arden disappeared again. Olivia didn't want to go.

"Olivia?" I called.

She cocked her head and raised an eyebrow, not knowing what to make of being called Ms.

"You're the prettiest girl I know."

She smiled broadly, strode over, and planted a quick kiss on my cheek.

"And you're the bravest guy I know. I'll see you in a few hours."

My face flushed. No, my body flushed. I could feel it. I turned and affected a slight limp toward the office, but then I diverted for the hallway to the outside. My house circa 2016 was much closer to the pool than the one in 1984. A quick run and the day's adventure would conclude. It turned out to be a very quick run because there was a price to pay for everything fella.

***

Scott Windham leaned against the back wall of the Landowner's Clubhouse, his right hand shoved down his damp shorts, cupping his balls slightly away from his body. His buddy Matt had pushed the Moped behind the clubhouse where it now leaned awkwardly behind an overgrown azalea just a foot away. That little shit had nailed him good, and everyone saw it. The only way to reestablish the pecking order was to issue a legendary beating that the kids would talk about for weeks.

It was a shame, really. He didn't mind Ray. In fact, he thought it was pretty cool to travel around the state just to race other kids.

Didn't matter, though. Couldn't put your hands on the man.

First Ray would go down; then Arden Miller would have to be dealt with because Arden would demand to be dealt with. Matt might be required for back-up on that one, though his availability in the summer was sketchy. He seemed always to get sucked into watching his drunken neighbor's kid. Rednecks, they were all the same. Of course, Chris would be of no use in a fight with his matching Izod shirt and tennis shorts.

Scott peered around the corner of the clubhouse just in time to see Ray break into a jog across the parking lot and down the grassy hill to Firetree Lane. Perfect. He rolled the Moped from behind the azalea and mounted it gingerly.

***

I was around the bend and well down Firetree Lane when I heard the unmistakable whine of the Puch two-speed engine.

Scott Windham was coming to beat my ass.

Last I knew, Mopeds had a top speed of thirty miles an hour on level terrain. The stretch of Firetree Lane I needed to cover was mostly level. I guessed that I had about a 250-yard lead, and I knew that my top speed when running a mile or more was between nine and ten miles an hour—my mother had paced me across the dam once in the station wagon. All this meant one thing: Scott would close the distance between us relatively quickly. How quickly I had no idea because I didn't know exactly how far it was to Cherokee Trail and because I suck at math.

So, the answer was to haul ass. My speed doubled almost instantly. Young Ray's heart thundered in his chest. His leg turnover was astounding. Was I really this fast once upon a time? The whine drew closer, and something dawned on me: the last 100-yard stretch of Firetree that I needed to cover was downhill. If I could maintain a respectable distance from Scott until then, I'd hit the downhill before him and shoot into 2016 untouched. Scott would continue across Sequoia dam circa 1984.

A dump of adrenaline—once expended—would leave you exhausted. So really the trick was to be used to it, to manage it, and to milk it for all it was worth until it left you useless. The whine drew closer. I looked over my shoulder to see Scott was already around the bend and fifty yards closer.

"I want you to know I'm coming, Ray. I want you to see me and think about what's gonna happen."

After a year of racing—and luckily for both of us—young Ray could very much manage his adrenaline, and he probably did it better than old Ray. I knew this because my legs got faster, and they stayed faster. I could see the downhill portion of Firetree just yards away. I would lean forward, gallop down the hill, and turn like I was on rails into Cherokee Trail.

Another glance over my shoulder revealed Scott to be within 100 yards of me. He was grinning, and then his voice seemed very loud.

"Keep looking you little shit. It's going to happen. I think your track season might be over."

I tipped over the hill and my stride became inordinately longer as I leaned forward and took full advantage of gravity. I felt the nausea, the weightlessness. More than ever before it felt like I was on a roller coaster. I focused on the street sign that said Cherokee. Scott was saying something else at the top of the hill, but his voice was fading out. I whipped around the corner through the shimmer and collapsed to the ground in 2016.

***

"Keep looking you little shit. It's going to happen. I think your track season might be over."

It was the second time Ray looked over his shoulder. He was scared, and he should be, but he wasn't slowing down.

The plan was to catch him right at the beginning of the dam. He would push Ray off the right shoulder of the road down the steep grade to where no one would see. In fact, he would get off the Puch, lean it against the guardrail, and kick Ray the rest of the way down that embankment until he settled at the bottom. Then the beating would actually begin. Ray had just disappeared over the hill. Damn that kid was fast. He'd be exhausted by the time the first punches flew.

Scott came over the hill and saw…nothing. Ray was gone.

What, had he made the jump to light speed or something?

Chris hung a right on Cherokee…nothing.

He's in the woods. He's hiding in the woods.

Up and down Cherokee Scott drove, peering over the shoulder and into the brush.

"I know you didn't just disappear, Ray. I know you can hear me. It's only a matter of time before I see you again."

***

It took me ten full minutes to catch even a semblance of my breath. There I was, a full-grown man sprawled out in the middle of the road. Had someone come by, they would have called 911.

My first thought was that Ray would be looking over his shoulder until the end of the summer. A beat-up young Ray was not good for him, not good for me, and it was most certainly not good for Rob. If I hadn't had a physically capable younger version of myself to run around in, all would have been lost. I had to be there when the time capsule came together. I had to figure out how to send a message to Rob that he would see in May of 2016 and actually take seriously.

My second thought was that Scott Windham must have been cursing a blue streak right in 1984, and that made me laugh. Prick.

My final thought was of what had happened near the deep end of the pool. I had yet to figure out the rhyme or reason regarding what the anomaly allowed. I had learned that I had access only to structures bordering the three-mile loop, but that was apparently all I had figured out. The question was why there were limits to begin with? Either let me travel through time or don't.

Why surround me with an electric fence?

That night I dreamed, and for the first time it was not of Ava. I dreamed of a dark theater and stale popcorn. We sat in the middle of a long, center row of seats, Olivia's right hand in my left. I watched the movie, but I kept stealing glances at her upturned profile. I had made a new memory. The best part was at the end. That's when young Ray got his first real kiss.

15
The Barn

One thing Rita liked about North Carolina was the magnificent tobacco barns. To some degree they reminded her of Ed. In fact, she could picture him standing on one of those rough-hewn beams, smiling at her, his cigar held loosely in the corner of his mouth.

This particular barn was tucked away in a stand of long-leafs and was thus surrounded by a reddish- brown bed of pine straw. The barn was both tall and wide, with the base skirted on three sides by a slanted roof that made it look like it had a covered porch. The center of the building rose three stories, and so Jim had a second floor put in, removed some of the drying beams, varnished some of the others in a deep mahogany color, and added track lighting to them. The dirt floor was filled in with cement and painted a rich bronze. Though it had not held curing tobacco since the 1980s, Rita still picked up the faint scent of what smelled like raisins.

The building's width was mostly to the left in what appeared to be an addition but was nonetheless part of the original structure. Here was an additional 1,500 square feet of space for Rita to stage her furniture. Each nook had its own adjustable lightning so Rita could recreate a variety of outdoor entertainment scenarios to make her wares—Jim's wares—more inviting. It was half-ass joie de vivre, and it was unnecessary. Whether it was in the barn or on the truck, every piece sold in a matter of days. The work simply made Rita feel more essential to the process. It was a creative outlet which occupied her mind, and she needed occupation, needed it badly. Only a quarter of the shipment ever fit into the barn to be staged. The rest lingered in the tractor trailer outside to be fetched according to serial number by two strapping lads Jim had hired to flank her during the selling days. She was done with only the second staging when she heard tires coming up the gravel drive.

***

Christopher Sedgewick enjoyed a Sunday drive, especially when it involved the country and a fine European sedan. It sure beat the hell out of the charming-yet-congested town of Cary, North Carolina—a place many in the surrounding communities refer to as the "Yankee holding tank." After growing up in Pinehurst, Cary was a bit of an adjustment, but it was where his clientele lived, and it was where he needed to schmooze and network.

Most of Christopher's clientele were ex-northerners who worked in Research Triangle Park, and Chris's job was to install, repair, and monitor software that governed the operations of their respective companies. Whether it was human resources software for IBM or systems integration software for GlaxoSmithKline, Chris installed it, taught the supervisors how to use it, and made sure it continued to run properly, doing hot fixes and installing upgrades when necessary.

It was good money, but it wasn't real money. The guys who wrote the software made the real money. If he could get one of these companies to use a program he had actually written, his foot would be in the door and life would change dramatically. Until then, he would need supplemental income so he could continue to run and play with the big kids on the weekends. That was why he was navigating the back roads of Ellerbe, North Carolina in an aging BMW, chasing down a lead for an old friend.

The tree-lined drive seemed to go on for days, and it was not easy to find. There was no sign, just a considerable parting of flora and fauna and freshly limbed pines. Presumably so that the trailers would clear without issue. Finally, he saw it, a curing barn with a gooseneck lamp perched above a sign that read Abian Industries. As he came to a halt and stepped out, a woman in her seventies emerged with her hand shielding her eyes from the midday light. Chris lit an amiable smile and adorned it with a cordial wave of his hand.

"Hello there."

"Hello there yourself young man. Are you perhaps lost?"

She was a New Englander; he could hear it in her voice, so that was one thing confirmed.

"No...yes. Kind of. I lived around here once upon a time, but I guess I don't know my way around like I used too. I was just taking a Sunday drive. A friend of mine lives not far from here, but really I like to putter around into antique and pottery stores off the beaten path."

"Well, you and my husband would have gotten along just fine. If you want pottery, you need to be up in Seagrove."

"Oh, I was there this morning," said Chris. "Didn't see anything that called to me."

"Well, son, I'm afraid you've struck out here too. This isn't a store per se. I just house and stage furniture for vendors we supply."

"So, nothing's for sale?" Chris put on a weary, disappointed face.

"Not unless you have a resale license."

"Nope. Sure don't. I don't even know what you just said. That's a beautiful curing barn, though. May I have a look?"

She studied him for a moment and then broke into a grin. "Oh, what the hell; I'm not doing anything important anyway, and I might just get you to move a few pieces for me."

"Of course, lead the way."

Chris was entirely confused, but spending an hour with a pleasant old woman wasn't the worst way to kill an afternoon. He'd have a look-see, and then he'd make a phone call.

16
KOA

Tom had guessed that Mrs. McCarthy was more than halfway through the ten grand with which she had left home, and that and intuition was what governed most of his search. She was driving a Toyota Rav 4 which got almost thirty miles per gallon on the highway. However, that wouldn't determine gas-station stops so much as a fussy toddler's need to pee.

So, Tom focused on ultimate destinations, which was why in the passenger seat of his Lincoln sat a map of Kampgrounds of America sites, and he had zeroed in on one in St. Augustine, Florida.

Florida was not only the next logical stop; it was probably the critical stop. Money was now tight. Going any deeper into Florida painted them into a corner. Mom could no longer flee west toward family without backtracking—not that family would be much help. The gist Tom got from his phone conversation with Mrs. McCarthy's younger brother wasn't that family members were unwilling to help, just that they were incapable of helping and/or diverting attention from their own self-destructiveness. It sounded like addiction, in one form or another, ran in the family.

"I'm in between jobs right now, and my small place isn't really set up for kids. I don't need any more legal trouble. Truthfully, sir, I don't know where they are—didn't know they had left Ray. But even if I did know, I honestly would not tell you. What did you say she had again?"

Every liar he had ever met used a version of that turn of phrase, thought Tom—Honestly, Mr. C, I don't know where he went…Truthfully, I did loan him some cash Mr. Cianci, but I don't know where he got to…

Tom had brazenly identified himself as a private investigator pursuing a mother and her child out of concern for Mom's "considerable illness." Tom hadn't elaborated on the illness part. He was very clear, though, about the laws that she broke. The best he could hope for was that the brother would place a call and sell him out because that would put on the pressure, and then Mom would either make a mistake, or she'd tumble to the only sensible conclusion: go home. It was already on her mind; Tom knew it. She was already rehearsing a contrite plea for help.

Deducing whether or not she was telling the truth would be Ray's problem. Tom's problem was shooing her northward and catching up before the monkey on her back started making all the decisions.

The KOAs in St. Augustine, Daytona, and Wildwood all offered tiny cabins for rent, and according to Ray, Mrs. McCarthy wasn't a "tent-and-campfire kind of girl." But she would be, thought Tom, if she was on the run much longer. Even at the height of the season, the cabins were relatively cheap because those who frequented these campgrounds were enthusiasts who loved making use of their own expensive equipment. St. Augustine was closest, and it's where Tom believed Mom would have her epiphany.

He edged the Lincoln around the narrow circular drive toward a log cabin announcing itself as the General Store. He reached for the legal pad that rested beneath the map, and he flipped to the notes he had taken in Savannah.

***

Morgan McCarthy was still kicking herself over not remembering to ditch her phone for a prepaid Samsung and then absentmindedly allowing Ava to play on the tablet. Truth was she should have gotten rid of that too, but Ava would have thrown a fit. Morgan had to settle for leaving the tablet on airplane mode from now on and hoped it would not ping a tower and leave a trail. She had made only one long distance call on the Samsung—to her brother. He was the only relative that even remotely had himself together, and Morgan needed someone to keep her abreast of where Ray was poking around. Ray would poke around, and he would find her, which was fine.

It's not that she didn't love him, and this wasn't about breaking up their family. It was about keeping him from destroying her reputation in the community by shipping her off to a facility. It was about buying time. She knew there was a problem. She knew it when she woke up in the car and found Ava soaking wet in the car seat. She had never felt that low in her life, and yet she still had her pills. Nevertheless, she would fix this herself. If Ray was not willing to forgive her, so be it.

The Samsung tweeted out its minuscule ring. She pulled to the side of the road to answer it.

"Hello, sis. You want to tell me what is really going on now?"

"Does that mean you got a phone call, Bryan?"

"You bet it does."

"Well, go on and fill me in on the line of bullshit Ray fed you."

"It wasn't Ray. It was an older guy, and he had an accent…sounded like he was from New York."

Oh shit.

Morgan knew little about Ray's family, but she was aware that the bulk of them lived in New York and New Jersey and that some of them were NYPD detectives.

"He also said that he was concerned about you because you were suffering from an 'illness.' What is that about?"

"What it is is bullshit. It is one of Ray's detective uncles or cousins on a fishing expedition."

"OK, that's fine. Then I guess you wouldn't mind telling me the real reason you took off."

Morgan considered this for a moment. Denying and not supplying information was one thing, making up a story was quite another, and this was not Ray's fault—not really.

"It's complicated."

"I bet the hell it is. If you're not willing to throw Ray under the bus, then I think this is your deal and not his. I'm simple, but I'm not stupid, or are you calling me stupid?"

"You're not stupid."

"Just answer me this then: why did you take the man's child? Dear god, he could have forgiven almost anything but that. What the hell were you thinking?"

Those words stopped Morgan cold, and they flooded her with dread.

This whole thing had been a mistake, and Ava was the biggest part. It had been an impulse, and her brother was right.

Ray could have forgiven her running away, but she wasn't sure he would forgive this, and that changed things quite a bit.

"I...I was thinking that I'd miss her and I didn't know how long this would take. I couldn't..."

There was a long pause. Finally, her brother spoke.

"Whatever it is, it's bad isn't it? Trust me on this. Go home and roll the dice with Ray. I doubt this detective is the only one looking for you. There's probably an Amber Alert out. Every cop between North Carolina and wherever the hell you are is looking for Ava. All you did was multiply your problems. Go home and piece it back together."

"I'll consider that. Keep me posted on what you hear and see. Check the news and Facebook, Reddit, Twitter...anything that will help me conclude this on my terms."

"OK. I will call you in a day or so. Bye."

Somehow, she had to bring this across a finish line without losing her family. The most pressing thing at this moment, however, was that she needed to feed the monster. She ached all over. There was a persistent ringing in her ears. She was stepping down her dosage. Well, that had been forced upon her. Her doctor in Rockingham had given her one last prescription refill and a lecture. Inside of two weeks on the run, Morgan was once again out of pills.

This meant meeting with some deadbeat and buying more at fifteen bucks a pill. College kids always had pain pills. It was a matter of taking Ava to an affordable lunch at an on-campus bodega sans wedding ring. She was an attractive woman who could very easily pass for a part-time student. She would make a pretense of reading a worn copy *The Republic* by Plato and wait. Sometimes she was not approached. Many times she was. They all wanted more than cash. They wanted to party. All they got was cash. Morgan would have to beat this thing before she ran out of money.

This was the process, and it had to run its course. She looked in the rearview mirror to see that Ava was absorbed in conversation with her Supergirl doll.

"I'm sorry, honey," Morgan whispered.

***

Tom looked over his list. Ray had informed him that Ava was obsessed with all the Disney princesses, but her interest in Elsa and Anna had waned a bit. She was more focused on Rapunzel because she too had blonde hair. Then there was Sophia, Elena of Avalor, and Ava's renewed interest in the cartoon fish, Nemo and Dory. Tom figured using the name Rapunzel would be quite a stretch, so he focused on the other two possibilities. He was pretty sure he had Mom's alias figured out.

Tom got out of the Lincoln and strode into the general store to find a middle-aged clerk in a NASCAR T-shirt.

"What can I do for you old timer?" he drawled.

"Well," Tom tried to tone down his Brooklyn dialect, "You can help me make sure I'm in the right place. I go to so many of these damn places that I get turned around."

The clerk laughed as Tom made a show of patting himself down for his glasses. He slipped them on and then studied his phone. He would have to leave himself some breathing room in case he was wrong, and nobody got more leeway than a confused grandpa.

"I am looking for a Ms. Britney Jean and her daughter Sofia."

"Let me take a look here sir."

The clerk opened a file on his desktop PC and scanned it for a moment.

"I have a Britney, but I don't register kids. What exactly is this about?"

Tom exhaled in exasperated fashion as he removed his glasses and stuffed them in the pocket of his white silk camp shirt.

"Ah, Christ. I can't keep the names straight. Britney's my daughter, and the girl is my granddaughter. They're hiding out from that abusive prick that I never approved of her marrying. I'm here to pay them up for another couple of days."

Tom pulled a money-clipped wad of cash from his khaki trousers.

"I knew it had to be something like that," said the clerk, shaking his head. "Britney and her little girl always pay cash day-to-day. That's a cute kid. They sometimes help with delivering mail to the campsites."

"What's the daily rate for the cabin?" asked Tom.

"Seventy-five dollars a night."

Tom unclipped the cash and thumbed through the bills.

"Here's for the next few nights. Which one are they in?"

"They're in cabin F7, a one-roomer on the lake. What is your name, sir?"

"Tom. That's my actual name. My daughter's name is not Britney, and my granddaughter is not a Disney princess, but I'm not telling anyone their names. In fact, if anyone other than me comes looking for them, call me at this number."

The clerk looked momentarily confused, but Tom wasn't going to give him any time to process. He only grabbed the clerk's Post-it notepad and wrote down a number. Finally, the clerk nodded as Tom tore off the note and stuck it to the clerk's palm.

"There's not going to be any trouble here is there, Tom?"

"Not while I'm around. They'll be moving on soon. You go ahead and call me if they run short of cash too."

The clerk nodded again.

"My sister was in a bad marriage. Damn shame it was."

Tom nodded back and then abruptly turned and strode out of the general store. He slipped into the Lincoln and put it in gear.

The meandering rock drive toward the lake was flanked on both sides by occasional cabins of varying sizes. The drive began a downgrade that looped to the right, and Tom could see what he presumed to be cabin F7 at the edge of one of the lake's small coves. He pulled in to cabin F4, which looked dark and vacant. Tom and his Bruno Magli loafers would hoof it from here. His only intention was to have a closer look and confirm what he already knew, but sometimes opportunities presented themselves.

Mrs. McCarthy's place was indeed a log cabin with an AC unit poking out of a window and a small porch jutting out into the water. The porch swing appeared to be moving. As Tom got closer, he could see a gangly figure rocking back and forth.

"What exactly do we have here?" asked Tom aloud to himself.

When he got within fifty yards of the cabin's short driveway, he could see the kid's profile: he was relatively handsome and in his early twenties. He was sporting an undercut with a swoop of longer hair piled on top. The jeans were faded and too long, the T-shirt also faded—a washed-out pinkish red. There were too many bracelets on the arm he had resting on the back of the swing. Tom wondered for a moment if Mrs. McCarthy had found some entertainment to occupy her days on the lam. Then he tumbled to an entirely different idea. Tom wandered up the drive and began climbing the steps. The kid was instantly on his feet and appraising Tom. Tom slipped into the confused-old-man routine.

"Hello there, young fella."

The boy relaxed and smiled.

"Hello."

"I was wondering if I had the right place."

"Well, ah, I'm just waiting on someone. I don't actually stay here. I'm not sure I would be much help."

"Who are you waiting for?"

The boy's face began registering concern again.

"Ms. Britney. She's a friend of mine."

"Ms. Britney Jean?" asked Tom animatedly.

"Ah, yeah."

"Fantastic. That is who I'm looking for!" Tom continued to mount the steps while slipping his hand into his right trouser pocket, fumbling but finding what looked and felt like an electric razor.

"How do you know her?"

Tom crested the last step. The kid was as tall as he was. Perfect.

"I don't. I just keep getting her mail. I have some right here."

Tom feigned a slight trip and put his left hand on the boy's right clavicle. His right hand then swung from his pocket and buried the Taser in the left side of the kid's neck and pulled the trigger.

The boy seized up in a full-body Charley horse and collapsed to the ground, trembling lightly. Tom commenced rifling through the kid's pockets.

"Now I have a feeling kiddo that you and Ms. Britney are not actually good pals. I have a feeling that you are a delivery man. Am I right?"

The boy uttered what sounded like a combination of a gasp and a growl as he stared wide-eyed at Tom. There was a sealed envelope in the kid's right pocket. Tom pulled it out and waved it in front of the boy.

"Sealed but with no address. To whom do you mail such a letter? I think I will see."

Tom tore it open to find several pills wrapped in cellophane. They were white and cylindrical and looked like the ones the doctor prescribed him after knee surgery. He couldn't read the tiny letters stamped on the pills, but he could feel them, and he was pretty sure he had a handful of Vicodin—or, as the kids called 'em, Vikings. Tom got within inches of the boy's face a looked him straight in the eye.

"I'm going to guess that you don't have a prescription for these, and I'm going to guess Ms. Britney has not paid you for them. Guess what? You're not getting paid today, but you're also not going to get arrested? Sound good?"

The kid nodded.

"In a few minutes, most of the effects of that Taser will wear off. I'm not gonna lie. You're gonna be sore, but you will be fully capable of going about your business. Part of that business is never returning to this place and never contacting Ms. Britney. Nod if you understand."

The kid nodded enthusiastically.

"Good because next time you won't even see me coming."

Tom removed a pen from his pocket and scrawled a message on the envelope. The cabin had a screen door and a formal entry made of lacquered cedar. The door was locked as he expected it would be, and so he pinned the envelope to the door jamb by closing the screen door on it. With this bit of business concluded, Tom turned, stepped over the sprawled figure of the boy, and jogged down the steps. He would park the Lincoln at the convenience store across from the entrance to the campground. He would sip iced coffee, and he would wait.

17
The Subcontractor

Monday morning, I sat on my back deck and stared at a pair of deer finishing off the hostas that I had planted the first year I bought the place. They're resilient little plants. Hostas come back every year, and every year the deer eventually find them and end them. My feet were perched on the railing, and my laptop sat open to Facebook while uncomfortably warming my thighs. Slumped beside me on the deck was the latest edition of *The Pilot*, the local newspaper in Southern Pines. A picture of Rob dressed in a tuxedo stared back at me from above the fold, along with the headline:

Architect's Death Ruled Homicide

RALEIGH, June 13, 2016—*The North Carolina Chief Medical Examiner's office revealed that Robert Erwin of Seven Lakes North died of blunt force trauma to the head last Tuesday evening, though he sustained a litany of additional injuries.*

I remembered the picture. It had been taken at a charity ball. Smack in the middle of four intersecting PGA golf courses is a working harness track with a retired barn-turned-banquet facility. I think that night we were raising money for The Humane Society. The article was sketchy on the details, and the list of injuries was not as thorough as the one Detective Spruill had related to me. It did mention that because Rob had been tossed in the water, the collectible forensic evidence was minuscule and hopelessly deteriorated. I couldn't help thinking about the difference it might have made had Eugene gone straight to the cops that night, but I could "what if" myself all day. It would not change anything.

As a result of Rob's death and my daughter's disappearance, my voicemail was perpetually full of messages, and I no longer bothered to delete them and make room for more. I didn't realize I had so many friends and well-wishers. Granted, several of those voicemails were from my mother.

After the memorial, Mom flew to New York to spend time with my brother and his kids.

She just "couldn't walk by Ava's room anymore until this thing ended." Mom's guest room was filled with Ava's toys and was decked out in full princess regalia. I guess I could understand.

Unless I passed out there, I rarely went into Ava's room here at my house.

On my laptop, a picture of who I initially thought was Olivia Allen at age eighteen grinned at me. It turned out the photo was taken a month ago. Sylvia Lee was whom I had found, and her mother, Olivia Allen, had taken the picture. Olivia's Facebook page was rather nondescript except for a panoramic cover photo of Florida's gulf coast. There was no profile photo, just a lot of random pictures of Sylvia and a pair of enormous tabby cats.

She lived in Callaway, Florida, which was near Panama City, and the page listed her as working for Bay County Department of Social Services. That figured, I thought. A DSS job catered to her intervening nature. That was if she was still anything like the Olivia I knew.

I clicked the button to send her a message:

Hello Ms. Olivia:

It's your old pal, Ray. I moved back to NC in 2008. Not much has changed in the ole Lakes. Unfortunately, it's been a rough summer for us here. It made me want to think of better summers and old friends. We lost an important part of our circle, Rob. Go ahead and check The Pilot, *and then I'll fill you in on the rest. Your daughter is beautiful. Good genes.*

Of course, I couldn't help trolling the internet for word of Scott Windham, and I found nothing. Of all the egocentric fools I thought would embrace social media, he would have been number one on my list. In retrospect, I guessed that was not a fair initial assumption. I mean, everyone grew up eventually didn't they?

I did find a LinkedIn page for Walter Windham, his father. Believe it or not, he was a still a practicing physician in Richmond County. He had to be in his mid-seventies, but he was still making his rounds at Richmond Memorial in Rockingham.

While ruminating on why old Walter would still pound linoleum instead golf course fairways at his age, my phone rang. Detective Spruill was not in the mood for greetings.

"I need you to meet us down at Rob's office. We need another pair of eyes and maybe some context on what we've found so far."

"Give me twenty minutes."

I put the phone down and looked again at the article, specifically the dateline, and I had an idea. I pulled up a digital calendar of June 1984 on my laptop. If it was June 13 in 1984, then I was wrong about time moving faster in 1984. It didn't move faster so much as it simply had its own timeline that didn't match up perfectly with this one. Monday, June 13 here was Wednesday, June 13 in 1984, which meant Young Ray was getting close to his big track meet. I seemed to remember putting the time capsule together in the days leading up to that track meet, which meant I needed to see what the hell Spruill wanted, and then I had to get on my running shoes.

***

It was the first time I had entered Rob's office since Rob had departed this Earth, and I got a little choked up. It smelled like the rarely-used leather chairs. The inner office held a massive banker's desk with a blotter and a small lamp. Diagonally to the left sat a small circular table where I wrote most of my very first novel. In the late afternoons, I would keep Rob company as he pawed through receipts and other paperwork. Back then there was no Ava, no wife either, and the house was sometimes just too quiet. Rob joked that he would put a small plaque on that table that read, *Here is where Ray McCarthy got famous for making shit up.*

On this day, Eugene Sawyer sat at this table buried in paper. Detective Howard Spruill sat behind the massive banker's desk with a manila folder open in his hand. There was a hanging file filled with additional manila folders lying flat on the desk, which I supposed was for me to dig into.

"Good morning," said Spruill without looking up. Eugene gave a half-hearted wave, also without looking up.

"Hello, gentleman. How can I be of assistance?"

Spruill closed his folder and slid the file on the desk toward me.

"I require your research abilities on this particular item which I myself cannot justify man hours for."

The file was entitled *Dropped Contracts*, and I had seen it before.

"Is this a wild goose chase?" I asked.

"It's your chase, and it's not wild. It's eliminating all possibilities. Your friend kept track of his failures. I find that interesting, and so I would like to know more about them."

I opened the file. Rob liked to assess where he was outbid and to deduce if he could have done more to win. He liked to keep tabs on the build in case the winner of the contract was a charlatan or to see if said company had put itself in over its head. Rob was that thorough, and he had swept in and finished builds for half-asses before. It was one of the reasons the best subcontractors made themselves available to him. There was always work, and there was a standard. That's all that was in the file aside from two or three builds where the client ran out of money. That was early on in Rob's career when he was accepting just about everything and not necessarily vetting his clientele. There was one folder with an amusing title: *The Jesus Builds*. I opened that one first. Rob had bid on a contract to construct a church in Ellerbe and later a church in Asheboro. He had wanted to get into the church-building game not out of any call to do the Lord's work but because places of faith are tax-exempt and congregations always seem to have money. Over relatively short periods of time, they also seemed to get bigger and require expansion of their facilities. He tried twice. He was outbid twice by the same company.

"Eugene, were you around when Rob bid on the Ellerbe church contract?" I asked.

Eugene looked up, smiled a wan smile while rubbing his eyes.

"Yep. Rob really wanted to get his foot in the door of the church game. We got outbid there and in Asheboro. Rob gave up after that."

"What do you know about Halo Construction?"

Eugene shook his head. "Not a whole lot except that all they do is churches. I can give you some details about the Ellerbe contact."

"OK, shoot."

"Well, Ray, you know Rob. He used good, timeless, cost-effective material that holds up. At 1.3 million, Erwin Construction outbid Bolton Builders, BVH Construction, and Daniel Adams. We all got low-balled by Halo who committed to doing it for under a million dollars. I'm not sure how they managed that, but I've been inside the Ellerbe Fellowship Baptist Church, and it's solid. They didn't cut any corners."

"Can you write off a loss like that? I'm assuming they took a loss."

"I don't think it would be difficult to see what they built some of their other churches for," answered Eugene. "I know they did the one in Asheboro for under a million."

Spruill shut this down quickly. "I think that's a solid project for Ray. Anything helps, and I need to eliminate possibilities, but I'm not overly enthusiastic about a pair of dropped contracts. Has this company intervened in your business on any other occasions?"

"I think not," said Eugene.

"Then I want to know more about this guy." Spruill turned his tablet around and showed us the smiling mug shot of a skinny redneck with shoulder-length hair and a cursive neck tattoo that said:

Optimistic

I laughed out loud in spite of myself. Spruill just stared at Eugene, waiting for him to look up and display recognition, and—I think—to see how that initial, natural reaction looked. "That tattoo is a great pick-up line in a dive bar," I said. "I bet he does well."

Eugene looked up, and Spruill got the reaction he was looking for. Eugene smirked and just returned his eyes to the file he was studying.

"I've seen that picture before detective," said Eugene. "I saw him listed on an old payroll."

"I've arrested this man."

"You and a few other people I imagine," said Eugene.

"I got Matt Roper on possession of opiates for which he had no prescription, but the record shows—"

"Yup," interrupted Eugene, raising his head to meet Spruill's gaze, "assault, and public drunkenness, and assault, and public drunkenness. I'm pretty sure I know how it reads. He was definitely a hard case, but I never saw that side of him. He came in here looking for work, and the truth is he was a talented painter, and none of his prior employers had a bad word to say about him. Rob ran his record of course. Rob checked out everyone, and Rob brought him in to talk after running his record. I was there."

"And what exactly did he say?"

"I'll never forget it," said Eugene. "He looked Rob in the eye and said 'Sir when I am on my own time I like to drink and hit on women. Those women always seem to respond, even if they already have a fella. Almost always, that fella takes exception to that, and almost always that fella has friends. I know how to do things. I always win.'"

Spruill stared at Eugene for a moment.

"What things does he know how to do, and did he ever hit on Candace?" asked Spruill.

"Other than what it says on his record, I have no idea what the man does on his own time," Eugene said, a little indignant. "He treated me, Rob, and Candace with respect. When Candace visited a building site—she was always dolled up. Everyone made efforts not to notice the short skirts. She would seek out Matt if he were on the job. I think they knew each other. They're both from Robbins. Matt always bowed his head a little and called her Mrs. Erwin."

Spruill and I looked at each other, and Spruill read my mind.

"Ray, have a look into Halo Construction. If nothing else I'd like to know how one can have an entire business which caters specifically to the faithful at a perpetual loss. If, in fact, they low-ball everyone on every job. I will have a more involved look into Mr. Roper. Are we clear?"

"Absolutely."

***

Candace Erwin put her Jeep Grand Cherokee in gear and backed it out of the garage for the first time since a sheriff's deputy came rapping on the driver-side window as she snoozed before the sun setting over Lake Auman.

It turned out to be the sunrise.

So be it. She'd been drunk. She'd been drunk a lot, but someone—more than one someone apparently—had beaten her husband to death. Not just her husband, but the most decent man she had ever known. He had put up with every pound of shit she had brought to the table. The least she could do was make an effort to find those responsible. She was not a drunk. Her mother was a drunk. It was a wonder she was still alive. She might even visit Mom later in that ratty, Section 8 apartment complex with the dirt courtyard and rusty playground equipment. Right now, though, it was back to the old stomping grounds. She couldn't help but hum the Garth Brooks tune.

'Cause I've got friends in low places, where the whiskey drowns, and the beer chases my blues away. And I'll be OK.

Candace took route 211 to 705 until finally, she was cruising on Middleton Street through Robbins 'brief downtown district, which consisted of a gym, a pet store, the IGA, and a handful of mom-and-pop business ventures. She turned right on Plank Road and then meandered down Belleview, not far from the Church of God and Prophesy. The road wound through a heavily wooded area, but about two miles past Collins Chapel Church, on a small hollow of land, sat a farmhouse under heavy renovation by its owner.

Matt watched Candace carefully negotiate his partially washed-out gravel drive and park. She stepped carefully around his boxer's heavy bag, held together by duct tape, that hung from a lower branch of a massive magnolia tree. Candace had just mounted the stairs when he stepped out the door.

"Hello there Mrs. Erwin." The gentleman bowed. "How might I be of assistance?"

"Well for starters you can knock that shit off right now, Matthew. I got serious questions to ask you, and I want honest answers."

Matt Roper's genial countenance instantly became one of worry. As tough as he was, he had never mastered dealing with Candace.

Candace took a seat on a varnished porch swing and watched as Matt followed her and took a seat on the porch floor and leaned his back against the house. He said nothing. He knew whatever she was about to say was probably well thought out. Interrupting her script would just further piss her off.

"I want names. I want names of every lowlife you do business with, whether it's weed, pills, or whatever," Candace said as she gracefully lowered her forearms to her knees and looked at Matt with big, angry eyes that did not blink.

"Now that doesn't make any sense." Matt shook his head sympathetically. "Your mister didn't have anything to do with the substances I sometimes side-hustle."

"No, he did not. The shit-stains you deal with are all broke, living in trailers paycheck-to-paycheck, and they're all hopelessly addicted to something. They take any job that comes along that'll put money in their hands and drugs in their pocket, and that includes beating the shit out of someone for a couple of bucks. Hell, I went to high school with probably half these morons..."

"Now hold on there," said Matt, his pride and anger rising a bit. He felt as if he was being lumped in with the "shit stains," and he didn't much care for that talk. "I may have alternative sources of income that folks like you don't much approve of, but that doesn't mean I hang out with these people or know what kinda other shit they're into. I keep to myself. I work for people like your husband. I fix my house. I occasionally entertain a lady friend, and that's it. Damn it, Candace, I spent almost every summer of my teenage years babysitting you while your useless Momma got shit-faced at her neighbor's house. How about a little respect?"

Candace's tone did not soften, but she did get off the porch swing and sit beside Matt on the porch floor.

"I know that. I know it. I'm not judging you. I'm asking for your help. Other than Rob, you're the only person who has ever looked out for me, and I need your help. Do you want me walking through these trailer parks looking for trouble?"

"No." Matt sighed. "Don't do that."

"Then let's make a list so we don't waste our time. I'm looking for people with bad habits, with warrants we can hold over their heads, people who'd beat your ass if you looked at them wrong or scratched their truck in a grocery parking lot. I'm gonna take that list to Detective Spruill. If anybody can make guys like that sing, he can. Maybe whoever we find had nothing to do with Rob's death. Maybe they just know somebody who got drunk and bragged. I just want to make a whole lot of people nervous. Then I want to sit back and see who sings. Or see who runs."

Matt helped Candace come up with a list of five individuals he had little interest in dealing with ever again. The truth was that Candace was right about most of the people he knew. Matt could have given her a list of ten, or even fifteen, pieces of trash that fit the bill she had described. He watched her Jeep lurch out of his gravel drive with a mixture of guilt and sadness because he knew the responsible party. Any one of those guys he mentioned could have been enlisted to help, but they weren't calling the shots. Matt went into his house and grabbed his phone off a newly-installed granite countertop and dialed.

"Hello, pal. What's the word in Robbins?"

"This is a courtesy call," said Matt.

"Is it now? I guess I should be thankful, but truthfully, you could have been more useful to me a few days ago."

"I don't want to know anything about a few days ago. I am just making assumptions here, and based on those assumptions, I figured you'd want to know who was sniffing around your door."

"I appreciate that. Then again, the health of my enterprise affects the health of your enterprise, so tell me what you want to tell me."

"First, the investigating detective is Spruill, who's a hard-ass."

"I've evaded him effortlessly for two years, but good to know."

"Second, Candace Erwin came by with a rather good plan. She wanted me to help her make a list."

"A list of what?"

"Of people on the hook so bad they'd be willing to take a side job that might end their days as free men."

"And what did you give her?"

"Guys I don't want to deal with anymore. Broke guys, violent guys. Most of them live in Vass."

"Also good to know. I don't believe I have any friends in Vass. Would you be up for a different paid gig, one that is not violent?"

"No."

"Reconsider the shit out of that, Matthew. Really. The dominance we've exerted over this portion of the Southeast is in considerable jeopardy, and I would like to make certain that the spectacular deterrent I orchestrated, did actually deter."

"What do you want?"

"I want you to steal some furniture."

***

With *The Jesus Builds* file sitting beside me in the passenger seat, I pulled my Frontier into the Short Stop gas station to fuel the truck and to caffeinate myself. From behind one of the nearby pumps, a familiar voice called. "What's goin' on Ray?"

"I've lost count of what's goin' on," I said to the air. "Who's that?"

Christie Ebel, one of my few childhood friends from the '80s who also returned to Seven Lakes to raise a family, stepped from behind a yellow SUV.

"Any word on Ava?"

"No, Not yet."

"It will work out, Ray. Hey, I read your book."

"Which one?"

"The first one where the two high school sweethearts grow up to marry other people, but then they reconnect. I forget how. But they meet up every summer at the Outer Banks for like ten years, having an affair for just a week each summer. Oh, and then he comes back one summer to find his sweetheart's husband instead. Did she have to die, dude?"

"Yes. I should have killed off that book. It did well, but I was treading on Nicholas Sparks territory."

"Well, I can't wait for the next one."

"I think it's going to be rather different from the other two, but I'll bring you a copy."

"Cool. See ya."

"Hey, Christie."

She poked her head back around the rear of her truck.

"If you ran into your kid self, what would you tell her?"

Christie considered this for a moment and then smiled. "Same thing I tell my daughter. Don't marry the first one."

"If you didn't marry the first one, you'd have no daughter."

"True. I guess it's best not to mess too much with that stuff. Everything works out the way it's supposed to. Is this your next book?"

Honey, it's because I could very well see you this afternoon.

"I have no idea yet, but I think you're right about second-guessing the past." *To some degree.*

18
Catch and Release

Tom sometimes had to remind people that at his age he was in the finding business, not the apprehending business. Anything more than that was stuff better left to younger men with aspirations. The thing was, though, people had to stay found.

Thus, there he sat, in his Lincoln, at the 7-Eleven across the street from the entrance to the Kampground of America. Via his Kindle, he musingly perused an online version of the Miami Herald while sipping iced coffee. The other tab of his search engine was on WebMD.

"God this guy's a pisser," Tom blurted out loud. His affinity for Carl Hiaasen had begun in the '80s when he'd spent two days at the South Florida Container Terminal watching those who were watching his container. The Lincoln was running for the air conditioning, sure. But it would also have to move quickly, and soon.

***

Morgan McCarthy steeled herself for what she considered her walk of shame. It was the routine of locking Ava in the car while she walked up to a strange person and purchased pain medication illegally. The depth of depravity and shame and the overall feeling of complete irresponsibility were almost paralyzing to a woman who considered herself rather intelligent and morally sound. The truth was, though, that she was scoring drugs from some hipster douche in a campground.

Morgan dabbed at her nose with a tissue. Her sleep was minimal these days, and she was coming down with a cold. She would complete this transaction, and she would make Ava an early dinner. As Morgan negotiated the long rock drive toward the cabin, she craned her neck to see if anyone was on the porch. She was only about five minutes late. She had gone two days without meds. That was inevitable, but that was also too drastic a step-down. Her aching neck and shoulders told her so.

Then Ava spoke up.

"Mommy, who are you looking for? Is it Daddy? Is Daddy finally here?

"No, Ava. I have to meet someone, and then we are going to make dinner."

"I don't want to meet anybody. I want to meet Daddy. I want Daddy on the phone now."

Morgan pulled into the driveway and put her head on the steering wheel, trying to hold in a sob. After a moment or two, she took a breath and composed herself. Her head remained resting on the steering wheel.

"Ava. We will talk to Daddy. We'll find a way."

"I know the way. Take out the phone. Take it out. I know how—"

"Ava!" Morgan turned to face her daughter who'd been shocked into silence and was now on the verge of tears herself. "I said I would find a way."

Morgan grabbed her phone out of her pocketbook and quickly exited the car. She climbed the stairs to the porch defiantly, as if to ward off the encroaching shame. There was no boy. There were no meds. She was pacing the porch and punching the boy's number into the phone when she noticed that the screen door was slightly ajar. She moved to investigate and found a folded envelope stuck between the door and the jamb. She pulled it out and saw the message.

Met your boy. Got your meds. Me, you, and Ava need to have a chat.

(718) 555-0963

Tom

Morgan's adrenaline dumped, and the all-over needling sensation was not unlike when one's foot or hand falls asleep. Immediately she racked her brain for names with which she was familiar. Ray's uncles had names like Joe, John, and Bill. His cousins were Mike and Jay and Justin. Shit! Which ones were cops? For the life of her, she could not remember a Tom, but this was probably the guy who had called her brother. Could Ray have hired a private investigator? It would have been more comforting had he been a relative. There might have been some measure of understanding. There was no telling what this guy's motivation was. She unlocked the door and began grabbing things as she entered: Ava's toys, random food, a casually strewn pair of jeans. It was time to go.

***

Tom had seen only one Toyota Rav 4 enter the KOA since he'd been sipping coffee and catching up with Carl. It was silver, and so he was waiting for that same vehicle to come tear-assing right back out of the KOA. He gave Mrs. McCarthy an hour to gather herself.

She came tear-assing out onto the Coastal Byway in less than thirty minutes, heading north.

North was good. Next, she would find Route 1, and then inevitably 95 North. Once she was on 95, he expected a call. She'd be fishing about his identity and motivation, thinking she had already put some safe distance between them. If she didn't call, he would call her. He didn't want her trying to score meds at a truck stop, and he had something for the kid. He would reassure her that he was here to watch and to keep her safe while she figured things out, and he would prove it.

19
The Captain

He sat on the porch watching the last of the winter runoff making temporary stream beds. The sound was soothing. The cabin still smelled of wood smoke. He didn't care for the wood stove, but running the generator meant burning fuel, and fuel was running relatively low. He needed to keep some gas for the truck so as to eventually make a run to town and refurbish his supplies. He hadn't been to town since November.

It would have made sense, when Dad died, to either move closer to civilization or to install some upgrades to the cabin. He and Dad had built this cabin, and he liked the fact that it remained timeless. Looking around, it amazed him that he and Dad had coexisted in little more than 1,100 square feet. Of course, Dad had it to himself off and on for almost fifteen years.

In 2005, the Captain, which was how some locals referred to him, left the United States Army permanently to see his father through what turned out to be the last year of his life. His mom had smoked herself to death in the '90s, but Dad had not smoked. He had not drunk, but he had worked outdoors every day of his life. The melanoma consumed him fast. In the last three months he had lost the power to speak, and with that went his will to live.

It was just the Captain now. Once, he had friends. He had graduated high school and gone straight to the sands of Iraq and made it out with all his faculties intact. He had plenty of friends.

In 2003, he went back to Iraq and returned with a few less faculties.

In '91 he had fought an army that did not want to fight back. In

2003, Iraq was up for grabs, and zealots were tearing it apart. Zealots fight differently. They fight brutally and without code, which meant he fought brutally and without code. Cancer had killed his dad, but it very well may have saved what was left of the Captain. He returned to Flathead County with little interest in correspondence and even less interest in socialization. The cabin had no discernible address, and the Captain never bothered renting a post office box.

After laying Dad to rest at the First Baptist Church, he had not had the wherewithal to go right back to the cabin. He rented a room above the Garden Bar, a cash-only establishment with a grand patio out back where he quietly sipped beer for almost a year. He couldn't remember where or when he had last possessed a valid driver's license, and so when the bartender asked for some identification on that first evening, the Captain offered his military ID. The barkeep, who sported a fresh shiner on his left eye, was merely being nosey about a haggard stranger who looked even older than his thirty-four years. He called the bar's owner to his side to assess the document's authenticity.

"Yup, that is an expired military ID, but that is the weirdest first name I ever saw. I'm just gonna call you 'Captain' for now. Give this man whatever he wants," said Mark, to whom everyone seemed to refer to simply as "Mister."

"By the way, I'm not sure I've seen you before."

He explained to Mark that he had been honorably discharged for some time and that he was taking care of a relative who had recently passed.

"Do you need a place to stay?" Mark had asked.

Captain wandered into his cabin still warm from the wood stove. His generator could power a small television and DVD player when he wanted it to and stacked neatly beside it lay a handful of documentaries on rock bands he once adored. On the shelf over the wood stove sat his mother's collection of horror books, some historical fiction set in World War II (Dad's favorite), and a sappy love story set on a beach.

During the summer, and sometimes in the fall, he would drop by the public library and sit at a computer for an hour or two. He would assess his funds online. He hardly touched his military salary over the years, and there was also his father's life insurance money. Sometimes he ordered a few items off Amazon, including ammo, but not for anything as ridiculous as a gun.

He'd ship a few Predator II carbon arrows and an extra package of Brodhead tips, the NAP Rednecks, his favorites, if only for the name. The Captain had not fired anything but a compound bow since 2005, and currently, he hunted with the Diamond Infinite Edge. To this day he still had packages shipped to the Garden Bar as if it was his home address, and Mark held them in the back office.

It would do him good to see Mark, he thought, but there was something else eating at him. He hadn't shipped anything. He had enough fuel for another couple of weeks, but still, there was an impetus to move, to speak to someone…anyone. He would get his hair cut and his beard trimmed. He'd have a look in the bookstore and perhaps catch up with an old friend.

He wandered down his little mountain to McCaffery Road and then walked north on Highway 35 to Winterhawk Storage. He fueled and jumpstarted Dad's Scout II Traveler. It rumbled to life without issue; only the tires were suspect in that he saw some dry rot. He proceeded South on 35 and eventually made the left on Bay Drive and connected to Bridge Street, crossing the narrowest slip of Bigfork Harbor.

The Garden Bar smelled of stale beer and fresh varnish. There was a baseball game on every television screen.

"Captain!" cried the bartender. "Long time no see. Mark's not here, but he'll be back. He went to the post office."

"Wheatfish."

"Wheatfish it is. Hey, the Braves are on that TV over there. Take a load off and enjoy."

After three beers and five innings of Atlanta getting clobbered by Cincinnati, there was no sign of Mark. The Captain was ready to move on. He left cash and made it as far as the door.

"Jesus, man, don't move. The curiosity is killing me!" yelled Mark as he barreled through the kitchen swinging door waving something in his right hand.

He turned from the door and walked back across the room, offering Mark a toothy grin.

"I'm not sure what you mean."

"I mean," said Mark, "you got a letter."

Captain Arden Miller did not have to stop by the bookstore to catch up with his old friend. His old friend had caught up with him.

"Only hope can keep me together. Love can mend your life, but love can break your heart. I'll send an S.O.S. to the world."

—The Police

20
Forget Subtlety

I parked the truck and ran with *The Jesus Builds* under my arm while fumbling with my house keys. It was almost noon. Never had I attempted to run through the anomaly this late in the day. There was no telling how late it was in 1984, and I knew today was the day. I would find them in the gazebo at the corner of Lake Echo, the one standing at the beginning of the dam with a dock and a boat launch.

I almost sprinted across the dam, eager for the weightlessness to ensue. I pierced the shimmer of air with more hope in my soul than I had dared allowed since Ava disappeared. I felt if I could save Rob, just set one thing right, then perhaps more dominoes would fall in the right direction. Dear God, just one win, please.

Young Ray's thoughts downloaded into me. He had managed to avoid Scott Windham. This was no surprise as I didn't have any new memories of being beaten up. Olivia Allen was very much on his mind. I couldn't blame him for that. I was able to learn also that his race was tomorrow, so I instantly cut my speed to an easy jog. As I did, something jounced about in the right front pocket of my shorts. I stopped and finally noticed the stillness in the air, and the odd pink hue of the light. The sky looked as it does sometimes when we were under a tornado warning, and it made me uncomfortable. I reached into my pocket and pulled out Luke Skywalker in his X-Wing pilot gear.

Today was the day.

There was also a scorecard pencil and a folded-up piece of paper, my letter full of prognostications, and possibly my last chance at saving Rob's life.

As I finally neared the Lake Echo dam, I could see their silhouettes hunched over the picnic table, the sun low across the lake. Rob saw me first and lit up.

"My god man, you own a bicycle. Give the running shoes a rest. Don't you race tomorrow?"

"Yup."

"How far is 800 meters anyway?" asked Arden, who continued to etch *Open 2004* on the outside of the PVC pipe.

"A half mile."

"That's it? Hell, all the miles you run, a half mile ought to be nothin'."

"They run it really fast," interjected Rob. "I saw Ray's last one. It's a two-lap race around a track, and it's over in a blink of an eye. Ray was right on this guy's shoulder and then shot around him like the Millennium Falcon going into hyperspace. It was awesome. Ray's mom lost her mind. If we weren't packing up to go to Carolina Beach Wednesday, I'd go watch this one too."

Arden looked up and offered an admiring grin. Then he looked at Rob the same way. It was as if he was taking it all in, this time we had together like he knew it couldn't stay like this forever. It hurt my heart a little, and suddenly I had an idea. I took a seat at the picnic table Rob and Arden had commandeered, and I unfolded my letter.

"Hey, I don't want to see that," said Rob holding up a hand. "What we wrote is supposed to be a complete surprise to us when we dig it up in 2004."

"We don't open it in 2004. We forget about it. You will open it in 2016."

Rob stopped tying his fishing lure. Arden quit carving. They stared at me blankly, waiting for more. It was the sound of my voice that had them transfixed. I sounded certain and real.

"Rob, we're still gonna bury this thing in the crawlspace of that house being built on Sequoia, right? I mean the house beside the big hill on Firetree Lane?"

Rob nodded silently.

"Well, you will come back here, and you will have a construction business. You will one day renovate that house, and that's when you remember the time capsule."

"Man, I told you, Rob," said Arden. "I told you he's gonna write stories for a livin'. I don't care how fast he is. Damn Ray, what happens next?"

"Rob, it is no secret that both our parents like it better up North, except for your dad. He'd stay here forever. The truth is though, maybe this year, maybe next year, you and I will go back North. All our relatives are there. As teachers, my parents make much better money up there. I will go back to New York. You will go back to Massachusetts. It sucks, but that's what's going to happen."

Arden raised his hand to speak as if school was in session.

"What happens to me?"

"I don't know. That's the problem. Rob and I will stay in touch. We like to write letters. You don't."

"You got that right," said Arden.

"That's a problem, but I have a solution. You're only going to have to write one letter. In fact, you've already written it. You're just going to have to update it when the time comes."

"I don't understand," said Rob, "and how do you know 2016 is when I find the—"

I interrupted Rob. I had to keep the information rolling before they both just threw up their hands and laughed off the whole thing.

"Rob, you and I will move back here—as adults, because we love it here—but it will take some time. We'll graduate high school, then college, start jobs, but eventually, we will drift back down here, but we won't know where Arden is unless he tells us."

"I don't plan on goin' anywhere," said Arden, once again transfixed.

"Plans change my friend, and because of that I am hereby instituting a new rule for the time capsule: Arden is the only one who may dig it up before 2004."

"Why would I do that?"

"To leave us a message as to where you went if you move, especially if it is out of the state of North Carolina."

"I've lived here my whole life; Daddy wouldn't dare—"

"Promise me." Our eyes met, and probably for the first time, I saw that Arden was a little afraid. "Promise us."

"OK. Done."

"So, what happens to me?" Rob asked in a tone that clearly said he was playing along.

"You and I both get married and have a child. We both have girls. I'll give you more details in a minute. I just have one more thing to add to this letter."

While I scrawled, Rob ruminated on what it would be to have a little girl around. Arden continued to look unsettled, which was fine by me. Someone had to take this seriously without writing me off as nuts.

I folded up my letter and handed it and Luke Skywalker to Arden, and Arden finally cracked a smile.

"Is our time capsule now under the protection of The Force?"

"Damn right," I said, and Arden cracked up. "Seal this sucker up, boss. Rob, walk with me a minute. Then you and Arden and I have to clarify some stuff."

"If it's about Scott Windham whoopin' your ass, I got that covered. It's not gonna happen as long as I'm around."

"I don't care when he finds me as long as it is not before the race tomorrow. Yeah, if he gets me, then you get him. You're the only one of us that even makes him nervous."

Arden nodded, and Rob and I walked a little way across the Lake Echo dam.

"Do you still watch the reruns of *In Search Of*? That show narrated by Mr. Spock?"

"Oh, you know it. I love that show, especially the one where they went lookin' for Bigfoot."

"Did you see the episodes on Nostradamus and his predictions?"

"Yeah. Creepy how much he got right. Oh, and he guessed Adolf Hitler's name! Except he missed it by one letter; He called him 'Hisler' instead of 'Hitler.'"

"It is creepy. I'll tell you something creepier. I think one of the reasons I write good stories is that I have some of what he had."

Rob stopped and turned to me. He was intrigued. He was too much of a sci-fi fan not to take me at least a little seriously.

"I didn't want to say anything more in front of Arden because I think this kind of stuff scares the shit out of him."

"It does," said Rob in a conspiratorial tone.

"I want you to listen to me. I see things that sometimes happen. They're just pictures, like short movies in my head that don't make complete sense until later. You understand?"

"Yeah. Yeah, I do." Rob was jazzed now. This kind of stuff was right up his alley. It was time to go for all the marbles.

"That stuff I was saying before about the when you find the capsule, that stuff about you having a daughter…"

"You weren't making it up."

"I wasn't making it up."

"I've seen your daughter. I've seen your wife. I've seen your office." Rob then turned deadly serious.

"Is my wife good looking?"

"Your wife is great looking, and so is your daughter."

"Mom and Dad?"

"Rita's still around. I can't see the Colonel."

There was a long silence, and we stopped walking.

"I can't see you either."

Rob's mouth dropped open.

"What I can see is a fight, a bad one. I don't know if it's a robbery gone wrong, or a case of mistaken identity, or what happened, but at least two or three guys are beating on you, and one of them has a club or a bat. You put up a good fight, too good. You get hurt real bad, and then I don't see you anymore."

"What happened?"

"I think if things stay the way they are, then you don't live past the age of forty-four."

"What, did you see a cake with forty-four candles on it or something?" Rob took a breath and looked over his shoulder at Arden who had finished sealing the time capsule and was now looking at us curiously.

"Hey," said Rob, "this is all guesswork now. We might have changed something just by talking about this right?"

"Maybe, maybe not, but I'm going to try two things here: first, that fight happens in the summer of 2016. It happens on your dock; you live on Lake Sequoia. A guy named Eugene comes to see you. They knock the hell out of him too, but I see him again. When those guys come for you, you hit whomever you have to hit to get away, and then you jump in the lake and swim clear across it if you have to. Do not run. You're slow as shit, and they'll have you blocked off anyway, but you can still swim like a fish.

"Second, I left instructions for you in my letter. When you find the time capsule, you obey those instructions to the letter. Got it? If you need more proof than that, then you're thick as a brick."

Rob gave a barely perceptible nod. He had now arrived at the same emotionally uncomfortable place we had left Arden in a few moments before, and so we headed back toward our buddy.

"What super-secret plans are you two lovers making?" Arden asked.

"Nothing really." I took the lead, and Rob followed. "I want Colonel Ed to take me out in the station wagon soon to measure out some different running routes. I'd like to stay out of Scott's way as long as possible, and if he does find me, I rather he didn't find me in the middle of a run when I'm tired."

"And if he asks his mom to do it, she'll know something's up," interjected Rob.

"I hear that," Arden said.

"I gotta go guys. I need to finish this little jog, eat, and get to bed early. "

"Where's the national championship gonna be at if you qualify?" Arden asked.

"Alabama."

"Alabama? Nothin' but rednecks there."

Rob and I exchanged a glance and then smiled a pair of tight, broad smiles that barely held in the laughter.

"What are you chuckleheads smiling at? Oh, you think I'm a redneck huh?"

"But you're our most favorite one," said Rob.

"By far," I added, and Rob and I busted out laughing. Soon even Arden was laughing.

"Screw you guys. I'm country. There's a difference between country and rednecks. Now my uncle, that there is a damn redneck. He's got a car in his front yard up on cinder blocks and got chickens livin' in there."

That comment put us into hysterics. It took a good ten minutes for us to calm down. Rob then gave me a short hug goodbye and wished me good luck. Even Arden hugged me. I jogged toward 2016 with that dangerous thing called hope flowing through me. I dared to think of a late afternoon on Rob's deck with Ava on my lap and Rob working the grill. Arden would be on Rob's dock and reeling in a fish.

I broke through the shimmer and turned onto Cherokee Trail in the year 2016. I was more out of breath than I should have been. My head throbbed. I dropped to one knee. An information download flooded me. There were too many thoughts of which to make sense. I retained memories of everything—every timeline: what had happened initially, new memories like movie night with Olivia…and what had changed. It was too much to process, but something had changed. I could feel it.

When I got home, the time capsule was gone.

21
Buyer Beware

Having booked a flight to the states, Colonel Jim did not have much time to chat with his plant manager. However, Manny Reyes had insisted they meet today. Perhaps Manny could take him to Mactan, and they could chat on the way.

Jim had more pressing issues than whatever production or labor problems Manny needed to sort out. The procedure was simple: Patio furniture properly reinforced with iron and other solidly built accessories should be shipped to the usual vendors. Everything else went to North Carolina.

At present, Jim was interested in the unauthorized buyer who had come to visit Rita on Sunday. Rita was convinced that he was some lost yuppie out antiquing. However, the barn was rather hard to stumble across.

If this man had come down Route 220 from Seagrove, he would have had to get off on the Route 73 exit and make two awkward lefts—one on Wallace Road, and then another on John Deere Road, which shares a stretch of Bowers Lane. Jim and the Bowers clan had an understanding of how much traffic there would be on that lane. There would be the occasional trailer and a considerable amount of traffic for a three-day stretch once or twice a month. In return, Jim had anteed up the money to reinforce the road's infrastructure. The Bowers knew Rita and her car. They had been told that anything other than transport trucks, was unusual. Furniture bidders drove trucks. They paid; they loaded; they left.

A BMW was unusual. Mr. Bowers Sr. had called Jim. Jim had called Rita.

Jim exited his battered Scout and jogged through the increasing rain toward the plant entrance. He entered Manny's domain with bluster and impatience. It was a sparse office with 1970s era wood-paneled walls which featured framed aerial shots of Cebu. Manny sat behind a large wooden desk.

"Manny I've got to catch a flight, so either make it quick or help me get to the airport while we chat."

"Please have a seat Colonel. This won't take long," said Manny, gesturing to one of the metal chairs which scraped across the concrete floor when they were maneuvered.

Manny's tone was different. Jim didn't like it. It was not the tone of a subordinate—which Manny was regardless of his fifty-one percent ownership stake. Manny had not risen from his chair when Jim had entered. It made him nervous, and he peeked back into the hallway to see if there was anyone behind him. There was no one, but there was a pair of Humvees parked behind the Scout. Jim promptly sat down while silently considering alternative exits from the plant. One hundred yards from the south entrance was a dilapidated storage shed with landscaping equipment and a small safe that secured a stash of funds.

"What's on your mind, Manny?"

"I would like to make an offer to purchase Abian Industries. Here is the figure I've come up with."

Manny slid a handwritten piece of paper across the desk. Jim had to get up to retrieve it. He picked it up, folded it, and then sat back down without giving it a glance. Jim stared at Manny, who merely stared back. Finally, he gestured to the Colonel to have a look. Jim had a look. Then he smiled.

"This is a fraction of what it's worth, Manny."

Manny did not smile. He reached into his pocket and then slid his National Bureau of Investigation badge across the desk.

"Not when you consider this, Colonel."

Jim nodded. Once upon a time he believed this day would come, but it had kept not coming, and so he assured himself that it never would. It did not matter. His assets were considerable and well hidden.

"What took so long Manny?"

"Actually, Benigno Aquino III was on to you, but since you strictly exported your product, he let you alone. Also, he couldn't bring himself to move on the man that taught him how to throw a curve ball."

Jim laughed out loud.

"Also, you've done much good for the inhabitants of this community. You own their land, but they live on it rent free, and you still pay them a fair wage at the plant. You've handled medical expenses for many of your workers. Some of them have named their children after you."

Jim lowered his head and stared at the floor. "I want them all to get the deeds to their respective properties."

"I figured," said Manny. "That is already in the works."

"What happens next, Manny?"

"You'll make your flight to the States, Colonel. In fact, I will take you, and we'll have an escort. Unfortunately, your long affair with the Philippines is over. Our current president's policy on entrepreneurs like you is rather extreme. Do not return here, ever, or you will find yourself the victim of a tarmac altercation similar to that of Benigno's father. Are we clear?"

"Crystal."

Your arrest and punishment would give President Obama yet another reason to involve himself in how we handle things here, and President Duterte does not care for Obama...at all. So, you will be allowed to leave."

"You can keep your money, Manny."

"As you wish, Colonel. And Colonel..."

Jim finally looked up from the floor and met Manny's eyes.

"You're in your mid-seventies. Most all of your friends are dead or retired. We have not coordinated with American law enforcement. Go home. Enjoy the family you have left. Live a quiet life."

"Let's go, Manny."

Jim was too busy to be sad. He would grieve. When it was all over, he would grieve for the loss of the Philippines, but both times and regimes change. This fact he had lived long enough to learn. Would times change before he was too old to travel? Well, that was up for debate. Jim, though, had spent a lifetime dealing with loss by throwing himself into his next project. His forced retirement was an opportunity to take a more hands-on approach to set right what had happened to Rob. God help whoever was responsible, for now, Colonel Jim Dorn had time to kill.

22
Meatballs and Meds

"I don't understand! Why did you put my toys in a box? What about dinner? I don't want chicken nuggets! I want to take a bath! I want to take a bath! I want my daddy! I want Da...ha…deee…"

Ava McCarthy dissolved into unintelligible sobs interspersed with intense coughing fits. It was what she did when she reached her limit, and she was most definitely at her limit. The problem was that when she got this upset, she usually threw up all over herself.

Morgan did not have time to pull over and change Ava and hose out a car seat. Her abject panic was at its hysterical precipice, and she was going to lose it if Ava did not calm down. With the on-ramp to 95 in sight, she pulled the Toyota off on to the road's shoulder and turned to face her daughter.

"Ava," she said in a slow, measured tone. "Ava, look at your mommy."

Ava had just finished another round of coughing and had stepped down to a shaky, not-quite hyperventilation. She looked up with eyes still bulbous with tears.

"Ava, we are headed back home. It will take some time. Mommy is about to get on the big highway."

Ava looked at her distrustfully, and that look broke Morgan's heart.

"Re-Re-Really?"

"Yes, honey."

"Why di-did you decide so fast?"

"I knew it was time to go."

"Can I talk to Daddy?

Morgan was out of excuses on that one, but then she had an idea. She was going to do it anyway, why not make it work for her?

"Daddy is a little angry right now; what I can—"

"Why?"

"Because we've been gone a long time."

"It will be OK. I can call him."

"Why don't we talk to a friend of Daddy's first?"

Morgan drove down the shoulder and merged into traffic while Ava looked quizzically at her via the rearview mirror. They drove in silence for roughly ten or twelve miles when Morgan shut off the car's Bluetooth and punched in the number.

***

Tom was four cars behind when he saw the Toyota meander on to the shoulder of the road. This was unanticipated, but this was also why he was four cars behind. He too pulled off the road and waited to see if Morgan went either north or south. Perhaps she was second-guessing her impulsive departure and considering her options. Maybe the kid was acting up—little Ava couldn't be anything short of bewildered right now.

Whatever the reason for the pause, it lasted less than ten minutes, and Ms. Morgan chose north.

Tom edged his way back into traffic and drove hurriedly until the Toyota was back in sight. If Morgan had made the tail, then she would take the next exit and probably head south. That didn't happen. Ten miles up 95, the expected happened: His phone lit up with a local number, and he supposed it was whatever disposable phone Morgan had purchased.

"Greetings," said Tom out loud.

"May I please speak to Tom."

"Speaking. Nice to make your acquaintance Mrs. McCarthy."

"Who the hell are you?"

"I am Thomas Cianci of Goshen, New York. Google me if you will. I am a friend of your priest, Father Baumann, and I have recently become friends with your husband, Ray. To answer your next question, I am not affiliated with law enforcement."

"Then what is your business with me and my daughter?"

"Only to ensure safe travels to wherever your next destination happens to be."

"And I suppose that you are going to ensure that the next destination is Seven Lakes, North Carolina?"

"That is the preferred destination young lady, but I am no longer in the business of forcing anyone to do anything."

"What exactly is your business, and who's paying you?"

"I've had a lot of businesses. I am now retired. Your pal the Colonel is reimbursing expenses, and I'm pretty sure that he'd like me to either drag you home or sell you out to the first lawman we happen upon."

Tom waited for what he said to sink in, and then added: "That is not what Ray wants, though, and Ray is calling the shots."

Morgan took a breath. She did not know whether to be relieved or more concerned.

"And what does my husband want?"

"I think he wants his family back safe. I think he knows what you are trying to do, and I think he hired me to make sure you get there safely."

That comment broke her, and she almost sobbed out her next sentence.

"And then he's going to divorce the shit out of me."

"Mommy, you said 'shit,'" interjected Ava.

"Shush Ava."

"I'm pretty sure that was his initial thought when you first tipped out the door, but I don't believe that's his agenda now. Was that Ava?"

"Yes, say hello. Hold on. Ava, I have a friend of your Daddy's on the phone. Do you want to say hi?"

"Yes, is Daddy with him?"

"No, but say hello."

Ava gathered the phone from her mom and gave a tentative hello.

"Who is this?" Tom asked.

"This is Ava Elizabeth McCarthy. Who is this?"

"This is your daddy's pal, Tom. Your daddy misses you very much, and he told me to bring you something."

"What? What did my daddy send?" Ava asked excitedly, and Morgan looked at her nervously through the rearview mirror

"Spaghetti and meatballs."

Ava's mouth dropped open.

"Mommy, this man has meatballs. We have to find him."

Tom cackled on the other end of the line. Ray's description of his daughter had been dead-on.

Morgan grabbed the phone from her daughter.

"You can't possibly think that I am going to stop and meet you in person."

"I'm not sure what you have to lose except for maybe meatballs and meds. I just said that I'm not here to apprehend you. I am here in a guardian angel capacity."

"Did you hurt the boy?"

"No, but he was very excited to leave my presence."

"Did you pay him?"

"Absolutely not. I'm your guardian angel, not his. Speaking of which, the Vicodin appear to be the regular strength, correct?"

"They should be."

"Which means each pill is five milligrams of hydrocodone and 500 milligrams of acetaminophen. How many of these did you take on average?"

"I took four pills twice a day, six hours apart. It takes way more hydrocodone than that to put you in the hospital."

"You realize that more than four grams a day of acetaminophen can shut your liver down right?"

"That is why I didn't take more than eight pills a day. I tried to be at least somewhat responsible."

"Honey when you start doin' math to see how much you can get away with, the responsible thing to do is check yourself into a facility," said Tom.

"That was not an option."

"So I've been told you believe. Didn't want the dirt of rehab stickin' to you. What do you think that Amber Alert did to your reputation?"

"And I'm sure Ray has only added fuel to the fire."

Tom was pretty much done with this broad's self-interested outlook. It was time to magnify her worldview, and he would look for an opening to take the steam out of her pissy little engine.

This was part of the plan: overwhelm her with the mess she'd added to, and then hand her a clean way out.

"There is something you should know about that. Of course, Ray's had to talk to cops. However, other than me, your pal the Colonel, and Father Baumann, Ray hasn't said anything to anybody about the reasons behind your departure, which I find to be impressive. Your husband isn't exactly famous, but he is well known in his parts, and the news people call him all the damn time. He should really get an agent or somethin' to run interference for him. Still, Ray's said nothin'. What's escaping you here, sweetheart, is that the back-door Ray took to track you down is an indication that he is trying to save your day and your image, not destroy it."

Morgan remained silent a moment.

"Well, I'm sure the Erwins are thoroughly aware of the situation."

"That's somethin' else you need to be brought up to speed on, dear."

"What's that?" asked Morgan.

"In addition to losing you and Ava for more than a month, your husband lost his best friend forever last Wednesday. He was killed in some sort of home invasion or robbery attempt."

"What? Jenna, Candace, Rita? Are they all right?"

"My guess is that they're far from all right, but they are in one piece. When you get done Googling me, you should Google that and get caught up."

"I-I don't know what to…" Morgan sniffled. Her voice had become thick.

"You okay, Morgan?"

"I have a cold."

"Although that is not out of the realm of possibilities, Morgan, I doubt it. You've enjoyed rather pleasant weather for the duration of your tour. I'm guessing you have some muscle aches too. When's the last time you had meds?"

"Two days ago."

"And what have you stepped down to as far as dosage?"

"I'm down to four pills a day."

"You cut it in half. Impressive."

"I told you I can do this."

"I know you can."

"Tell you what. I've got your meds, and I'm going to give you two so you can travel easy and maybe get some rest tonight, and as I said, I've got dinner. These meatballs aren't getting any warmer sitting in my front seat, and I doubt you have a microwave in your car."

"What do you want me to do?"

"Pull off at the next truck stop and pull alongside the first vacant gas pump. Then dinner and evening meds will be served. After that, I will continue up the road a piece, maybe find some dinner myself."

"Where are you?"

"I'm right behind you."

***

Morgan did as she was told. Tom, what was his last name?, was right. At this point, there was nothing much to lose. If the man wanted to, he could notify the highway patrol where she was right now. Cianci! That was it. She would most certainly Google him to see with whom she was dealing, right after she learned more about what happened to Rob. Guilt swept over her. God, Ray must be hanging on by a thread. She would beat this. The least she could do now that the damage was done was to come home free and clear of this pill baggage. She was almost there. Somehow along the way she would have to prepare Ava for the truth about Uncle Rob. It would be her first direct encounter with loss. She was aware that people went up to heaven, but until now that place had been reserved for grandparents and great uncles she had never met.

A knock on the window brought her back to the present. She found the visage of what she estimated to be a seventy-something man with a tanned, ruggedly handsome face and Roman nose that looked to have been broken long ago and never set right. She lowered the passenger side window.

"Good afternoon, Morgan," said Tom. He then looked over the seat at Ava with her blonde ringlets and smiling eyes. "Hello, Ava Elizabeth McCarthy."

"Are you the meatball man?"

Tom smiled.

"I am indeed the meatball man." Tom extended a large Styrofoam container and plastic cutlery through the window and lowered it into the passenger seat.

"Now there's plenty enough for everyone, but don't eat all the meatballs. I've been warned about you Ava."

Tom waggled an index finger at her. Ava continued to smile while shaking her head.

"I do not know what you're talking about."

"Ha!" Tom threw back his head and laughed.

"And this is for you, Mom," said Tom and handed a Chewbacca PEZ dispenser through the window.

Morgan lowered her head and smiled sadly.

"Nice touch," she said.

"Cheer up," exclaimed Tom. "You're winning. This'll be over in no time. Give me a call when you're on the road tomorrow and brief me on your cash situation. Drive for a while tonight, but don't sleep in the car. You need cash now?"

"We're OK. Thank you."

"By Mr. Meatballs."

"It's Tom," said Morgan.

"Goodbye Uncle Tom."

"Ha!" Tom laughed. He made as if he were tipping an imaginary cap. "Goodbye, Ms. Ava." He theatrically twirled his keys and lost them on the third revolution. They flew toward the rear of the Toyota and skidded across the ground.

"Oops. I used to be better at that. Arthritis."

Morgan smiled and looked down again at the PEZ dispenser. Ava laughed with delight.

Morgan watched the old man through the rearview mirror as he ambled to the back of her car towards his keys. He stooped, then stooped again, coming up with his keys on the second try.

23
Three Angry Men

Howard Spruill was pissed. Had he not just had this same conversation with Ray McCarthy a few days ago? And now he had the wife of the deceased interrogating persons of interest, which yielded a list of repeat offenders with whom Spruill was well acquainted. Sacrificial lambs they were. Oh, he did not doubt that at least two of them were capable of beating someone to death, especially Kyle Seymour who had put both his ex-wife and her new boyfriend in Moore Regional Hospital. He was paranoid, bi-polar, and drug-fueled. He had bankrupted two construction companies as a result, but he was no one's lackey. Neither were the other folks on Candace Erwin's "list." All she did was let Matt Roper know that he was on the sheriff department's radar.

He had given Candace a project similar to Ray's—snoop through her husband's home office records and bring him anything of interest. She had accepted the challenge, and Spruill was confident that that would keep her busy and out of harm's way—more confident anyway than Ray's research would keep him out of harm's way. Ray didn't have to look for trouble. It seemed to know where he was at all times.

One blessing was that Jim Dorn was out of the country. The last thing he needed was a retired, self-important colonel up his ass. Conversely, Rita Erwin never called. She had retreated into herself, and Spruill desperately wanted to come up with something to offer her as progress. Not to mention that this was the first murder to occur in his sector of Moore County since he had joined the force. He was the drug guy. The deaths on his small-time watch had been accidental and self-inflicted. For these reasons and more, he pulled his cruiser into the sandy main drag of an officially nameless trailer park in Vass. Older deputies commonly referred to it as "Whispering Acres," The younger ones called it "The Narrows," a reference to the shit neighborhood Batman had to deal with in Gotham City. Spruill was interested in only one resident—parolee Darryl Richards.

He had busted Darryl on three occasions—possession or possession with intent to sell was the usual charge. It was always either weed or pain pills. Darryl was currently engaged in a righteous effort to remain clean and productive, but this was mostly because no one would sell to him anymore. Darryl was harmless, but he was also careless and stupid, and he would roll on his own mother to get out of trouble.

On his left Spruill noticed a dilapidated double-wide with a newly constructed deck and a Ford Super Duty pickup out front—Kyle Seymour. It would have been better if Kyle had not been home. He shouldn't be on a Tuesday morning, but there was no explaining Seymour's behavior, even Kyle couldn't explain it. A pair of fingers briefly parted a window blind and then disappeared. On his right, a screen door rattled as a storm door was slammed shut.

"Hello everyone," said Spruill to himself. "Good to see you too."

Darryl's single-wide sat at the end of the main drag before the trail made an abrupt bend to the left where two more condemned-looking structures sat draped in pine straw and occupied by squatters. Darryl was out the front door shirtless before Spruill even got out of the car.

"This is no good boss."

Spruill stepped out of the cruiser.

"You're looking rather thin, Darryl. What'd you say?"

"I said this is no good; you comin' here like this. I ain't in no trouble."

"No, you're not Darryl, not yet anyway. Why are you so thin?"

"I ain't been workin', so I ain't been eatin' so good. You can't be here," said Darryl with a furtive glance up the street.

"I can be wherever my job takes me, Darryl. I did not build your reputation."

"No, but you can make it worse."

Spruill stepped close to Darryl and lowered his voice. "I need your help Darryl, but I don't want to make your life difficult. Grab your fishing pole after I leave and head right through these woods to Camp Easter Road. You remember where I first busted you sellin' weed on the Northeast side of Crystal Lake?"

"Well, yeah."

"I'm going to meet you there in twenty minutes. Then you and I are going to have lunch in Lee County. You need a sandwich."

"Ummm…"

"Darryl, you and I are going to have a sandwich in Lee County, or I am going to come right back here and let your paranoid neighbor guess what I'm up to. Got it?"

"Got it."

"Now make a show of telling me off, go back inside and slam the screen door, unless you think slamming the door will make the whole damn trailer collapse around your ears."

"I ain't had nothin' to do with that!" yelled Darryl. "Leave me the hell alone. I been clean for six months!"

Darryl threw up his hands and marched back to the door of his trailer. He slammed the screen door shut only for it to bounce back open and sit agape, slightly off its hinges. Good enough. Spruill got back in the car and headed out.

***

Jim Dorn sat in the back of a McAllister's Deli in Raleigh, tired and frustrated after being twenty-four hours in the air, taking stock of his existence. Tom Cianci had left him a voicemail. Not only had he found Morgan and Ava, but he had made contact and was shadowing them up the 95. It was good news, but it left him nothing to do, so he opened his laptop and pulled up the screenshots from the Abian Industries tree-mounted cameras, of which there were three.

Luckily the kid had pulled up rather close to the barn, and so Jim had a view of the front, rear, and passenger side of the BMW as well as a wonderfully clear shot of the auburn-haired lad who got out of it.

He did a license-plate lookup on Search Quarry. There would be a record of his actions, but this may very well come to nothing, so who cared? Jim couldn't buy the idea that the kid had stumbled upon the barn. It was too hard to find. Equally hard to process was what the young man, or his handler, hoped to learn or accomplish. Until yesterday, Jim believed he had one of the most secure and under-the-radar operations in the world.

Christopher Sedgwick was the owner of the mysterious beemer, and Jim had to admit that the name most certainly fit the foppish urban professional from the security stills. One thing was also sure: he was not exactly a kid at almost forty-four years old.

Before he made a definitive move in any direction, though, Jim would set in motion some contingencies, and so he dialed up Wyatt Halsey down in Wilmington.

"Air America," answered Wyatt.

"Very funny," replied Jim.

"What are you doing back in the States this soon old friend?"

"The shipment en route to you now will be the last one, Wyatt."

"Are we compromised or are you finally retiring?"

"We are compromised overseas."

There was a considerable silence before Wyatt spoke again.

"How are we here in the States?"

"They have no desire to alter our life here, and I believe them. However, I am going to look into what may or may not be a concern of a local nature."

"What do you need from me?" asked Wyatt.

"Once customs is done with our container, and it is on its way up 74, I want you to fly the Cessna into Moore County airport and top it off when you get there. Before you do that, though, rent us a house up Moore County, and make sure it is not in an area where our comings and goings would be noticed. Use the Abian credit card. Incidentally, unless someone decides to check, you're the only one who knows I'm stateside, and I'd like to keep it that way for a while.

"I'll get on the rental," said Wyatt. "Where we flying to?"

"The TTX. It has a range that will allow us to visit Provo correct?"

"Yes, it does. Are we gonna be conch farmers?"

"You can choose to be. If so, my house is there is yours. From there I may go visit Uncle Victor, and you are more than welcome to join me."

"These sound like contingencies Colonel."

"At our age, such things are a must. I'll see you soon."

Jim ended the call. The last time he had visited his home in the Providenciales of Turks and Caicos was to get the house ready for Ray to use on his honeymoon. That was more than five years ago. Since then it had only one had one tenant who gave up the lease a year ago. There was a service he used to clean the house monthly, tend to storm damage, and to maintain the landscaping. He assumed it was in good shape. Speaking of storms, it was the beginning of hurricane season in the Caribbean. That might necessitate additional contingencies.

Jim turned his attention back to the security stills. Mr. Sedgewick's rear passenger-side window had a barcode on it similar to those he'd noticed on both Ray and Rita's vehicles. He zoomed in and barely made out the words "Carolina Vista."

Another Google search revealed that Carolina Vista was a townhome complex. Mr. Sedgewick lived right down the road in Cary, NC.

"Why don't I sort you out right now?" said Jim to Chris's grainy image.

***

I remembered every detail—about her, about that night.

Rob and Candace had ditched me at yet another charity event in Pinehurst. I leaned on the corner of the bar in a rented tuxedo that looked like it was wearing me. I usually cleaned up nice, but on this occasion, I should have spent more time with the measuring-tape lady. It helped that I had ditched the jacket and was standing in vest and bow tie with my sleeves artfully rolled up, a poorly-suppressed grin on my face.

On the parquet dance floor before me a fifty-something executive from Eaton Golf Grip was shimmying himself red-faced with a trio of ladies I hoped were his wife and two daughters.

She approached in a gown with a slit up the right thigh. Her hair was blonde. The gown was red.

"Exactly what are you grinning at?" she asked.

I turned to find blue eyes—big, sparkly ones which gave me pause. I recovered by extending my hand toward the sweaty executive as if to say "behold."

She almost spit out the sip she had just taken from her drink.

"Since I caused that, I'll buy you another."

"What are you drinking?" she asked.

"Scotch."

"That is a serious drink, an older-man drink." I turned to the bartender. "I'll have a Scotch and a Fuzzy Navel for the young lady."

Morgan turned to the bartender.

"Make that a vodka tonic, and I'll get the old man's Scotch," she said with a wink in my direction.

The bartender laughed and went to work.

"What song are they dancing to?" I asked.

"'Womanizer' by Britney Spears."

"Perfect."

"Should I put in a request for some Bon Jovi? Will that get you out there?" she asked, raising one eyebrow.

"As far as '80s bands, I was more partial to The Cult."

"I don't know them. I was enamored with Guns 'N Roses."

"How's that? 'When Appetite for Destruction' was released, you were probably just learning to write your name."

"Videos. I loved Axl Rose's snake dance."

"Let's see it."

"Not a chance."

"You can't love the snake dance and not have your own rendition of it. It has to be good; you've been working on it since you were a toddler."

Our drinks arrived, and we toasted.

"I am Ray McCarthy. Nice to meet you…"

"Morgan Anderson."

"Ms. Morgan, I too have a version of the snake dance. Let's have a talk with the DJ. Then we will sort this out like gentlemen."

She laughed and took my arm.

Her snake dance was better.

I still loved my wife.

Damn it.

For the first time since Morgan had taken off, I had dreamed of her. So, needless to say, Tuesday morning I woke up conflicted. I had been rolling off a substantial reserve of anger, and that had worked for me.

Said dream was on the heels of me ransacking the house for most of the evening in search of the time capsule. Who would take it? Well, no one. Without it, I had no idea what I had changed as a result of my last trip through 1984. Oh yes, I could dial Rob's number and see if he was among the living, but I didn't have the balls to do that without a little more information.

Mostly I was afraid of learning that nothing had changed.

But something had changed.

I remembered getting the time capsule from Colonel Jim. That didn't mean anything, though, because I retained memories both old and new. Everything was in my head—everything and nothing. I would have to wait and see what new wrinkle presented itself and proceed from there.

I thought of young Ray. Right now, he'd be busy up in Durham, jogging, stretching, and psyching himself up, and that gave me an idea. I too would keep busy to keep sane. I decided to look into Halo Construction.

Halo was controlled by a holding company in Charlotte called Universal Imports, a ridiculously vanilla name that sounded shady as hell to me. Then again, I was looking for shade. I was in a shade mood. Such a business relationship did explain why Halo could perhaps operate at a perpetual loss. If Halo went under, the holding company would not be liable and would write off the whole thing.

However, when I looked up when Halo was registered as a business, I found that it had been around for almost seven years. I guessed that the holding company (if Halo had always low-balled everyone and operated at a loss) either used Halo as some kind of tax shelter because they funneled money into it endlessly to keep it alive, or they used it to launder money. That last revelation may have been me looking for shade again. It just all sounded a little off.

There were no definitive answers just by poking around public records and perusing the internet. There was the Ellerbe Fellowship Baptist Church on Wallace Road in nearby Richmond County—the first church project Rob had bid on and lost to Halo was only twenty minutes away. Halo was registered as a business that originated from Richmond County.

Road trip.

Suddenly my phone lit up.

"Hello, Mr. Cianci."

"I found 'em, kid. Now what?"

***

Spruill parked his cruiser at the local post office and doubled back on foot through the woods flanking Mill Creek. He would keep tabs on Darryl's progress through the woods toward Crystal Lake. Worst case scenario was that Darryl would hightail it on his liquor-cycle and lay low somewhere for a few days. If Spruill didn't lay eyes on him inside of fifteen minutes, he'd assume Darryl had made a run for it on his motor-scooter.

This was not the case. Spruill ducked behind a tree when he spotted Darryl trudging through the undergrowth carrying his obligatory fishing pole and no tackle box. What was more interesting was the six-foot-four inch, 300-pound shadow less than 200 yards behind him and advancing quickly: Kyle Seymour.

Darryl muttered to himself and remained oblivious.

Kyle and his younger brother Travis had been a popular wrestling tag-team throughout the Southeast. Initially part of Matt and Jeff Hardy's OMEGA Championship Wrestling crew until the Hardy's signed with World Wrestling Entertainment. The Seymours bounced to a variety of wrestling promotions from the late 1990s until the early 2000s.

Whereas the Hardy's were hell-bent on being great entertainers, Kyle and Travis were hell-bent on being famous. Hell, they thought they already were famous, and the recreational excess of drugs came quickly. They often could not remember their in-ring choreography, and as a result, many of their opponents got hurt.

Also, their oratory and acting skills remained something to be desired. Travis relied heavily on tired clichés. Kyle spoke little. Nevertheless, they rocked their shtick of good-natured behemoths who thwarted the antics of heel wrestlers wreaking havoc. The Seymours were a crowd favorite. They even attracted the attention of WWE talent scout Jim Ross. Ross, however, quickly deduced the Seymours as doomed to remain a regional act. Even that gig came to an end when Kyle kicked his ex-wife's ass and threw her boyfriend from a second-floor balcony into a hotel swimming pool.

Ironically, the ensuing years had seen Kyle deemed the more responsible of the brothers.

He was able to pull himself together for long stretches and build businesses which employed Travis. When Kyle fell off the wagon, though, it was spectacular. Travis was being dragged behind the wagon, his big brother desperately trying to haul him on board. It was only a matter of time before he slipped off and disappeared into the gutter.

And now Spruill watched this less-than-stable T-Rex—the responsible one—advancing toward Darryl. Spruill had his Glock 19. The TASER was in the car. That was not good. If Kyle got out of hand, he would have to subdue him physically or shoot him. He had time for neither the paperwork nor the period of mandatory administrative duty that came with plugging someone.

Kyle picked his pace up to a jog and closed the distance between him and Darryl. Spruill put his hand on his pancake holster and waited. Darryl finally spun around when Kyle was no more than 100 feet from him.

"What the hell do you want?" yelled Darryl, desperately trying to make his fear sound like annoyance.

He should be scared, thought Spruill.

"I wanna know what you're up to you little NARC," said Kyle, calmly striding through the remaining distance between them.

"What the hell does it look like? And since when am I a NARC?"

"It looks like you're going fishing without a tackle box and without a bucket to hold your fish. It looks you just had a quick chat with Detective Spruill."

Kyle placed his right paw on Darryl's scrawny shoulder. Kyle's neck began at his earlobes, and his shoulders looked like grapefruits. A slightly distended belly suggested little interest in cardiovascular pursuits, and Spruill hoped there was some tactical advantage there because Kyle looked like he could body slam a refrigerator.

"If you saw that, you saw me tell him off," yelled Darryl. This time he sounded convincingly pissed off.

"You're gonna tell me what that was really about. You're gonna tell me that or I'm gonna throw you around these woods until you can't get up."

Spruill stepped from behind the tree and strode toward them with purpose, which visibly startled Kyle.

"It was Darryl being non-compliant, Kyle. He was so non-compliant that I wondered what he was up to, so I followed him. Now I'm wondering what you're up to."

Spruill sounded like a teacher losing his patience. Darryl exhaled audibly and looked infinitely relieved. Kyle had recovered from the initial shock of Spruill's appearance, but he was still nervous. He was not used to being advanced upon, especially by a man whom he outweighed by 120 pounds or more, and that made him snap.

"I have told you people to leave me and my family alone, damn it!"

Kyle released Darryl and went to meet Spruill.

"This is not about you idio—" Spruill started.

Kyle grabbed a fistful of Spruill's button-down shirt with his left hand. His right arm reared back to commence a haymaker assault. Spruill then quickly adopted a boxer's angular stance and grabbed Kyle's right bicep with his left hand. Spruill wrapped his right hand around Kyle's left wrist, the hand that held Spruill's shirt, and pulled himself closer to Kyle's chest.

He turned his head down and to the right, tucking in his chin.

Kyle's first shot was a good one, but it glanced off the side of Spruill's turned head. So did the next three. Spruill kept his left arm extended, pawing for Kyle's bicep. His slight reach advantage took much of the force and speed out of the haymakers. In the meantime, he kept shuffling to the right. The two of them looked like a pair of middle school kids in their first awkward slow dance.

Kyle was frustrated. Spruill was too close for a clean shot to the face, and Spruill kept moving him in a circle, so he was perpetually off balance. He would have to switch tactics.

Spruill bided his time. He waited for a pause in the haymakers. Guys of this size always reverted to grappling. He would wait until he felt Kyle shift his weight forward instead of away.

He felt it. Kyle attempted to lunge right with the haymaker hand, most likely to grab Spruill's belt and throw him to the ground. That maneuver guaranteed that most of Kyle's weight would be on his right leg. Spruill picked up his own right leg and brought it down on the inside of Kyle's right knee.

Kyle howled and folded sideways to the ground. Spruill drew his weapon and immediately mounted Kyle, pistol whipping him twice. He was going for a third when he saw the glazed look in Kyle's eyes. Spruill holstered the Glock, rolled the behemoth over, and cuffed him.

"Holy shit, I about pissed myself. I thought we were both goners," said Darryl.

"Stay back. He's dazed, not out."

"What if he had got your gun."

"He couldn't have fired it, Darryl. It recognizes my handprint only."

"When the hell did that come about?"

"Shut up Darryl."

Spruill rolled Kyle face-up and patted him on the cheek.

"You OK sunshine?"

"Just take me to jail," Kyle moaned.

"Not today shithead. We're all going to lunch."

24
Road Trips

"No."

"I absolutely did find them, kid. I met them yesterday afternoon at a gas station. We came to an unspoken agreement," said Tom.

"How is Ava? How did she look? Is she eating OK?"

"She ate well last night. I brought her meatballs from one of my favorite haunts in St. Augustine."

Florida. They made it to Florida, and then Morgan ran out of ideas.

"What agreement?" I asked.

"I made it clear to your wife that I know what she is trying to do, and that I am here in a guardian angel capacity until she is ready to come home."

"And what exactly is she trying to do and how does it involve my daughter?"

"Taking your daughter on impulse was a mistake I believe she regrets. She is trying to beat this addiction herself. She's cut her dosage in half. She's winning. I'm going to make sure she crosses the finish line. She is also afraid that she will come back clean and sober only to get arrested and divorced."

"I am not going to have her arrested. I am still on the fence about divorce."

"Get off the fence. You're not getting divorced," said Tom.

"Aren't you the guy that told me to 'adjust my marital arrangement when this is over?'"

"You're not doing that. This is going to work out for you."

And just like that, it was decided. I would give Morgan the benefit of the doubt. When she came home, we'd try to put the pieces back together.

Tom explained that he had interrupted a delivery and scared the shit out of some kid. In one fell swoop he got Morgan to contact him while establishing control over the meds. He was tracking Morgan with a magnetized GPS device he had slapped on to the gas tank of her car. It was impressive and a little scary.

Though Morgan still had money and could buy more meds if she wanted, she seemed to be content with meeting up with Tom for her reduced dosage, probably took some comfort in not being alone, and in having some non-invasive guidance. I had a feeling that Ava found Tom most entertaining.

I knew what Tom was trying to do. He wanted to go back to Morgan with a message that home would be a safe place to land when this was over so she could focus on the task at hand.

Tom also wanted me to clear my head of at least one thing so I could cross my own finish line.

Tom was a good guy, regardless of what Google said about him.

"Tom, have you briefed the Colonel on all this?"

"I left him a voicemail. I will probably not pick up when he calls back. I don't want him trying to control a situation that is already under control."

Well, Tom had been a quick study on Uncle Jim, and I agreed that the Colonel would only muddy the waters by forcing the resolution that he himself had envisioned.

"It doesn't matter. He's still in the Philippines."

"That's a good place for him. I gotta go kid. Morgan is out of her hotel and on the move up 95. I like to stay relatively close."

"Thanks, Tom. I can't tell you what it means to know they're safe."

"I know. Now don't get yourself in trouble poking around up there. The people who killed your friend are not professionals. They were violent and sloppy, and they simply lucked out. They are wanna-be professionals, and that kind is a lot more dangerous. Take care."

Tom hung up, and I sat in foreboding silence for several minutes. Then the doorbell rang, and I about jumped out of my seat.

I carefully approached, trying to get a look at the figure on the other side of the frosted, beveled glass. I could see nothing but a shadow, and so I just opened the door.

Father Baumann.

"Well Father, I am both surprised and not surprised to see you," I said as I opened the door.

"Hello, Ray. What do you mean?"

"I mean I was just talking to Tom. I think you two are on the same wavelength."

"We've known each other a long time. What's the word on Morgan and Ava?"

"He found them and is following them up 95."

Baumann smiled.

"Father, I'm headed out to the Ellerbe Fellowship Baptist Church. Why don't you ride with me and I will fill you in on Morgan and Ava?"

"I think I can do that. I was just at Rita's house checking up on her. Will you also fill me in on why we're going to Ellerbe?"

"Yes. It has to do with Rob. How's Rita?"

"Her New England resolve to carry on has served her well, but it is faltering. Parents should not be predeceased by their children. It guts them like cancer, and it is very difficult to overcome. The only thing she is looking forward to is some kind of closure."

"I am on a closure mission."

"Does Detective Spruill know about this mission?"

"Detective Spruill gave me this mission."

"Very well. I know Pastor Lowery. Let's go say hello."

***

Father Baumann listened to me relate Tom's location of Morgan and Ava showing little-to-no surprise, as if Tom finding them was the inevitable conclusion for which had been waiting.

"Father, if you don't mind me asking, how do you know Tom?"

"He would sometimes hide out in the church where I was an altar boy."

"Hide out from what?"

Father Baumann glanced at me. When he didn't say anything, I turned to find him staring at me like I was a complete idiot.

"Never mind, Father. You don't have to spell it out. He's a good man."

"He is indeed," said Bauman. "Tell me how you want this to proceed."

I had briefed Father on the particulars of Halo Construction and its holding company Universal Imports, and he had a unique perspective.

"A few years ago, I wouldn't have thought twice about a huge company doing what equates to charitable acts through a non-profit division, but in the age of mega-churches where faith has become big business, it doesn't make any sense."

"No, it doesn't," I said. "Spruill doesn't think much of this angle, which is why he is using it to keep me busy, but I have a feeling there is something to this."

"If only because there don't seem to be any other explanations," interjected Baumann.

"Exactly."

"Well, Ray, I'll break the ice. I play golf with Pastor Lowery. Sacred Heart could use some renovations to its classrooms. I will simply tell the good pastor we are here to have a look at Halo's handiwork."

"Is there anyone you don't play golf with?"

Father Baumann didn't miss a beat. "Golf is how business is done in the Sandhills, and yes, I have never played golf with you."

Business. Everything was business, even Jesus.

Ellerbe Fellowship Baptist Church was a modest brick structure with a seamless, sprawling addition to the left of its main entrance. There was also an additional free-standing hall on the other side of the parking lot. I couldn't tell one way or the other if the work quality was good, but it seemed like the Baptists got a lot of bang for their buck. Baumann had called ahead and let Lowery's administrative assistant know we were dropping by. Apparently, he got the message, because Lowery was out front waiting for us.

"Hello there Father Baumann! We are overdue to hit the fairways together!"

"Yes, sir we are. Thank you for seeing us."

Lowery was probably in his mid-fifties, sandy-haired, and with a booming voice that emitted from a slender, diminutive frame of five feet, seven inches.

"Lois said you wanted to see our classrooms. Well, Vacation Bible

School is in session as we speak, so we'll have to peer into the classrooms through the windows, but that will give you an idea of the dimensions. Are you Ray McCarthy?"

"Yes, sir."

"My wife is reading your book…the one on the beach."

"*Return to Summer*," I said.

"That's the one. She'll be so excited. I wish I had her copy with me. How do you know our Yankee Father?"

"I am a member of his flock. Tell you what, before we leave I will jot down a little note for your missus if you have a pen and paper handy."

"That'd be very nice of you young man, very nice. How can I help you?"

"Ray knows his way around these parts better than I do, so he's assisting with navigation. I wanted to lay eyes on the workmanship of Halo Construction. They built your classrooms, correct?"

"Yes, but that was just before I became pastor here. I can tell you that we've had no problems with the classrooms. They are spacious; the HVAC unit is efficient. The flooring holds up rather well, and that's about all I know other than it was a hometown boy who did the building."

Bingo.

"There is very little information on Halo other than pictures and a digital form to fill out so as to begin the estimate process. Who owns it?" asked Baumann.

"His name escapes me, but he's a local and a member of this congregation too—so I'm told."

"I don't understand."

Father Baumann placed a hand on my shoulder and said, "Like you, this gentleman's church attendance gets more sporadic the older he gets."

Pastor Lowery let out a low, resonant chuckle.

"That is, in fact, the case, Father. He was a regular attendee as a child, but I have never met him, even though he lives just a few miles from here. I know that the congregation was very pleased that he was doing the renovations and that they thought he did a great job."

"Perhaps after looking at the classrooms we can find his place if only to have an address to send a letter of inquiry," said Father Baumann.

"I here-tell you can't miss the contractor's house. It's a horse farm with no horses—lots of property that falls away from a big white home."

***

Baumann and I made a pretense of looking into the classrooms for about twenty minutes. I mentioned to Lowery what the bid on this job had been, explaining that we had to see for ourselves the quality of the work. Lowery too was amazed at the low bid, but then he smiled and said he was sure that some "Good-ole-boy networking was probably in play." Before we left, I wrote his wife a quick letter thanking her for reading the book. It was the first of two letters I would write that day.

Not five miles farther down, we found a sprawling horse farm devoid of grazing livestock. Atop the acreage was a plantation-style home with four columns and a deep veranda. A series of tiered brick steps led from the circular drive to the plateau of lawn upon which the house rested. The house was so incongruous with the surrounding farms, Baumann wrote down the address.

This was the house of a builder. This was the house of a builder who did well. Clearly, there was more to this guy's story. Baumann and I got out of the car and walked to the fence and stared at more than 300 yards of lawn framed by the two parts of the U-shaped driveway that led to the main road. To the left and right of the house were fields. In one of the fields was a pair of horse barns. One looked as if it had been converted into a guest residence.

"Both you and Rob are landscaping enthusiasts, but I'm not sure either one of you would be excited to take care of that much grass."

"No, I'd have to have..."

Just then we heard the firing of an engine and a man riding a large zero-radius mower appeared on the drive.

"One of those."

Baumann grinned as I continued to stare. The mower began its slow advance toward us. Baumann decided it was time to get back in the truck, and still, I stared. There was something familiar about the paunchy, middle-aged man piloting the mower. I took my phone out of my pocket and brought it up to my ear as if I had pulled over to take a call, or as if I were calling a tow truck.

The man's gaze remained on his mow line, but I recognized the perfectly tousled hair, which was now entirely gray. He got closer, and I made out the lantern jaw and dimpled chin. The eyes sagged, and his neck was a bit fleshy. He looked like Tom Brady—if Tom Brady retired and went on a steady diet of beer and cigarettes. Finally, he looked up, and our eyes met.

I was staring at Scott Windham.

I waved, and he casually waved back. I quickly turned and made my way around to the driver's side of the truck, got in, and fired the engine.

"You look like you've seen a ghost," said Baumann.

"I have. I know that man."

It was there and then on the side of Route 73 that I had a revelation about getting bounced from certain places when running through 1984. There was no reason to jog down Cottage Grove Lane after Art Dykeman. There was no reason to play shark in the deep end of the pool. The anomaly's purpose was to show me what I needed to see, and what I needed to see was Scott Windham.

I was certain of it.

25
Call Him

Jim Dorn left McAllister's Deli and did a quick check of his cash situation: two grand and some change. That'd be enough for now. He was aware of the blatant trail one's digital meanderings left behind, which was why the battery was now out of his phone, and his debit and credit cards were locked in the glove compartment of his SUV.

He pulled into a Best Buy and dropped eighty-seven dollars on a Uniden handheld police scanner and then stopped in CVS and purchased a box of latex gloves and a shower cap. Just before getting back on Route 40, he saw a Lowes hardware store and grabbed a box of zip ties, a hammer, and a pair of ratchet straps.

He followed his GPS to Carolina Vistas. A more in-depth look into Christopher Sedgewick revealed that he was originally from Pinehurst and was currently an independent software guru serving the companies in Research Triangle Park. That gave Jim an idea.

Jim rolled up to the gate only to be greeted by a man roughly his age. He lowered the driver-side window.

"Good afternoon, young man," said Jim.

The guard smiled.

"Either you're someone's grandparent, or you're lost, nothing but young urban professionals in here."

"I am neither, but I need one of those young, urban professionals to fix my laptop. It's all seized up with a virus. I am looking for Christopher Sedgewick."

"Oh, well he's your guy for that stuff, and you were right to come here first. He sets his own hours, but he's out, probably at the at the Academy Street Bistro having one of his three-martini lunches."

"That sounds like my kinda man."

The guard coughed out a laugh. "Head down Chapel Hill Road the way you were going, and in two miles hang a left on Academy Street. Let me lift the gate so you can come in and turn around."

"Much obliged, sir," said Jim who promptly raised the tinted window and ended the conversation before names were exchanged. If Seven Lakes had taught him anything, it's that gated communities, if their security cameras worked at all, discarded the footage quickly. There was no need to make more of an impression on the guard.

***

"Mary Anne, you make the best martini I've ever tasted."

Christopher Sedgewick sat at the expansive bar of the Academy Street Bistro hunched over his chicken pesto panini. A pendant light hung from the creme-colored, tiled ceiling and illuminated his crow's feet.

"Well Mr. Sedgewick, you can't feature something called 'Martini Tuesdays' and not make a hell of a martini," said Mary Anne. "Is there anything else I can get you?"

"Just a little salt if you would."

"No problem. Be right back."

With a wink and a smile, Mary Anne turned and sauntered off. Christopher did not need the salt; he needed another look and his twenty-five-year-old bartender's pert little bum. It was exquisite. He sat there marveling at it and feeling like newly-minted money. His hair was freshly colored, his cologne judiciously applied, and his teeth professionally whitened. He and his old pal in Moore County had just settled up for the variety of errands and favors Chris had completed over the last two months. Life was again good. After lunch, he'd run home, do a little work, and then take a nap. At around 7 p.m., he'd casually stroll into the little club Mary Anne liked to go to after work and buy a round for all her friends.

It was time to move on from his side gig. He knew little about what his buddy was up to, but what he did know made him uncomfortable. Creating accounts and moving money around for him was easy, and by itself, it appeared merely devious. Writing encryption software and spying on people was a bit more alarming. If it all came crashing down, he'd like to be able to look someone in the eye and say, "I didn't know, but it looked weird, and I stepped away." So that was the plan.

He never even heard the old man approaching. Suddenly he was just there standing next to Christopher at a bar that was empty save for the two of them. Then his hand was resting on the back of Chris's neck.

"How does one acquire a drink around here?" the man asked.

"One waits for the stunning waitress to return," said Chris.

"Well then, it sounds like it's worth the wait."

***

Colonel Jim took the second stool down from Sedgewick. He could smell the pissant's Drakkar Noir. It orbited him like the rings of Saturn. He sized Chris up. Sedgewick was a little shorter than Ray but about the same age, and that made Jim wonder. The man-boy wore an expensive pastel-colored golf shirt and pressed khaki pants without pleats. The shoes were nothing more than Florsheims, but the watch, there the boy splurged. The watch was a Rolex Submariner, not the top of the line, but not cheap. The BMW parked outside was the same one from the security stills. It looked to be a few years old and in need of tires.

Christopher Sedgewick reeked not only of moderately-priced cologne but of a man living above his means, a man who had some money but who pretended to have more.

Mary Anne returned with a smile.

"Young lady, if martinis are served here, I would like one. I'll also buy this young man his next round as he was correct that you were most certainly worth the short wait."

"Would you like that shaken or stirred, Mr....?"

The colonel approximated a remarkable impression of Sean Connery.

"Ed. Ed is my name. The martini? Shaken, of course, Mary Anne, and dirty as you can make it."

"You got it, Mr. Ed."

Sedgewick began to laugh and then turned to offer his hand.

"I'm Christopher Sedgewick, software engineer, Ed. What brings you to Cary?"

"A long plane ride resulting in a profound need for a martini."

"Noted. Nice to meet you."

Jim turned to Sedgewick and eyeballed him quizzically, still channeling Sean Connery, if only by facial expression.

"What is it a software engineer does, Mr. Sedgewick?"

Sedgewick commenced a grand sweeping gesture with his right hand toward the northeast corner of the bar.

"In yonder distance is Research Triangle Park. Regardless of the company, there are a variety of computer systems in there running a variety of shows, and they need instructions. Those various systems sometimes need to be able to talk to each other as well, and then they need more instructions on how to do that. I am the provider of instructions."

"That," said Jim, "sounds rather lucrative."

"Not as lucrative as you may think. What is it you do, Ed?"

"Antiques and sometimes pottery."

"That sounds not lucrative at all."

"You'd be very much surprised young man. People are always trying to buy back time— a memory or an object that represents a better place. Maybe they want something that no one of their generation has, a chair or a bar that looked like it could have belonged to Don Draper, who knows?"

"Not my thing, but I see where you're coming from."

"Not your thing huh?"

"Not in the least."

"Even if I had some vintage Star Wars toys still in the package?"

"Well, now you have my attention."

"You're the right age, and now they are going to make a slew of new movies. It's good business to track down the toys. You Gen-Xers supposedly have the disposable income now."

"Disposable income?" Chris laughed. "That's a myth."

"I'll tell you what," continued the Colonel, "I have plenty of disposable income but limited tech knowledge. I've got a virus on my computer holding my files hostage, and I get endless notices of an expensive opportunity to rectify the issue."

"That's a ransom virus. Where'd you pick that up? I picture you doing nothing more on your laptop than checking email and stalking eBay."

"It's probably the Filipino porn I've been looking at."

Chris spit out some of his martini. "You, sir, are a piece of work."

"So I've been told, but back to the issue at hand: I'm going to pay your tab here, and then I'm going to give you another 500 dollars to take that virus off my computer."

Sedgewick smiled. It was indeed a good day.

"You'll have to follow me back to my condo, Ed, but I can have your laptop back to normal in twenty minutes, and I'll even establish a data cloud for you so you can back up your files from here on."

***

Detective Spruill, Darryl Richards, and Kyle Seymour had to be the oddest trifecta of patrons ever to darken the door of the Applebee's in Sanford. Spruill sat on one side of the booth nursing a Diet Coke. Darryl's nervousness had taken a back seat to the first whiff of fried foods. He had already inhaled half his burger and was going to town on the French fries. Sitting next to Kyle's enormousness in the booth, he looked almost stuffed into the corner.

Exuding defeat and sadness, Kyle held his glass of Mountain Dew to his forehead where he'd been pistol whipped. It was he who spoke first.

"I'm sorry I put hands on you, detective. I have no excuses."

"What was your excuse when you launched your ex's boyfriend off the second floor of the Days Inn years ago?"

"Drugs. It was always drugs. My ex was on them too. Break-ups are hard enough as it is. People get mean. Drugs amplify everything. I'm not on drugs anymore, but my brother is. I wanted to find him before someone like you did."

"Kyle, I don't want your brother, but we'll get to him in a minute. In fact, I want to help you find him. Can either one of you tell me about Matt Roper?"

Darryl lit up. "The Prince of Pain. Oh yeah. He's a drug dealer."

"Who the hell is the Prince of Pain?" asked Spruill.

"Roper," Kyle interjected. "He was a promising cruiserweight boxer for a long time. He won the state title and defended it for quite a while. Had a few professional fights, did well."

"Then what happened?"

"Drugs. He got off them, but not before he lost everything, so now he sells drugs to make a living. That and he's a damn fine painter. I've hired him a couple of times."

"We still call him the Prince of Pain, though, 'cause all he pretty much sells is pain killers," said Darryl.

Spruill sat back in the booth and took in the sight of his two guests. Then he considered his next words carefully.

"Darryl: I need you to stay off drugs and get a job. Kyle: I need you to keep your temper in check and stay clear-headed. Do you really want me to find your brother? The chances are high that he's into something that is no good and that I can't ignore."

Darryl withdrew into himself and stayed silent. Kyle looked down at the table. Slowly he returned his eyes to meet Spruill's. Then he gave a barely perceptible nod before he spoke.

"I think it's at that point, detective. I haven't seen Travis in a month. The last time I did see him, though, he was high as a kite. He's been hooked on pain killers for years, but the high I saw him on was much different. I don't know what he's doing for money, but it has to involve drugs. He needs them, and it's all he knows now. "

"It sounds like his appetites are changing—chasing a bigger high. That's a bad road to be on," said Spruill.

"Everyone I know who has ever run down that road is dead," Kyle said. "That's why I'm going to help you find my brother."

Spruill nodded and looked at Darryl.

"Are you done with your food?"

"Yeah."

"Good. Time to get you back to the house. Kyle and I need to go for a ride."

***

Colonel Jim tipped an imaginary cap at the guard as he followed Christopher Sedgewick through the gate to his condo. He selected a parking slot a few spaces away from Chris and regarded the homes. They had been designed to look like Brooklyn brownstones, and thus he wondered why the builders hadn't worked that into the name of the place. Rob would have.

"I'm sorry, son," Jim whispered to himself. "I am going to find out what happened, but first I need to see what this man is about. You don't want to see this."

Jim exited the SUV and raised his index finger to Chris, indicating he needed a moment. Chris called to him.

"It's 106, Ed. The door will be open. I gotta get inside. It's hot as hell out here."

Jim nodded, smiled, and waved. Then he opened the back hatch of the SUV and dug inside for a small duffle bag. He pulled on a pair of latex gloves and tossed the zip ties and the hammer into the bag with the pair of ratchet straps.

Jim put on the shower cap and entered the condo. The layout was simple and open: wooden staircase on the left, great room on the right. In front of him was a short hallway to the kitchen where Sedgewick stood at the sink.

Perfect.

Jim hooked the duffle bag around the knob of the stair railing. He soundlessly made the distance to the kitchen in seconds, placed a sleeper hold around Chris's neck, and tilted the fool's head forward. Chris struggled for only a moment, and then he slumped to the floor.

Jim saw that the kitchen sink was wide and deep and featured a retractable faucet. He also saw that the kitchen table was long and quite tall. He would have to prop one end of the table with dishes or books, so it angled down to the sink.

This will do nicely, thought Jim.

***

Chris awoke to bewildering discomfort in his arms and shoulders. Then he realized his hands were bound behind him and rested at the small of his back. It felt like his chest and legs were strapped down. There was a bigger problem though. His head was in the sink.

Suddenly a man in a shower cap stood over him.

"Hi Chris," said Jim.

Calmly, Sedgewick responded.

"Hi, Ed. This got really weird, really quick. You some kind of pervert?"

Jim placed a cloth over Chris's mouth and nose and turned on the faucet.

It was unbearable. Chris immediately went back to when he was twelve and swimming in the lake. He had made a joke at his buddy Matt's expense, and Matt had held him under for what felt like forever.

Finally, the water stopped, and the cloth was removed. Chris erupted into a fit of coughing.

"Aw god, I think I'm gonna puke."

"I wouldn't recommend that," said Jim. "And to answer your question, no, I'm not a pervert. I have deduced though, sir, that you are a liar."

Jim returned the cloth and turned the water back on. After two interminable minutes, it was off again. This time Chris did puke.

Jim reached inside Chris's mouth with his gloved hand to spoon out some of the puke and flick it into the sink.

"Easy there kid. You can't move your head too much, so I'll help you. I can't have you going out like Jimi Hendrix before I get my information. Chris sputtered and coughed.

"What information?" croaked Chris.

"Do you remember what I said I did for a living?"

"Antiques I think."

"Correct. And do you remember your level of interest in antiques?"

"None," slobbered Chris.

"Correct again," said Jim. "Why then, young man, were you at my barn in Ellerbe and telling my proprietor that you were looking for antiques and pottery?"

"Oh shit."

"Oh shit is also correct."

Jim replaced the cloth and let the water flow.

Chris returned to that day in the lake. Matt had let him up, and all he heard was Scott laughing. Then back down he went. He had barely gotten half a breath.

Jim turned off the water and removed the cloth.

"Who told you to go to my barn?"

Chris hacked and coughed and snotted. Finally, his wind returned. He looked at the man called Ed, who was now holding a hammer. He felt the cold metal of the hammer caress his naked toes.

"Son, it's a simple question. This can get worse."

"Stop. Please. OK. One question though..."

"Shoot."

"What's with the shower cap?"

"Probably excessive," replied Jim flatly. "I watch a lot of *Forensic Files.* I don't want any DNA evidence lying about if I have to kill you."

Chris actually laughed.

"You don't have to kill me. I don't much care for my old pal, and I question what he's into. I won't even call the cops."

"I know you're not going to call the cops because you will either be dead or 500 dollars richer."

"You're still going to pay me?"

"You'll have earned it. I might even pay you more."

"His name is Scott Windham. He lives near that area."

"I want to know what it is you do for him, and after that, I want you to do one more thing before I cut you loose."

"What's that?"

"Call him."

***

The hay fields quickly gave way to great stands of longleaf pines on Samarcand Road in Eagle Springs. Lingering like a ghost behind a curtain of those pines was Samarcand Manor. On the 230-acre campus of this defunct correctional institution was a squalid cottage that Travis Seymour sometimes called home.

Samarcand Manor had opened as a facility for young women in 1918. In 1931, some of those young women tried to burn it to the ground. In the 1970s it became a co-ed facility catering to runaways and kids who were one step away from jail. The coincidence was not lost on Travis.

Not only was he figuratively a breath away from jail, but he was literally less than a mile from the firing range where correctional officers now trained.

The cottage listed on the southeast corner of the campus. It was a makeshift, half-forgotten storage facility accessible by a service road pock-marked with washouts and choked with brambles.

Travis slept during the day to the handgun staccato. In the evenings he was serenaded by a concert of bullfrogs and June bugs in the nearby tepid pond as he cooked. He needed a source of income. He did not like working for other people, and the person he worked for was losing his grip.

The cottage was essentially one floor save for a rickety staircase that led to a pilot-house room that functioned as a small attic. Hidden among the stacked steel bed frames, the rotting lampshades and the baskets for collecting strawberries, was a rather large suitcase. In it hid the Ephedrine, the acetone, the rock salt, the batteries, and a litany of other ingredients. The rest of his equipment he stored in a hole under the ancient outhouse in the backyard.

Meth was easy to make but hard to disguise. The swamp-ass odor of the pond helped to cover his tracks, but ammonia was an overpowering scent, and that was a hard smell to justify emanating from a vacant shack. Travis kept his batches small. After all, this was just an experiment, a test run. His boss might not appreciate a full-scale freelance operation. For the time being, he was still chained to the boss.

Travis had been up for days and was nearing a crash. In the corner of the great room was a mattress covered by a sleeping bag and a rolled-up fleece that served as a pillow. He looked at it hard and then pulled out his phone to set an alarm for 10 p.m. Tonight he would cook.

It was the hum of an engine with the air conditioning on that Travis heard first, then the low screech of branches on paint and the pneumatic hiss of struts absorbing the shock of tires plummeting into the washouts. It was the sound of a vehicle hesitantly negotiating the service road.

Travis did not bother to look out the window. He grabbed his phone and bolted out the back of the cottage through the corpse of a screen door on rusted hinges. He made his way to the tree line behind the pond. Less than a mile through those woods rested his truck, the only functional piece of equipment in an abandoned scrap metal yard. First, though, he would wait and see why the cottage was of interest to anyone.

***

"You're kidding me," said Spruill.

He and Kyle sat in the sedan before the coded gate of the Samarcand Training Academy.

"I am not, detective," said Kyle.

"The whole campus is fenced in. How does your brother come and go?"

"It's probably the last original cottage still standing—where some of the kids would bunk. It's on the back corner by a quarter mile of service road that runs right to the side of the house. No fence there. Service road is hard to find. If we do find it, we'll probably have to walk it."

"Show me," said Spruill.

It was a tufted hump of dirt that revealed the service road. Profound ditches flanked the blacktop, and suddenly there was an interruption in the steady trough of ditch on the left side of Samarcand Road. Spruill parked in the middle of the road, got out, and let the brambles tear at his slacks as his feet found the ruts of what used to be a road. Then he got back in the car and plunged the Crown Victoria into the overgrown mess. There was only about a hundred yards of uncertainty before the road opened up and revealed itself to be a genuine pathway big enough for a vehicle. Washouts jounced the sedan dramatically, but soon the ghost of a cottage appeared.

"Is there a back door?" Spruill asked.

"Yes."

"Go up and knock on it. Make sure Travis knows we come in peace and that we need his help. Then come back out and indicate to me whether or not he's on the premises."

Spruill watched Kyle disappear around the back of the house. Five minutes later he reappeared and motioned for Spruill to follow him, and Spruill obliged.

Spruill knew everything he needed to know about Travis Seymour the moment he stepped into the cottage.

"He's sleeping here," said Kyle shaking his head. "He made a little pallet over there in the corner with a sleeping bag. Man, that pond smells. I don't know how he stands it. Smells like bad eggs."

"It's not the pond."

Spruill took in the plank-board floor, the disheveled dust, and the rat droppings. He moved to the staircase, tried the first step, and decided it was sound. In the attic: more dust, bed frames, baskets, assorted furniture, and a large suitcase.

Spruill saw the disruption of dust leading to the suitcase. He matter-of-factly strode to the suitcase, laid it down, opened it, closed it, and walked down the stairs. Kyle spoke first.

"What's up the stairs?"

"Your brother is cooking meth within shouting distance of men training to be corrections officers. It is both amusing and concerning."

"I was afraid of this."

"Your brother is a meth head. Not only do I smell the ammonia, but upstairs in a suitcase are most of the necessary ingredients. I've got an opioid epidemic in this county and a heroin problem. I don't need meth re-entering the scene. Your brother has to go down, but not today."

"Why is that?"

"This is not a full-scale operation. It couldn't be—not located here. This is a meth starter kit. He's using it, and he's probably selling some of it. I'd rather watch him for a while. In the meantime, you can try to talk him out of it. We both get what we want. I learn his connections, and you get a chance to get Travis to do the right thing."

Kyle nodded.

"Now show me where he might hide a vehicle. Obviously, it's off-campus somewhere, and he walks into the cottage, but it can't be too far."

Kyle led Spruill to the edge of the pond and pointed toward where the woods recommenced.

"Through those woods I think there's a junkyard with its own crappy little road that leads back to pavement."

Both of them heard it and looked at each other. It was the unmistakable bell of a phone trying to activate Siri.

Spruill sprinted around the right side of the pond and made for the woods, drawing his weapon. In the woods he proceeded tree-to-tree, taking cover and assessing where next to move. The tree limb came down on him like an avalanche. He was unconscious before his face hit the forest floor.

***

Kyle found Travis standing over Spruill. Spruill was out; his gun spilled into the pine straw not far from his right hand. Travis eyeballed it.

"Travis don't you dare!" yelled Kyle.

Travis looked up at his brother, momentarily startled. Startled quickly turned to a look of disgust.

"You're telling me what to do? You? You bring a cop to my door, and now you're gonna to tell me what to do about the cop."

Kyle stayed in his big-brother voice, calm and commanding.

"You are cooking meth in the middle of cop land, and you're surprised a cop finally showed up? You idiot. I am trying to control this situation for you. He was not here to arrest you."

"Says you."

"Yeah says me. I asked for his help."

"To find me?"

"Yes. I knew you were into something bad, and I was right."

"That's not why he's here, Kyle. You're being played."

"What are you into? Why meth? Why are you trying to be a meth dealer?"

"I'm not a meth dealer. I'm just looking into my options. I don't like working for other people."

"Who? Who don't you like working for? What are you into? Come with me. We'll get out of here. We'll leave the cop right here. "

"You came with him, Kyle."

"Then take me with you. We'll go to my trailer, grab a few things, and we'll disappear. We'll get off the drugs for good, start over."

"It's too late for that. Stay with the cop."

Travis turned and jogged deeper into the woods. When Spruill came to, he found Kyle with his back against a tree staring into the distance.

"Why did you really want to come here?" Kyle asked in little more than a whisper.

"Did Travis hit me?" Spruill retrieved his weapon.

"Yes. Why are we here?"

"You asked me to find your brother. He's part of a crowd I'm looking into anyway."

"Does this have anything to do with the dead architect?"

"It does."

"Is that why you asked about Matt Roper?"

"Yes. The architect was beaten to death. Matt was a professional boxer, and he had a connection to Rob. Your brother has no connection to Rob, but he runs in the same circle as Matt, makes sense to see what he's up to."

"You think my brother could kill someone."

Spruill exhaled, rubbed the back of his skull, and sat against a tree.

"Kyle, your brother is the size of a dinosaur and is running around hopped up on meth. Yes, the thought crossed my mind that he could kill someone."

"He wants to get away from who he's working for. That's why he's trying to cook meth."

"Who is he working for?"

"He didn't say. If I were you, I'd start with that."

***

Travis didn't waste any time. He found his truck and jumped inside. He knew that Kyle knew the scrap yard and had seen the direction he was running. He knew it would be a matter of minutes before Spruill or some other cop came and blocked off the road to the scrap yard. He had another problem though. He was homeless again. He hated what he had to do next. He pushed on the center button of the phone.

"Siri, call Scott."

26
Ray McCarthy

Father Baumann and I drove in silence. Never once did I get the feeling that he was waiting with baited breath for me to elaborate on the man riding the lawn mower.

He was. After about fifteen minutes, he broke.

"As your priest, I'd be doing you a disservice if I did not inquire as to why you look like you've just had a stroke."

It was a solid assessment. I was indeed disoriented, and yet I was certain of at least one thing. However, there was a big piece of the puzzle missing. Why, after all these years, would Scott Windham want anything to do with Rob? And for God's sake why would he want to hurt him? Yes, they were both builders whose companies crossed paths no more than twice. Scott's company won both bids, so what? It certainly didn't bother Rob that much, and Rob sure as hell didn't know who owned Halo Construction.

"That man, Father, his name is Scott. He bullied Rob and me as kids. I've not seen him in decades."

"And you're sure it's him?"

"Yes."

"And?"

"And…I don't know. I think he's involved with what happened to Rob. I feel it in my gut."

Father Baumann thoughtfully studied the terrain as we entered the rural edge of Moore County via the wooded Jackson Springs, ultimately landing again in the land of lush fairways and US Open Golf Championships.

"When kids are abused, even if it's just run-of-the-mill bullying, many times they still see their abuser through the eyes of a child. Regardless of how they've aged and adapted, it can be quite traumatic."

Instantly I began an internal debate as to what and how much to tell the good Father. I settled on revealing to him as much of truth as I thought he could handle.

"I'm sure that's accurate Father, but that is not what I'm going through."

"You're going through a lot," he said.

"Yes, but I have a handle on it. I'm not sure you'd believe me if I told you the source of my certainty."

We came to a stop at a traffic light. I could feel Bauman staring at me again. I turned, and this time I found a smile in his eyes.

"You'd be amazed at what I'd believe, Ray. Try me."

***

When I finally did my homework on Tom Cianci and Father Baumann, it was a toss-up as to which one of them was more interesting. Baumann entered the military right out of high school, which perhaps explained the no-bullshit way he carried himself. To this day, though, Tom tells me that Baumann had been like that even as a kid.

Once honorably discharged, he immediately enrolled in Saint Joseph's Seminary in Yonkers. Baumann was one of the few priests his age well-versed in psychology, and he continued to study it online through the University of North Carolina at Chapel Hill.

In retrospect, I'd wish I'd told him the whole truth. Instead, I told him that I'd been dreaming about traveling back to 1984 and hanging out with both Rob and Arden. He listened and did not interrupt. By the time I was done, we were sitting at the bottom of my cul-de-sac in front of my house. Bauman responded succinctly.

"Ray, obviously you miss your friends and that time in your life. You should find Arden. You should make peace with the fact that Rob is gone, and that there is no way to undo that. However, do not discount everything your dreams are showing you. I don't think it is a coincidence that after all these years you dream of Scott Windham and then you find Scott Windham. If it will bring you peace, then jump down that rabbit hole and follow it to its end. Just don't get yourself hurt."

Why do people keep telling me not to hurt myself?

"Will do, Father, and thanks."

Baumann got out and hopped into his own truck. I laughed out loud when he turned his ignition and the stereo screamed AC/DC's "Back in Black" at a barely tolerable decibel. I pulled the truck around the cul-de-sac and headed for the mail house, which was near the pool. I couldn't remember the last time I'd emptied my mailbox, and I was sure there was a nasty-gram in there from the postmaster lecturing me on the subject.

It was a cloudless day and insufferably hot; the cicada's whined and declared it so. The heat in the mail house was worse. All the windows were open, and a simple box fan thrummed in one of them. I opened my mail slot to the inevitable:

Mr. McCarthy:

Please be dutiful in checking your mail each day as we have a limited number of package mailboxes to store shipments and bulk deliveries. These boxes are not reserved to store mail that piles up. If need be, we can hold your mail at the West End post office.

That was actually tamer than I was expecting. I fumbled my fingers through the mailbox to come up with the key to one of the package cabinets and found cabinet F4.

Damn, that was a lot of mail.

The letters tumbled out: advertisements, bills, offers to refinance my everything, and a rectangular, brown box just over a foot and a half in length. I dropped everything and sawed open the seal with my truck keys.

In a bed of Styrofoam peanuts was the time capsule.

It had been opened at one end and loosely duct-taped back together. I opened it and found Rob's letter. Things had indeed changed.

Ray –

You bastard! How did you pull that off? You are one of a kind, my friend.

So, on May 15th I'm putting a Carolina room on the deck of that house you love. I go down in the crawlspace to see where the ducts lead and it dawns on me: we buried the time capsule here! Oh, I had such plans for this thing. I was gonna reveal this sucker to you on a special occasion, whether it was a birthday or some sort of anniversary. Can you imagine when I opened your letter and found your current phone number on the bottom of it? I was shocked, and then I almost wet myself laughing. I didn't remember telling you that we were renovating that house. When did you think of this stunt? Well, I wasn't going to give you the satisfaction of a phone call, so I decided to mail it.

Maybe when all this craziness settles down with these wives of ours, you, me, Jenna, and Ava can sit on the deck and relive the old days. Have a look-see. There are some surprises in there. Enjoy your trip through time, Highlander. Glad you made it to The Gathering with your head intact!

Pals for life,

Rob

While reading, I had drifted downward and taken a seat on the on the musty indoor-outdoor carpet that floored the mail house. My eyes became glassy.

He just didn't remember.

Who could blame him? For me it was yesterday. For Rob, it was thirty-two years ago.

I dug farther into the time capsule and pulled out my letter. There at the bottom was my plea:

Call me as soon as you read this. We need to talk.

910-400-5555.

I should have written something more specific, something that would have jarred his memory about the conversation we had that day. I was lost. This whole situation was lost. I thought maybe I should follow Baumann's advice and make peace with the situation.

Baumann's advice...

Again, I dug into the time capsule and found Arden's letter. Line by line there was nothing new from the last time I had read it, but then, at the bottom:

Destination: Bigfork, Montana

April 14, 1997

***

I tore into my house, the time capsule under my arm. I left the keys in the door and the door ajar. I found the laptop on the kitchen table on but asleep. I poked it and let it come to life while I frantically searched for the handset to the landline phone. My cell reception at the house was lax, and this was too important. I went to the base, hit the search button, and listened to the beeps echo off my pitched ceiling. Finally, I found the handset in the folds of the couch.

I googled Bigfork, Montana. The town looked small enough that there was a chance in hell that everyone knew everyone else's business. I found the number for the post office on Holt Drive and dialed. It rang seven or eight times. At this point I was waiting for voicemail, but then…

"United States Post Office, Bigfork."

"Hello, this is Ray McCarthy of North Carolina. To whom am I speaking?"

"My name is Marjorie."

"Marjorie? Nice to meet you; I need your help."

"OK, with what?"

"We've had a death in the family here in North Carolina, and I need to track down a friend…"

"And you don't have a specific address, do you?" interrupted Marjorie.

"No, but he has an unusual name. His first name is Arden, full name Arden Miller. I'm going to assume he is an off-the-grid-type of guy."

"Well," exhaled Marjorie, "We have a lot of guys like that up here, and they range from nut jobs who want to form an anti-government militia, to guys who just like to hunt and be left alone."

"Arden would be in the latter category. He would not be averse to having a P.O. Box or coming to town from time to time."

"Neither was Ted Kaczynski against coming to town and using the mail. Sure your guy is not a nut job?"

"Ted Kaczynski? The Unabomber? I'm not sure I follow."

"They caught Ted just southeast of here in Lincoln."

"Arden is not a terrorist. He's a country boy."

I heard Marjorie typing away on a keyboard and mumbling to herself—I think she was repeating Arden's name.

"I just searched the database. He doesn't have a post office box. Seems like I've come across that name before, but it was months ago, maybe even a year. It had something to do with a local business."

I thought of my options. I figured I had only one and that I better make it as simple as possible to ensure some form of compliance.

"Marjorie, do you perhaps have a fax machine?"

"We do."

"My printer is also a copier and a fax machine. If I fax you a letter to Arden in a few minutes, and you figure out either where he lives or where he frequents, will you get it to him?"

"Why would I do that?"

"You'll understand when you read the letter. Will you promise me? I swear if you find my friend I will fly into Bigfork and buy you dinner personally."

"You'd have to fly into Kalispell, big shot, and then you'd have to answer to my husband. I wonder if your friend might be the guy who sends stuff to a local bar. Maybe he lives or works there. Anyway, it wouldn't be too much trouble to call."

"Thank you, Marjorie. Thank you very much."

Marjorie recited her fax number to me and then asked a question for which I was not prepared.

"Mr. McCarthy?"

"Ray," I answered.

"Ray then. How long since you've seen this fella?"

"Years. I didn't know where he was."

"I thought in this day and age you could find almost anyone anywhere. Why wait until somebody dies?"

I was silent for what felt like an eternity, and Marjorie let it play out.

"I don't know, Marjorie. I just know I regret it."

"I'll find him, Ray. Don't you worry."

On a piece of printer paper, I wrote a note to Arden. He deserved more than that after all these years, but time was of the essence. I faxed it off to Montana and was waiting for confirmation when a memory downloaded into me. It was really just a picture of me with my hands raised.

Rob wasn't the only person for whom I'd left a message.

I left the printer and went into the guest bedroom where there was an entrance to the attic. I pulled down the stairs and turned on the light. Two or three boxes back were my trophies and medals. I dug inside and pulled out the Nike shoe box full of ribbons. I picked up the ribbons and flipped them over, looking for the ones from June. It found it. The air in the attic was oppressive, but my core was as cold as steel in November. It was a needling sensation that trickled from head to shoulders to gut—adrenaline, pure adrenaline.

AAU Regional Championship Durham, NC June 1984

Race: *800 meters*

Time: *2:20.18*

Place: *First*

Young Ray had listened, and he had come in first instead of third.

Grab the lead or stay in lane two.

More of the memory flooded into me. I had grabbed the lead and never let it go. Coach Carter had pleaded from the fence in the third turn of the first lap for me to settle down, but instead, I ran faster.

I climbed down out of the attic and caught a chill as I re-entered the air-conditioned bedroom. I sat on the bed, the ribbon in my trembling right hand. That aloof seductress known as hope crept into my soul once more.

I will try again. I will find a way to make him understand, and I will save him.

What I should have been concerned with was saving myself.

27
Rob Erwin

Rob Erwin let the silence between him and Eugene sit for a moment. Eugene had been babbling on about the Carolina Panthers' recent draft picks, where the Braves now ranked in the National League East, and the work quality of some of the new subcontractors.

There was something on his mind, and Rob had a feeling as to what it was, and that made him sad. There seemed to be no end to this situation, so he would have to bring it to an end himself. Eugene was a good man. He'd let him say what he came to say no matter how long it took. Rob would keep Eugene. He'd get rid of the wife.

Rob clipped his phone to his shorts and returned to tying off the boat.

"Boss there's something on my mind, bet you can tell. I'm having a hard time puttin' words around it."

He turned to face Eugene.

"Whatever it is Eugene, just say it. It will be all right. I've been through this kind of thing before. It will be a little tougher with you, but it is what it is."

Eugene looked down, deflated and ashamed. That was when Rob noticed the two men stepping onto the dock. He'd been so absorbed with this moment that he had not seen them descend the lawn. One looked relatively familiar. The other man looked like he had stepped straight out of a comic book. He was even bigger than Eugene.

The familiar man abruptly dropped his right arm, and from his hand shot out a black rod, some sort of collapsible baton.

"Eugene!"

The man with the baton cracked Eugene across the back of the neck as he was turning around. Eugene folded, and the muscle man stepped to Rob.

Rob did not hesitate. He figured such men were used to fists flying, so he round-housed the man's left knee and followed with a straight right hand to the face that absolutely connected. The kick had more of an effect than the punch. The man grunted and stumbled as he let fly a right hook that all but crushed the right side of Rob's head.

Rob dropped to one knee, and the behemoth advanced. Again, Rob did not hesitate. He drilled the man in the solar plexus. That bought him some time as the man stumbled back and gasped for air. Rob stood up, and the baton came down on his left knee. He heard something crack and then it was his turn to fold to the ground.

The behemoth recovered, picked Rob up by the neck with his left hand, and then pummeled Rob with three quick body shots via his right hand. Rob saw the baton let fly and raised his left forearm to block it. There was another crack, bones breaking. Rob throat-punched the behemoth and turned to face the man wielding the baton, only to meet the baton head first, and then he was back on his knees. Then another shot of the baton landed.

"OK Rob, you're about done," said the familiar man. "Being a successful builder, I'm not sure why you would take on such a dangerous side hustle, but that's done too. Hopefully, whoever is helping you will take the hint and fold up shop. Otherwise, we're going to have to go visit Rita."

Rob's vision darkened and bells rang. The man's words sounded garbled. This was bad.

He could not take another shot like that. Then, out of nowhere…

Swim. Just swim.

Was that Dad's voice or Ray's? Maybe it was both.

It was a fine idea.

Rob rolled on his side, not knowing which part of the dock he was on. He flickered in and out of consciousness. One awkward revolution and he plunged into Lake Sequoia. He sunk like a rock toward the bottom of the drop-off.

No matter what, swim. Just swim. Clear across the lake if you have to.

As he sank, the water got cooler, and Rob's cobwebs began to clear. Swim? He could do that. Stay underwater for a few hundred feet to get clear of the dock and the thugs, then backstroke it.

In his mind, he was twelve again, and he focused on that. Rob again flickered in an out consciousness and began to worry that his lights would go out completely. Stay with me, Ray. How far is it to the island? Dad had measured it once. It was 880 yards or a little over 800 meters.

The half mile—wasn't that your race Ray? Come on, Ray. I'll race you to the island. I can't outrun you, but we're neck and neck in the water. Where's Olivia? She's faster than both of us. Let's make this interesting. Last one to the island has to climb up into the little wooden tower and declare out loud that their ass has been whooped.

Well, there goes Olivia out to an early lead. Looks like we might both get beat by a girl, but I'm not climbing the tower buddy. You're doing that. You're gonna have to do that in front of your favorite girl.

Ray's pulling ahead of me. Guess it dawned on him that coming in last would not be cool. I've got you in my sights buddy. Yup, pulling alongside you...there you are. I see you're taking a breath with every stroke—very inefficient my friend. That'll cost you.

Ray? Ray, it's getting dark. Stay with me, Ray. I'm not...

Rob ladled his arms back robotically. His kicks became spastic and half-hearted. The left leg was useless. The bulk of his backstroke was being propelled by his arms, which were tiring, and the left one was screaming. His vision became a black and white television screen with bad reception. He pictured his dad fiddling with the antennas of the old Zenith, and sometimes his vision cleared.

Instead of Ray's voice, it was now Ava singing inside his head.

Just keep swimming. Just keep swimming. Just keep swimming like Dory, Uncle Rob.

Rob rolled over on his belly to mark the distance. He would breaststroke the rest of the way to keep the island in sight. If his consciousness began to falter, he'd return to the backstroke where there was a better chance he'd stay buoyant and breathing air until the lights came back strong.

The lights flickered again with 400 yards to go, and again with 300 yards to go. He flipped over on his back and focused on breathing. Less than 200 yards from Sequoia Island, the lights went out.

28
Arden Miller

Hello old friend.

I hope this letter finds you faster than we found the time capsule. Rob unearthed it last month, and he held on to it...wanted to make it a surprise. I see you kept your promise. I knew you would. I wish after all this time I had better things to say, but here goes.

Rob is gone. It's just you and me now.

Someone killed him—killed him right here in Seven Lakes, and I am going to find out who it was. Yes, the police are on it, but that isn't enough.

Rob had no enemies. For a while, I thought this was all just a case of mistaken identity, but it wasn't. I need you pal. Come as fast as you can. I live at the end of Shadywood Court in Seven Lakes North, that house that looks like a cabin. Call me when you get this: 910-400-5555.

Ray

Arden read and re-read Ray's letter as he sat on the tarmac of Kalispell City aboard a United Fight bound for Colorado. At Denver International, he would have to sprint to make his connecting flight to Raleigh-Durham.

He had not wasted any time.

Mark obviously had not read the letter. All he knew was that Marjorie from the post office had called the bar all in a panic looking for "The army fella named Arden," and that Mark needed to get a message to him "straight away about a mess in North Carolina."

Mark was intrigued and had driven straight to the post office to collect the letter. Marjorie had read the letter and suggested Mark deliver it immediately. Mark was halfway to Arden's cabin when he remembered to call his bartender and tell him where he was going.

"He's here!" said the bartender. "He's here watching the Braves game."

"You're shitting me," said Mark.

"You want I should put him on the phone?"

"No, but don't let him leave. I'm turning around right now."

***

Mark burst through the kitchen swinging door out of breath.

"Jesus, man, don't move. The curiosity is killing me!"

"I'm not sure what you mean," Arden said.

"I mean," said Mark, "you got a letter."

Arden had read the letter and was speechless. He looked at Mark as if the man would instruct him what to do. Finally, Mark read the letter.

"Is this your buddy? The author?"

Arden nodded.

"Who is he talking about? Who is Rob?"

"Erwin," Arden finally managed to speak. "Rob Erwin. The three of us were pals growing up in North Carolina."

"Sit down, Captain. I'm gonna get on the computer. You have to go. Do you have a credit card?"

Arden handed over his debit card from American Bank.

"I'm going to research flights for you. We'll try to get you traveling by late this afternoon."

That was less than three hours ago.

Arden had driven to the cabin and thrown a few days' worth of clothes in his army issued backpack. He could not remember the last time he'd been on a commercial flight, so Mark had briefed him on what to expect as far as security. He didn't have a phone, but he resolved to get one when an opportunity presented itself.

For the moment Arden was enveloped in discomforting quiet, and he took stock of his loss.

He had waited too long. Now one of them was gone.

Still, there was Ray, and if Ray was as obsessively determined as he'd been as a kid, then he would track down the answers he was looking for to the bitter end. Ray would put himself in harm's way, no doubt about it.

Losing Ray would be unacceptable. It was all he could do to…

A memory was intruding on Arden's train of thought, something his mind was struggling to piece together. He again unfolded the letter.

I hope this letter finds you faster than we found the time capsule. Rob unearthed it last month.

Arden saw himself in the gazebo by Lake Echo, tediously carving on a piece of PVC pipe.

Open 2004

Ray had been bullshitting about something…

We don't open it in 2004. We forget about it. You will open it in 2016.

"Damn if Ray didn't say that to Rob!" said Arden out loud. He then quickly looked to his left to see that the only person sharing his row of seats had already fallen asleep.

Ray had said those exact words right before he had looked him in the eye and made him promise to write a note if he left North Carolina.

And Arden had most certainly kept that promise. It was spring 1997. He was on leave from the army to bury Mom and to help Dad pack up the house. Dad had put it on the market a month prior when the doctor said the end was near. He was not going to stay there a day longer than he had to. He just couldn't handle the memories. Most of the furniture remained in a storage facility in West End. When Dad was nearing his own end in 2005, Arden set the monthly storage payment on automatic draft from the account they shared.

He and Dad had been to Montana in '89, '92, and '94 to hunt elk. They had eaten supper a few times in Bigfork.

In '97 Dad didn't even have much of a plan. Dad was going to drive to Bigfork and figure out the rest when he got there. On his last day of leave, Arden had crept into the crawlspace of the house of Firetree Lane in the middle of the night, feeling like a complete idiot and praying to God that the family sleeping above him didn't wake and call the cops. With a flashlight perched between his teeth, he scrawled what he assumed to be his ultimate destination on the letter he had written thirteen years before. A promise was a promise after all. It was the last time Arden set foot in Seven Lakes.

He would land in Raleigh and retrieve his rental car. Then he would find a sporting goods store and gear up. He would scout around and get the lay of the land before calling Ray or knocking on his door. Arden didn't believe in coincidence. He was not sure what he believed when it came to what Ray had said in 1984. He felt now like he felt then: nervous. Actually, it was more like the heightened-sense anxiety that he'd become accustomed to in Iraq. He wasn't returning to North Carolina to bury a friend. Arden was pretty sure that he was returning home to protect one.

29
Recalculating

Morgan McCarthy was not an idiot, but she felt like one. She had made it all the way back to Hardeeville, South Carolina Tuesday evening and selected the Red Roof Inn as an accommodation.

Ava put up a short fight about sleep, going so far as to put on her swimsuit because she saw the hotel had a pool. She had fallen asleep with the one swimmy she had managed to struggle on to her left arm. She snoozed in the fetal position on the queen-size bed

Morgan seized the opportunity to do research—first pulling up articles in *The Pilot*, *The Fayetteville Observer*, and the *Raleigh News and Observer*. The description of Rob's injuries made her sob.

Some of the articles mentioned Rob's connection to Ray, and Tom Cianci had been right, Ray had spoken to none of them. An enterprising young reporter at *The Pilot* wrote a story about Ray dealing with both his best friend's death and his missing daughter, and he had done so without a single quote from either Ray or an Erwin.

Morgan then googled Tom Cianci and found a Wikipedia page devoted to him. Apart from some outrageous entries, the theme was simple: three decades of organized crime.

According to the page, Tom now boarded and raised horses.

How had Father Baumann hooked up with this character?

Morgan closed down her tablet and stripped Ava of her bathing suit and swimmy. On went the night-time pull-up and an *Elena of Avalor* nightgown. Ava didn't so much as blink.

Outside a dying sun cast pastel light behind an encroaching thunderhead, and Morgan lingered in the window thinking of the sunsets she and Ray had caught during their evening walks across the dam. What was to be in their future? Could it work? Could he forgive her? Resentment can be buried for a long time, but it almost always surfaces and becomes a poison that easily slips into any argument.

The pills.

It was time to take them. The ache was coming back, and there was no way to sleep with the ache. She found the Pez dispenser in her purse, and Chewbacca coughed up two Vicodin.

Humiliating.

She would follow the course she had set. It was the only way to get through it.

***

"Mommy. Pool."

Ava was straddled across Morgan's chest. Her pee-filled pull-up was discarded on the floor, and her bathing suit was back on. The kid had a wicked case of morning breath.

"Oh…geez…Why not? OK." muttered Morgan, rubbing her eyes.

"Yay!" yelled Ava.

"Inside voice Ava…and you have to brush those teeth first. For the love of God brush those teeth."

"God doesn't care if I brush my teeth."

"Yes, he does because he gave you the teeth. And even if he doesn't care, I do. Brush." Ava dismounted and headed for the small bathroom.

"We can only stay an hour at the pool, Ava. We have to check out at eleven." Ava popped back out of the bathroom.

"Is today the day we see Daddy?"

"No, a few more days."

"What about Tom?"

"Probably." Morgan had driven three hours and had been mindful of the traffic behind her. Never once had she noticed the same car behind her for any significant duration.

She and Ava spent exactly an hour at the pool. Ava whined a bit but then trudged toward the lobby as if to the gallows, still dripping. Morgan walked quickly to keep up. They entered the lobby to find Tom Cianci sitting on a sofa in pressed tan slacks and a burgundy bowling shirt.

How did he do that?

"Uncle Tom!"

Tom laughed with delight and had no time to get up. Ava ran to him and hugged his knees, leaving wet spots. Tom patted her on the head and reached for a Styrofoam container. "Good morning ladies. I have breakfast."

Ava cocked her head and looked at him quizzically.

"Mr. Tom it is way too early for meatballs."

"Ha! It's never too early for meatballs, but these aren't meatballs. They are breakfast burritos."

"What's a burrito?" Ava asked.

"It's delicious. Have a seat."

Tom took the small towel off Ava's shoulder and placed it on the couch. Ava plopped right down beside him. Tom then stood and handed Morgan a coffee.

"And how are you, Ms. Morgan? Sleep well?"

Morgan smiled.

"Well enough. I took your advice and did some research. Found a whole Wikipedia page devoted to your family."

"I'd take all that stuff with a grain of salt, young lady. Anyone can log on to that site and add whatever they want."

"So, you didn't retire and join Ringling Brothers as Cianci, the fire-breathing clown?"

"An entry by my own hand, Morgan." Tom smiled. "I like to keep 'em guessing. The retirement part is true. I raise horses. Sometimes law enforcement pays me a visit at the farm."

"For what?" asked Morgan.

"Advice."

Morgan nodded. They both looked at Ava who had opened the container and was now elbows deep in burrito.

"My goodness, Mommy this is good."

Morgan and Tom both laughed, and Tom rose to leave.

"I will leave you guys to gather yourselves and check out. I will see you later this evening. When our adventure is over, I want you guys to pay a visit to Brooklyn with me. There's a restaurant there I think you might enjoy. Meatballs galore. Oh, before I forget..."

Tom handed her another Pez dispenser, this one adorned with the head of a Stormtrooper.

"I love Star Wars," said Tom. "This one only has a single pill. It's time to step it down. Tonight, I'll give you two pills so you can sleep comfortably. You're doing well. You're young and strong, and you'll be off this nonsense in no time. Do you remember the last time you got up to face a day without this monkey on your back?"

Morgan shook her head.

"Well it's coming soon, and it's going to be a great day." Tom kissed Ava on the head.

"See you tonight kiddo."

"See you tonight!" replied Ava.

It was hard not to like Tom Cianci. He was endearing, and he carried himself with ease and confidence, but the fact that she had to be chaperoned across the finish line bothered her. It was indeed a comfort having him there, and it sure beat the hell out of going in search of meds, but it bothered her—especially the fact that he always knew where she was.

She collected Ava, brought her upstairs, and put her in the shower. Then she opened the tablet to do one more Google search.

30
Time is a Thief

"I coulda been a contender. I coulda been somebody, instead of a bum, which is what I am."

Matt Roper rolled out of bed, planted his feet on the wood floor, and massaged his temple. He had fallen asleep watching Turner Movie Classics, and Marlon Brando echoed in his head.

Like Terry Malloy, Matt had chased the short-end money, but he never took a dive. In fact, he was an undefeated cruiserweight contender.

Was.

That was before Oxy, before cocaine. That was before he went on the hook to Scott. Scott would say that he saved him, gave him a job, but what Scott really did was put the last nail in the coffin that held Matt's aspirations.

"I could do something else," said Matt out loud to his empty house.

He didn't use anymore. He still had a name in Raleigh. The gyms knew him up there, but some would still consider it a leap of faith to hire him. They would eyeball him warily and wonder if he'd drag down their up-and-comers.

That would not happen. Matt would keep the kids on the right path and live through them. He would pay a visit to Title Boxing Club in Cary and gauge the reaction to his presence. He and the owner went way back. A good word from him and news would spread that Matt was back and healthy and looking to work. He'd do whatever job anyone would give him, and he'd wait for his chance.

First, he had to tie up loose ends, handle Scott's little errand, leave things nice between them. Then he would begin liquidating assets. He knew the tobacco barn in Ellerbe. The best approach would be on motorcycle, parking it in one of the scrub growth fields off Wallace road, and then hoofing it across the Bower's farm. No way he could drive down Bowers lane; he was certain that they would sell out to the Erwins any vehicle they didn't recognize.

Hard to believe a man like Rob Erwin had been messing with anything this dark, but nothing surprised him anymore. He had liked Rob. Rob had been good for Candace.

Scott had told him to grab anything—a lamp base, anything he could carry easily and stuff in the saddle bag of his Triumph Bonneville. This was essentially a smash-and-grab job.

There might be cameras, so he'd have to cover up with a hoodie. If there were an alarm, it'd be a silent one. There was no way the Erwins would want to draw attention to the barn with some caterwauling screech.

Scott had sent their old pal Chris to do some reconnaissance, and he'd reported that not only was the barn still in business, but it was stocked to the rafters. The only entryway was through the double oak doors hung on steel strap hinges and secured by a massive deadbolt. There were no windows, and a concrete floor had been poured. Chris noted, however, that the outside was all original tobacco barn circa the 1950s. A good portion of the wood and mortar had been replaced, but some of it was still in need of replacing, especially the southeast corner. A crowbar and a mallet in the hands of someone who spent his youth working in such rickety structures was the way in.

Matt stood up, wandered into the master bath, and studied himself in the mirror. From the neck down, he looked as he remembered: a v-framed lean torso, long muscular arms attached to bulging shoulders. From the neck up there were changes. Strips of silvery gray had woven themselves into his shag of blonde hair. Smile lines were more pronounced, and a hollowness had settled into his cheeks. Time was no longer his friend.

"Let's get this over with," said Matt to his image.

It would be several hours before sunset. Matt would get his things packed. By Wednesday morning, he could be ready to go. He'd drop his stolen goods with Scott, and he would split without so much as a word, spend a week in Cary. If the gyms up there gave him the cold shoulder, he would head to Wilmington. If people didn't want him to train youngsters, he'd referee. There had to be a way back in. Everyone deserves at least one do-over. There had to be more to his life than this.

***

I had nothing. No ideas. If the time capsule didn't work, if looking Rob in the face as a kid and telling him that he would not live past the age of forty-four didn't work, what was I to do?

Get the hell out of the house. That is what I had to do. I think better when I drive. Just start by getting in the truck and pointing it in a direction. As I exited Seven Lakes North, I had an idea. I made a right turn on MacDougall Drive, drove past Boles Funeral Home, and meandered into the Seven Lakes Cemetery.

I instantly regretted it. Spectrum News had bought out Time Warner Cable, but they had not yet repainted the trucks, and they apparently were not going to replace any of the on-air talents because I recognized Linnie Supall setting up for a live shot near the memorial wall, and she had looked at me. Her eyes followed the truck all the way to where the encroaching woods bordered the rear of the cemetery, where Rob had purchased two plots: one for him, one for Candace.

Rob's plot was dug out and vaulted. This was news to me. If Candace was this far along in the preparation, surely a service was set, and surely someone would have called me. Tomorrow would mark a week since Rob left this earth. On a whim, I pulled out my phone and dialed Rob's number. On the third ring, a familiar voice picked up.

"Hello?"

"Hello, Jenna. What are you doing answering your father's phone?"

"What are you doing calling my father's phone?" she asked.

"I'm standing beside your dad's plot in the cemetery wondering why it's dug out and ready to go as if his services were imminent."

There was an exhale, and I already knew the answer.

"The funeral is tomorrow. Mom put a notice in the paper. She's still pissed at you. That's why she didn't call, something about an argument you guys had on the way home from Carthage."

"Jesus! That does not justify anything. And since when are we making this a big public deal? I thought we were going to do this privately."

Jenna paused, and I felt the mood change.

"Uncle Ray?"

"Yes, honey."

"I was home that night. I was here. I could have looked out the window, called the cops, ran out there, something…" Her voice broke. "I was watching an iHeartRadio concert on my tablet. I had my headphones on in my own stupid little world."

I raised my voice. This had to be nipped in the bud.

"Jenna, don't be ridiculous. The whole thing happened too fast. Even Eugene couldn't make a difference. Had Eugene seen anything, he'd have ended up in the water too. What do you think would have happened to you if you had revealed yourself? How fast do you think the police would have gotten there? The answer is not fast enough. You're not the only one who saw or heard nothing. You guys have neighbors. Spruill interviewed all of them—nothing. Trust me, dear. I have what-ifed this thing in my mind for a week. There is no course to a better ending, so stop it."

Silence.

"OK," she finally whispered.

"Come visit me. I'll give you an update on the Ava situation."

"Are they coming home?"

"Slowly but surely."

"At least there's that."

I got Jenna to give me the info for tomorrow—a short, sunset service at the Chapel of the Pines followed by an internment service for just the family and delivered by Father Baumann. I turned around to find an attractive, thirty-something African-American woman with rather toned arms pleasantly smiling at me.

"You're Ray McCarthy."

Shit.

"Hello, Ms. Supall. I recognize you too."

"How are you holding up?"

"It's been a rough summer so far Linnie. I'm not sure what else to say."

"You have quite a fan base for your books, Ray. I looked at the Facebook page—not your personal one, but the one you established for yourself as an author. There's a landslide of messages, and they are quite touching."

"That's nice to hear, but the truth is that I have stayed away from that stuff. One of my young cousins runs that page for me."

"It's going to be hard to lay low these next two days. I saw the Raleigh station's news truck at the Exxon. Would you consider a quick interview with me? The allure of being first to get you on camera will then be gone, and perhaps the others won't be all over you so much."

"OK Linnie, but here are the rules: I'll comment on my daughter first, then Rob. I will tell you how I'm feeling about all this. Then I'm out. Don't press me on my answers. When I'm done, I'm done."

Linnie smiled her broad smile.

"Deal."

We retreated to the V-shaped memorial wall in the middle of the cemetery because that was where the crew was already set. Linnie made a quick call. A crew member assessed the natural light and judged it sufficient. There was a countdown, and suddenly Linnie was beside me, microphone in hand, and we were live.

"This is Linnie Supall from Seven Lakes Cemetery where tomorrow final services will be held for local architect Rob Erwin who was tragically killed in what appeared to be a home invasion last week in this quiet, gated community. Beside me is none other than author Ray McCarthy, who is grieving the loss of his best friend while dealing with the disappearance of his daughter. Ray, how are you holding up, and can you give us an update on your daughter?"

I kept my eyes on Linnie. I had yet to get used to staring at a camera.

"All things considered, I'm OK. Numb. Numb is a good word. None of this seems very real, and it probably won't feel real for quite some time. Regarding my daughter, she is still out there. She is not home, but I would not characterize her as missing anymore. Law enforcement here and across state lines has been spectacular, but I think they have done all they can do. I think from here on it is a family matter that we will have to bring to a close privately. Hopefully, we can put the pieces back together."

"Does that mean you have spoken to your wife?"

"I have not, but I will."

I gave Linnie a firm look that said I was done with this part, and she took the hint.

"What can you tell us about the investigation into Mr. Erwin's death?"

"Not much. It was a vicious altercation. My friend has no enemies, but I think someone attacked him on purpose. I don't think it was a robbery. It was maybe a case of mistaken identity."

"Is that what detectives believe as well?" asked Linnie.

For reasons to this day I don't understand, I turned from Linnie Supall and stared into the camera lens, speaking to it with cold comfort as if I'd been doing it all my life.

"I don't speak for law enforcement. They are following every lead and keeping a lid on what information they gather, as they should. I believe that there was one person behind this, one person who brought along some thugs for assistance. Whatever issue this person thought he had with my wonderful friend, he was not brave enough to confront Rob himself. I imagine that he is now cowering in some hole, and I have faith that detectives will soon flush him out."

I continued to stare at the camera. Linnie let a beat or two go by, and then wrapped it.

"Ray our thoughts and prayers are with you and the Erwins. Thank you very much for taking the time to speak with us."

"Thank you, Linnie."

I walked off back toward the truck.

Halfway back I felt a hand on my elbow. I turned to find a concerned-looking Linnie Supall.

"Are you sure you're OK?" she asked.

"I'm pretty far from OK, but I'm getting there. Ava coming home will be a good start. Maybe when this is all over, I'll come find you for an interview. That was kind of...therapeutic in a way."

Linnie Supall nodded, and I continued quickly to the truck and drove away. Time was running out. I had the distinct feeling that once Rob was in the ground, my opportunity to set things right went with him. Time was no longer my friend.

31
VRBO

There was a catastrophic thump, and Morgan looked over her shoulder toward the open door of the bathroom.

"I'm OK!" yelled Ava gleefully.

"Ava," Morgan asked, "Are you playing with Mommy's shampoo bottles again? Last time you dumped half my shampoo down the drain."

"Ahhh, nope. Nope, I'm not."

Morgan returned her gaze to the tablet where she had an ongoing Google search of GPS tracking devices. This had to be how Tom Cianci kept tabs on her.

There was a litany of devices—some that plug in, some that have a battery, some that track a vehicle in real time, and some that had to be retrieved and downloaded into a computer. Morgan zeroed in on a rechargeable one with a battery life of roughly a week. It also tracked in real time. It was no bigger than a flip phone and could be slipped into any crevice of a car's interior.

Tom had leaned into the car to deliver the meatballs, but if he had tossed it into the backseat or the floorboards, she would have stumbled across it by now. Morgan and Ava spent a lot of time in the car and thus Morgan kept it meticulously clean.

Plus, how did Tom intend to retrieve and recharge it if he had tossed it in the car?

Unless…what if he had multiple devices and was just going to toss in a new one? That did not seem reasonable. It would increase the chances of Morgan finding one of them.

She navigated the website of this particular device. One could access the tracking map through a PC or a phone. Of course, there were a variety of accessories and upgrades, and one of those accessories was a magnetized, weather-proof case.

Gotcha.

Morgan flashed back to her first meeting with Tom at the gas station. He was twirling the keys, and then they let fly.

Oops. I used to be better at that. Arthritis.

Oops my ass, thought Morgan. Clever bastard.

Morgan touched her News app to see if there were any updates on the Erwins. It blossomed to life and filled the screen with an announcement. Then she was looking at her husband in-person for the first time in more than a month.

Morgan quickly plugged in her headphones. She did not need Ava hearing her Daddy's voice, and Ava did not yet know that Uncle Rob had gone to heaven.

"Numb. Numb is a good word. None of this seems very real, and it probably won't feel real for quite some time."

Christ, thought Morgan, he looks so thin.

"I think from here on it is a family matter that we will have to bring to a close privately. Hopefully, we can put the pieces back together."

Morgan repeated the line to herself two more times, momentarily lost in thought.

He still loves me. He's pissed, but he loves me.

Then Ray was staring directly at her, and he appeared to be all but threatening Rob's murderer.

Morgan knew that tone—knew it well. He'd pay public lip service to law enforcement on camera, but Ray was following his own trail, and he would never let it go. For a second, she wondered if his comment about her was lip service as well, but she thought not. Ray wanted some part of his life whole again. He had to want that. Morgan wanted it too. One thing was for sure. She had to get home. She had to look after Ray, but not before she was herself again.

Morgan pulled up Vrbo.com and typed in a particular North Carolina address.

The response from Vrbo came back: "This property is temporarily unavailable due to renovation." Morgan knew there had been a plan for renovation, but she doubted renovations had commenced.

"Ava, time to get out honey. We need to hit the road."

Morgan was checked out on time. She strapped Ava into the car seat, loaded the bags, and felt all over the gas tank of her Toyota Rav 4.

Nothing.

She got down on the asphalt, rolled over on her back, and scooted under the car. She studied the gas tank and saw it immediately—a small black case sticking to the tank like a tumor. She tried twice to pull it off. The third time was the charm. On the back of the case were two silver discs—magnets, powerful ones. Morgan pried open the plastic lever. In a bed of foam sat the GPS tracker winking its green beacon of light at her.

"Son of a bitch."

She had to give it up to Tom—he was casual and smooth and smart. It was time to inform him that she too was smart. Just so everyone understood each other. This was important for two reasons. First, she would not be pressured into solving her issues; she would do it on her timeline. She was her own person, and she wanted her self-respect back. Secondly, she wanted Tom's respect. She had a feeling he would remain in the lives of the McCarthy family even after this saga came to an end.

Morgan figured Tom knew she should be checked out by now, so she could not leave the device behind. Instead, she stuck the tracker right back on the gas tank. She drove three hours to Whiteville, North Carolina, a direction she assumed Tom would find encouraging, and made a long pit stop she presumed Tom would not consider unreasonable. The ache had seeped back into her bones, and so she took her last pill. There would be no evening meds. She would have to step it all the way down.

32
The Rabbit Hole

Colonel Jim Dorn proceeded down US 1 South wearing Ray Bans that masked the guilt and anger weighing on his soul and radiating from his furious stare into the late-afternoon sun. He had turned on his police scanner to make sure Christopher Sedgewick hadn't had any second thoughts about their arrangement. Sedgewick had endured waterboarding like a champ and with an admirable sense of humor, but Sedgewick was neither brave nor a coward. He was simply adaptable. He had sold out his employer quickly, but the Colonel suspected that Christopher had wanted out from under his employer for some time.

The boy could not tell him what specifically his boss was into, but there was no need. Chris had been told to seek out the barn, and when Chris described the kind of digital obfuscation he was employed to create, no other questions needed to be asked.

The phone call was nothing more than the Colonel poking Scott Windham with a stick.

"What do you need Chris?"

"I need you to tell me who Colonel Jim Dorn is," said Sedgewick.

"Colonel Jim? He's got to be what? Seventy-something now?"

"Looks pretty good for seventy. Looks pretty pissed too."

"He's grieving. Like most people down here know, Rob Erwin was killed. Jim Dorn is the best friend of Rob Erwin's father, the deceased Colonel Ed Erwin. How did he find you?"

"Rita told him about my visit to the barn. The barn has cameras. He found out where I lived."

Silence.

"One more thing Scott. It's his barn. Colonel Jim Dorn owns Abian Industries."

More silence.

"What does he know?"

"I took his money and told him that my employer had always worked through a third-party contact. I did not know who he was or what he did. I just created software and ran errands. I was at the barn to see if Abian Industries was still in business."

"That's quite a lot."

"I thought I did a damn good job, Scott, considering that the Colonel was threatening my life. What have you gotten me into?"

"Nothing. Calm down."

"Did you kill Rob Erwin?"

"No."

"Don't ever contact me again Scott."

Dorn had slipped Sedgewick a grand for his trouble. Money meant nothing to him anymore. It had to be ninety degrees in the cabin of the SUV. Dorn just kept driving, sweating through his linen shirt and staring at the highway. He had put the battery back in his phone.

Finally, he turned it on and dialed Wyatt Halsey.

"What's our status?"

"Hello Colonel. I'll be in the air in twenty minutes. It's a short hop to Southern Pines, just over forty minutes."

"Good. Where are we sleeping tonight?"

"That proved to be more difficult than I had anticipated," said Halsey. "There are three different golf tournaments going on in the Pinehurst area; the pickings were slim. I settled on a pair of rooms at the Inn at Eagle Springs, a bed and breakfast near…"

"Samarcand," interrupted Dorn. "I know of it. It's perfect, an under-the-radar place where no one will second guess the comings and goings of a pair of old men."

"That's what I figured. We'll say that we're up looking at properties, going to build houses out in the country to which our wives and we will retire."

"Men like us will never have wives," said Dorn.

"This is true, but I don't want people thinking we're life partners."

Jim cracked a smile. Wyatt was the only friend he had left in this world.

"Jim, what are your intentions here?"

"I have the name and address of the man I am certain killed my godson. Tomorrow we are going to acquire the said target and then go for a ride."

"There's another service for Rob tomorrow, followed by his burial."

"No one knows I'm back in the States, and I'm going to keep it that way. I've already been to Rob's memorial. The funeral is for the Seven Lakers, and I would rather dig a grave than watch my boy lowered into one."

"How long has it been since you killed a man, Jim?"

"Too long."

***

Howard Spruill sat at his desk in Carthage staring at the arrest record of Travis Seymour. He was pretty sure Travis had delivered unto him a mild concussion, and he had planned to go to FirstHealth and get checked out, but time was of the essence.

Travis had changed.

Though he had been arrested plenty of times, always drug-related, it had been a long time. Unlike his brother, none of Travis's arrests were for physical altercations.

Travis had just assaulted a cop without a second thought. Travis was experimenting with meth.

Spruill had seen this pattern of behavior before. When an addict-turned-dealer who normally makes stupid mistakes suddenly goes a long stretch without getting pinched, it usually meant one of three things: The addict was in prison somewhere else; the addict had gotten clean; or the addict had gone to work for somebody who did all the thinking for them.

Individuals experimenting with product production do so to either use the product or to go into business for themselves. With methamphetamine, it was usually both. Travis was not clean, and he had told his brother Kyle that he wanted to get away from whom he's working.

Travis was dangerous. Travis was now spooked, and he would run to someone for protection. Travis himself was capable of killing someone, but he had no connection to Rob Erwin.

Matt Roper, a professional boxer, who looked like he could still be a professional boxer, did have a record of violence and drugs. He did have a connection to Rob Erwin through Candace. Candace had said that they grew up together. Rob had hired Roper multiple times.

Matt's assault charges were uninspiring—bar violence with multiple opponents. There were bruises and concussions and lots of wounded pride, but that was it. Matt was not a killer.

Matt was a drug dealer who had a supplier. Was it possible that Travis and Matt answered to the same person? There were only so many big fish in the relatively small pond that was Moore County, North Carolina. What did this have to do with Rob Erwin? All the muscle was there, but there was no connective tissue.

Spruill's phone lit up. He didn't hesitate to answer it.

"Nice interview Ray. I just saw it streaming online. Is there anything you want to tell me?"

"She caught me in the cemetery, Spruill," Ray said. "There are news trucks all over the place; it was only a matter of time. They're going to bury Rob tomorrow, but that is not what I'm calling to tell you. I followed up on the little errand you assigned me."

"And?"

"Halo Construction operates at a perpetual loss and is owned by a holding company in Charlotte called Universal Imports."

"OK," said Spruill patiently. "What do they import?"

"Lots of things. I'm looking at it now online. One of the things it imports is pharmaceuticals. Do we not have an opioid crisis in our county?"

"The whole state, the whole country, has an opioid problem Ray. Get to the point."

"Halo Construction is operated by Scott Windham. This is Scott's only recorded employment for the last seven years, operating a business at a perpetual loss. His father is in his seventies and still works for Richmond Memorial Hospital in Rockingham."

"Perhaps," said Spruill, "Mr. Windham's dad supplements him financially, and that is why the old man still works."

"Perhaps," I said, "Scott dispenses pharmaceuticals and launders the money."

"That's quite a leap, Ray."

"Did I mention that Rob and I both knew Scott Windham and that he hated our guts?"

"That is the first thing that you've said that actually has my attention. When's the last time you saw him?"

"This morning mowing his lawn near Ellerbe."

"Were you stalking him?"

"No, I had Father Baumann with me. It's a long story. I was just looking for a man who built a church. Turns out it was Scott."

"OK, describe Rob's interactions with Mr. Windham over the years."

"He bullied us mercilessly throughout the 1980s."

"What?"

"Rob and I lived here as kids and Scott was our personal torturer."

"Ray…" Spruill took a breath. "As adults, what were your interactions with Mr. Windham over the last year?"

"We haven't seen him since the '80s."

"It's true that we have some unidentified supplier in this region, and a pharmaceutical import company with ties to local business is something I will follow up on, but…" Spruill exhaled. "Do you remember what I told you when you went and interviewed Eugene?"

"No, but I remember that you sent me down this rabbit hole."

"I told you to look into Halo Construction. I said nothing of going to bother people. When you visited Eugene, I said there is a reason I don't write books. There is a reason you don't wear a badge. Stay away from Scott Windham. I'll be in touch."

Spruill hung up and grabbed his keys. He was going to find Matt Roper.

***

Arden Miller purchased a cell phone during his short layover in Denver. A young lady gave him a quick tutorial and had downloaded three applications for him: E-Mail, Google, and iTunes.

"These," she had said, "are some essentials," and then she had helped link his email account to his phone.

Arden had an iTunes account. He had created it on the library computer in 2005. Dad had given him an iPod Shuffle as a welcome home present.

"In case yer still gonna get up each morning and do that PT bullshit," said Dad. "Here's somethin' to put yer tunes on."

He had not accessed iTunes in years, but now that he had his email account in hand, he could reset the login. Scrolling through his music had been like stumbling into a time warp: Iron Maiden, Black Sabbath, Motorhead, Metallica, a few Rush tunes. Ray had gotten him into Rush.

Back on the plane Arden had plugged in the headphones and clicked on "Tom Sawyer."

No, his mind is not for rent
To any God or government
Always hopeful yet discontent
He knows changes aren't permanent
But change is

Arden felt the bi-polarity of excitement and grief pulling at him. He would soon be home with his guys.

Except he was down a guy.

The flight attendant put a hand on his shoulder.

"Sir, would you like something to drink?"

"No ma'am, but could I ask you a question? I understand there is internet on the plane. I'm new to this phone. How do I get on it?"

"Oh, that's easy. Press the app that says settings and then select Wifi."

"What is airplane mode?"

"That's what you put your phone on during takeoff and landing. You don't want your phone sending out a radio frequency signal during those times."

"Why's that?"

"Might mess with the flight instruments."

"Jesus..."

"You're fine now. Go to settings, Wi-Fi, and then select...yes, that one right there United Wi-Fi. They'll bill the same card you purchased your ticket with. Just shut it down when you hear we are making our descent."

Arden tapped on the Google application and typed in Field and Stream, finding a store in Cary. He clicked on the website and began perusing the hardware. He felt naked without his stuff, but there was no time to learn the protocols of checking hunting gear onto a plane.

He found a Diamond Edge SB-1 Compound Bow comparable to his own, a six-pack of Bloodsport arrows, and a package of Rage Chisel Broadhead tips. All and all, he'd be out close to 800 bucks. Fine. He'd leave everything with Ray, and he would come back in the fall during hunting season. The Broadhead tips were probably overkill for the kind of game he would encounter in North Carolina, but not in Montana, and eventually, he'd figure out how to travel with this stuff.

He pulled up the website for *The Pilot*. There was a funeral for Rob tomorrow in Seven Lakes, and then the burial. There were a few articles on Rob and a picture. The sandy hair was now more gray than sandy, but he would recognize that face anywhere. He still looked like Rob. He still smiled like Rob. He could see him lumbering across the dam of Lake Echo carrying his fishing pole.

The tears came without warning. They simply slipped and tumbled. Arden dug his thumb under the neck of his T-shirt and lifted it to dab at the wetness. In a matter of hours, he had been reunited with his past only to learn that some of it had been stolen. It was tough to process.

***

Howard Spruill turned right on Plank Road and found the work-in-progress that Matt Roper called a house. His pick-up was in the driveway—finally a break. The late-afternoon sun was brutal and frustrating, a hazy perpetrator of stillness.

Spruill got out of his sedan, saw the heavy bag hanging tiredly from the magnolia tree. Grass was sparse at the base of the tree and tree roots abounded. He figured Roper must have wonderful footwork to not fall on his face while punching that thing. Spruill felt down his lower back to touch the pancake holster. He made it to the first step when Roper came out of the screen door and on to the porch.

"What can I help you with, sir?"

Spruill looked up at him from the base of the steps. Roper's tone was easy going, but his stance was guarded and firmly in front of the door. He did not want Spruill inside the house.

"Officer Spruill. It's been a long time."

"It hasn't been that long."

"What can I do you for?"

"I want to have a chat."

"About what?"

"Well, not the fact that you're a drug dealer. I want to talk about the architect." Spruill casually climbed the stairs and took a seat in a rocking chair as this exchange played out. Roper kept a poker face that in and of itself was telling.

"Look, officer—"

"Detective."

"Detective then. I have been an addict and a dealer. I am not that anymore."

"I believe you are no longer an addict, but like I said, I don't really care about anything else except for the architect right now."

Roper considered this for a moment and then finally let out a breath and took the rocker next to Spruill.

"I've known Candace all my life, used to babysit her. Her mom was a drunk. It's a wonder she grew up at all, much less went to college. After college, she came back here. She had no direction, was falling back in with her high school crowd. Eventually, she got a job at the Credit Union. Rob was a good place for her to land. Everyone liked him."

"Not everyone."

"I don't know who the hell couldn't like him. I certainly did. He threw me work all the time, even had me over to the house for dinner."

"For the record, I don't think you had anything to do with his death."

"For the record, you are right," said Roper. "What the hell are you here for then?"

"What's with the giant duffle bag by the front door? You were guarding that door like it was Fort Knox."

"It's my fight bag." Roper sighed. "Gloves, headgear, interval timer… all that stuff."

"I thought you were done with boxing."

"Boxing was done with me 'cause of the drugs. I'm done with drugs, and now I'm hoping to find a way back into boxing. I was going to head up to Raleigh tomorrow and visit some of the gyms, see if I can find work training…something. If they won't have me up there, I'll try Wilmington."

"Who supplied you with drugs to sell?"

Roper cocked his head and looked at Spruill like he should know the answer.

"The drill is the same all over, detective. You never see or talk to 'the guy.' You deal with all kinds of lowlifes that run interference and blinds for 'the guy.'"

"Give me a lowlife then."

"You know all of them, Spruill."

"Is one of them Travis Seymour?"

"You stay away from that fella, Spruill. He'll wreck himself before too long." Spruill nodded.

"Are we done here?" Roper asked.

"One more thing," said Spruill. "I'm a great believer in reboots. I am a pretty good facilitator of them as well." He fished a pair of business cards out of his wallet. "If the gyms in Raleigh won't have you, call this guy. We went to UNC Wilmington together. He runs a gym near Southport, and he wants to expand his mixed-martial arts program. He doesn't have a whole lot of money to sink into this program, so he needs an all-purpose guy, someone who can train and referee and tend to injuries."

Spruill handed him the card, and Roper looked dumbstruck. Spruill held up the second card.

"This one is my card. You're right. Everyone liked Rob Erwin. It makes no sense. That means until we figure out why someone came after him, his whole family is still in danger— Rita, Candace, and Jenna. I need to look under every rock. You call me and tell me about a rock I might look under if you think of it."

Roper looked Spruill in the eye and said nothing. Spruill left the card on the arm of the rocker and left without another word.

"Things on your chest you need to confess.
I will deliver. You know I'm a forgiver.
Reach out and touch faith."

—Depeche Mode

33
Come Together Over Me

We circle the roundabout to Wannamaker Drive, the spires of the University Chapel thrust toward a slate gray sky. Everything feels heavy. In my truck, we are silent until finally, she says, "I think we're here early enough that we can park in the circle."

We have this down to a science. It's a series of trips with a pair of industrial hand-trucks I borrow from U-Haul. She is so tall and so blonde. I'm still not sure from where the tallness comes.

We park, and she leaps out of the truck. Friends have already been spotted. The air is relatively cool, a suggestion of fall to come. Again, I feel the weight, and I realize it's anxiety.

Everything will be so quiet now.

"Dad, come meet Ah Lam; she's here from China. I met her last year."

I shudder to life in my rocking chair on the front porch, my computer half closed on my lap. It's evening. When I fell asleep, the sun was just starting to set. I couldn't remember the last time I consumed alcohol, so I must have just been tired. It's amazing how when the void is filled, the vice seems to silently ebb away.

I may or may not be able to save Rob, but at least Ava will be home, eventually.

There was no way I was attending the church service for Rob at 9 a.m. Most of the Seven Lakes community would be there, spilling out into the parking lot of the Chapel in the Pines. No one would know whether or not I was there amidst that sea of humanity.

Instead, I would run what I felt was my final race, and this one would be a come-from-behind victory. I would chase down my friend and never let him go.

What was that?

Never let him go.

Dear god why had that not crossed my mind before? Would it work? Would the anomaly even allow for such a thing to occur? Did it matter?

Hell, no it did not. I had tried everything else. There was absolutely no reason not to take Rob by the hand in 1984 and literally drag him into 2016. I envisioned only two possibilities: Rob being bounced to his ass like I had been at Cottage Grove and at the pool, or Rob Erwin walking into 2016.

Or you holding hands on Cherokee Trail with an embalmed corpse because that is what Rob is in 2016.

Jesus help me.

It would be a little later in 1984 but still early in the day. It was the perfect time to catch Rob fishing in Longleaf Lake. It was his summer ritual. First, he'd cast into Sequoia; then he'd walk a few hundred yards up Overlook Drive, cross Firetree Lane, and try his luck in the lake that bordered the community pool.

There was nothing to lose.

If I failed, I would attend the graveside service set for 11 a.m. Boles Funeral Home sat less than 400 yards from the cemetery entrance, and so Candace decided that we would meet Rob at his final resting place.

Or you can throw him in the back of the truck and bring him yourself.

I shook off that thought. I would make the attempt regardless of the possible outcome.

The decision was made; the deliberation was over. I opened the laptop and saw Ava's smiling face smeared with cake. I tapped the spacebar, and the windows I had opened appeared before me. I clicked on Facebook and saw that not only did I have a message, but I had a new friend request as well.

Ray –

How are you holding up? I've read everything I could find, including the articles about your daughter. My folks are on the West Side of Seven Lakes, but it's time for them to move on. I was planning a trip up there to explore their living options.

I think of you guys all the time. I guess we let daily life get in the way of a lot of things, like keeping in touch. I'm driving up tonight. Will I see you at the services? Keep your phone on you, and I will message you on Facebook and let you know where I am.

Love,

Olivia

For better or worse my heart skipped a beat, but it was hard to discern why. Yes, it was Olivia Allen, and apparently, she still had a power over me that I couldn't explain. There was something else, though, a much-needed boost. I had resolve, and I had a measure of hope. However, my faith in my ability to set things right was waning. I needed a sign, and I decided to take Olivia coming home as a positive one.

My cargo shorts buzzed.

I had wedged my phone into one of the pockets that were a little too small to accommodate the brick. I wiggled it free to see a 303-area code. Where the hell was that? If this was a reporter who somehow got my number, so help me…

"Hello?"

"Hello, old man."

"Who is this?"

"You wrote me a letter, dummy."

"Arden?"

"Damn right."

"Arden Miller! Arden Miller is on my phone? Ho-lee shit! Where are you?"

I leapt out of the rocker and started pacing the grass of my front yard. My heart was racing, and my skin was electric. I listened to Arden laugh, and I saw that toothy grin. Tears tumbled out, and I began to laugh.

"I'm in Southern Pines. I'm gonna grab something to eat and crash at the Days Inn. I'm whipped. I got your letter and got right on a plane."

"Remind me to call Marjorie and tell her I love her."

"How are you, Ray? Are you holding it together?"

"Yes, barely but thoroughly. I'm much better now. Book only one night at the Days Inn. I have an empty house. We have a lot to talk about."

"Yes, sir. I have a few questions about that time capsule, and where is your little girl?"

"I think the situation with my wife is in the process or working itself out. The time capsule is a story in and of itself."

"Correct me if I'm wrong, but I seem to remember you lookin' Rob dead in the face and sayin' Rob was gonna dig it up in 2016."

"You are not wrong."

"And Rob dug it up this spring."

"He did indeed."

"What the hell Ray? Was that just a coincidence?"

"No."

"I'm to believe there's somethin' else at work here?"

"You believed it enough to dig it up yourself in 1997…thank god."

"A promise is a promise, Ray."

"Damn right. Hey, are you going to the church service?"

"You know I don't do church."

"I know, neither do I. I will call the guard shack and make sure they let you in the gate. Meet me at my house at about 8:30. I'm the last house on Shadywood Court. I will catch you up on everything. Then we'll go to the graveside ceremony together."

"Roger that. Ray, what happened?"

"I think the past caught up with our friend, but I have not yet figured out why it bothered to do so. Tell you what, dress comfortable, like for a walk."

"Hey, I had to make peace with running when I joined the army. I still do it, how about you?"

"Oh yes. You and I my friend are going on a run. Get some sleep. I can't tell you how good it is to hear your voice."

"Good night buddy."

I would test my theory first thing in the morning with one of my most favorite reinforcements by my side. Arden and I would find Rob, and the three of us would walk into 2016 together.

I was barely done with that thought when the phone rang again. It was Tom Cianci.

"Hey, Tom."

"I'm sorry kid. I lost 'em. I found my GPS tracker stuck to a gas tank in Whiteville."

34
Furniture

Colonel Ed Erwin and Rob were packing the tan Oldsmobile station wagon to the point where there was only a pocket of seat-beltless riding space near the right rear door of the folded back seat. A pile of Batman comic books and a Capri Sun sat ready and waiting. A cacophony of fishing gear sat atop the luggage and poked out from under the piles of carefully folded bedding. Rita set the thermostats at seventy-five degrees and locked up the house. Ed exited the garage and pulled the door down with a bluster of cigar smoke.

"Come on gorgeous, sunshine awaits!"

"I'm walking out the door, Ed."

Rita was resplendent in a simple sundress. Her sandy hair voluminous yet short cropped and favoring Princess Diana. She paused on the steps while Rob scrambled over the bedding into the car. She loved to watch Ed notice her.

"Whoa, baby," said Ed. "Perhaps we should go back into the house together and make sure all the windows are locked."

"Whoa, baby!" called Rob from inside the car.

With nothing more than a dismissive hand gesture and a smile, Rita got in the passenger seat.

Rita Erwin awoke alone in her darkened cottage, which was still and quiet save for the subtle wind whistle of cool air emanating from the vents in her room. She remembered that trip to the beach. It was somewhere in the mid-1980s before Ed had to spend a month at Fort Benning.

The dreams came like clockwork. It was the same when Ed had died.

Snapshots and home movies of another life played out in her mind until her mind said enough and snapped awake. Rita turned over and focused on the small light she left on in the bathroom to orient herself. Then she looked at the clock: midnight. Today she would bury her only child. Rita got up, and her feet found her slippers. She picked up her tablet to find it flashing. *Unauthorized Access Detected.*

Her breath caught, and she tapped on the flashing link. The barn had been broken into fifteen minutes ago. Where was the sound? The damn thing was supposed to flash and make a noise!

She could not have been sleeping that soundly.

But Rita had a bigger problem. There was no one to call. Jim was still in the Philippines. He would get the same alarm on his tablet, so why had he not called? It was noon in the Philippines. Perhaps he had. Perhaps he was calling the cops. Well, there was no reason to count on that. He could have been on the production floor and not even heard or seen the alarm.

Rita's hands scrambled about her nightstand, turned on the lamp, and found her phone.

She opened a drawer, found her purse, and pulled out a business card.

***

Howard Spruill should have been sleeping, but there he sat in his second-hand, leather Barcalounger watching ESPN with the sound muted and thinking about Travis Seymour.

Travis had to be attached to this somehow. He was unhinged and violent, and he was being guided. Spruill thought about Ray and the sketchy holding company tied to Halo Construction. On a whim, he had run a check on Scott Windham and found nothing—not even a speeding ticket. Rob Erwin's memorial in Pinehurst had yielded a lead in the form of Eugene, but Spruill doubted tomorrow's service in Seven Lakes would yield anything useful. It would be no skin off his back to instead travel out to Ellerbe and see if Scott Windham was home and had a good explanation for where he was Wednesday evening one week ago, or to see Windham's reaction when he mentioned Travis's name.

If Windham wasn't home, Spruill would look up building permits in Moore, Montgomery, and Richmond Counties to see where Halo was currently working. Everyone gets anxious when cops knock on their door, but they are particularly anxious when cops visit them at their job. In fact, most people are eager to talk and get it over with when a uniform comes for them at work.

They are focused on discretion and not necessarily their story. It can trip up some folks.

Spruill's phone lit up. It was Rita Erwin.

"Hello, Ms. Erwin."

"Good morning detective. I am very sorry to wake you, but I have a dilemma. The alarm has sounded in our furniture warehouse on the country outskirts of Ellerbe."

"I would call 911 Mrs. Erwin."

"I've called you detective. I find it odd that my son is killed and then our barn is violated a week later. It is where we store our furniture, which is not cheap. If I text you the address will you meet me there?"

"Mrs. Erwin the last thing I would advise anyone to do is to purposely enter property where criminal activity is suspected. Please do not go there."

"I'm already in the car and on the way."

"Mrs. Erwin, do not go onto the property. Stay pulled to the side of a main road until I get there. What are you driving?"

"I'm in a Buick four-door sedan. I will meet you on Wallace Road just off of Route 220. Thank you, detective."

Rita hung up before Spruill could advise her further. What the hell was wrong with these people? Ellerbe was in Richmond County and beyond his jurisdiction, but this was property belonging to the family of a recent murder victim, plus a seventy-something woman was now headed out there all by herself.

Spruill found his shoes and his gun and badge and headed out the door. He closed the door of his sedan as the address of the warehouse popped up via text. Living in the Foxfire community, he was roughly twenty minutes away from where Rita was headed. Spruill fired up the radio and contacted dispatch. Dispatch acknowledged his intentions and patched him through to the Richmond County Sherriff's Department.

He found Rita on the side of Wallace Road and rolled down his window to look at a face of frightened resolve.

"Mrs. Erwin, lock up your car, get in the passenger seat, and give me the keys to the barn."

Rita guided him to Bowers Lane where a Richmond County cruiser waited for them.

Spruill flicked his lights and lowered his driver-side window.

"Patrolman?"

"McNair."

"Patrolman McNair did dispatch brief you on the situation?"

"Break-in at a furniture warehouse owned by the family of a recent murder victim, yes sir."

"Can you follow us in, and may Mrs. Erwin sit with you in your cruiser while I have a look?"

"Yes, sir."

Spruill found 200 yards of gravel drive littered with newly-fallen pine straw. Fifty yards short of the entrance, Spruill pulled off to the side, and Officer McNair followed.

"Which key opens the door?"

"It's the one with the electrical tape on it. We change the locks regularly, and so I have to do something to identify the new key."

"Have a seat in Officer McNair's cruiser and don't move from it until you see me step out under that light and give the thumbs up."

Spruill exited the sedan, drew his weapon, and quickly made the distance to the darkened right corner of the barn in a half crouch. He continued to creep the perimeter of the barn until he saw the dislodged boards and the chunks of aging, crumbling mortar on the ground near the southeast corner. He backtracked to the front door, opened it with the key, and moved in fast and low.

He cleared both floors and emerged underneath the gooseneck lamp to give the thumbs up. McNair and Rita got out and approached.

"Patrolman McNair you'll find the structure breached near the southeast corner. Looks like a pair of boards were dislodged with a crowbar or something. Rita, come inside but don't touch anything. There's a ton of stuff in here. A pair of chairs and a table was knocked over upon entry, but see if you can tell what is missing. Then you'll have to file a report with Officer McNair."

Officer McNair was gone within the hour. Rita had managed to identify a missing lamp only because she had put it there just days ago. Spruill had questions.

"Mrs. Erwin…"

"Call me Rita."

"OK. How much was that lamp worth again?"

Rita pulled out her tablet. "It's listed at a thousand dollars."

"That little table lamp?"

"Yes."

"I'll take your word on that one. I don't know much about furniture. What about the patio set over here?"

Rita clicked and swiped and handed the tablet to Spruill who studied it a moment and then looked up in awe.

"You're kidding me."

"Not only am I not kidding you, but every piece gets sold every time. This place will be cleared out next week as will the stuff outside in the truck."

Spruill took out his phone and snapped a few shots of the patio set, making sure to take close-ups of the workmanship. Rita could hear the woosh of the pictures being sent to someone. Then suddenly Spruill dialed a number which no one answered. Spruill dialed again, and then a third time.

"Damn Howard, what are you thinking? It's almost two in the morning."

"I'm sorry Dale," replied Spruill, "but you're the only person I personally know who could explain this to me. "

"Are you workin'?"

"Yes. I sent you some photos."

"I'm lookin' at 'em."

"Can you give me a ball-park figure of what a patio set like that is worth?"

"Gimme me a minute."

"What is this about?" asked Rita, looking concerned.

"Dale runs a furniture repair shop on Juniper Lake Road—sofas, tables, patio furniture, you name it. I simply need more information before my assessment."

"Assessment of what?"

"The nature of this enterprise."

Dale returned to the conversation.

"Whatcha got there is a non-cast, not wrought, basic aluminum patio set. It's powder coated, which will drive the price up, but basically, you can find that stuff on Overstock for a grand or less. What's that one goin' for?"

"You would not believe me if I told you. I'm sorry to wake you, but you've been very helpful. I'll explain later."

Spruill hung up and looked at Rita for a moment. She was scared and frustrated. Her eyes were glassy, probably from lack of sleep. Spruill needed to make a call here, and so he did. He folded his hands into hers and spoke slowly.

"Regardless of what it costs, I need to dismantle that patio set."

Rita remained silent in confused dismay. Finally, she met his eyes and cautiously nodded in the affirmative. Spruill promptly strode from the barn back to the cruiser. He popped the trunk, pulled on a pair of latex gloves, and retrieved the Klein 42-inch bolt cutter and a pair of pliers.

As he walked back, Rita appeared in the doorway.

"What is going on?"

"I've seen this before, just not with furniture. "

Spruill overturned the patio chair and positioned the bolt cutter around the weld joint of the leg. It sliced through as if it were butter. He used the pliers to squeeze back open the crimp the cutters had put in the aluminum. He pulled out his penlight. The hollow of the leg was filled with a substance that looked less-than-adept at reinforcing an aluminum chair. Again, he strode from the building and returned to the trunk of the sedan.

Spruill unrolled a piece of plastic and spread it on the floor of the trunk. He unfolded his pocket knife and scooped out a sliver of a dense brown substance resembling clay, smearing it on the plastic.

Next to nasal atomizers of Naloxone, for the perps who happened to be overdosing when he and the fellas kicked in the door, Spruill kept a box of NIK System test kits. The kits were essentially a colorless liquid reagent.

He opened one and let it drop on his little pile of clay. Slowly the brown turned a reddish gray. Spruill exhaled slowly. This was a narcotic, and judging by its appearance, a morphine base that in and of itself was ingestible. More importantly, though, it was the beginnings of heroin.

Spruill bagged his evidence and closed the trunk. He looked to Rita who had taken to sitting on the steps under the gooseneck lamp. She wore a blue chambray shirt with the sleeves rolled up and white denim pants. With her thumb and middle fingers of her right hand, she continuously spun the wedding ring on her left hand in endless revolutions, as if conjuring divine assistance. She looked to him with a face that needed answers. She looked as if she should be making peanut butter sandwiches for her family. She seemed completely alone.

"Rita, where is Colonel Jim Dorn right now?"

***

He could only see what transpired under the lighted doorway, but he saw Detective Howard Spruill, some uniform, and he saw Rita. Whoever broke in knew what was in there.

Whoever broke in knew there were cameras and thus somehow entered from the back.

Spruill walked in with bolt cutters and then walked out with a piece of something. Colonel Jim Dorn closed the laptop and sat in his darkened room at the Inn at Eagle Springs. The clock was now ticking.

35
The Family Windham

Dr. Walter Windham, MD padded down the third-floor hallway of Richmond Memorial Hospital toward the nurse's station to inform Leslie where he was headed. What had once been his pride and joy—the pain clinic—was now the bane of his existence. As an orthopedic surgeon, the clinic had been his endgame. He would get out of the operating room and manage and advise younger men and women adept at treating everything from arthritis to sports injuries.

But that was before the trend. Windham should have retired a decade ago, but when Linda died he simply did not know what to do with himself, so he kept working.

Once upon a time, the answers were simple: precise surgery, injections, physical therapy—a thoughtfully prescribed regimen to manage and alleviate pain. At some point, though, doctors got into bed with pharmaceutical companies and started putting Band-Aids on problems in the form of pills. Inevitably those patients would land on his doorstep looking for a clean slate and a new script.

Initially, the answer was no. Quickly, though, he began to discern the hopeless from the retrievable, but he would still not write another script. Then there was a new wrinkle: synthetics from Mexico, like Fentanyl. Now the average Joe could get their hands-on drugs meant to ease the pain of cancer patients staring at the end of life. Infinitely more dangerous this stuff was, and anything from Mexico was of suspect quality.

"I'm headed to the zoo, Leslie."

Leslie knew Windham meant the clinic and smiled sympathetically.

"It's a nice day Dr. Windham, let the young'uns handle it. Why don't you go play Pinehurst? How many courses do they have now?"

"Nine I think. I've played most of them. At my age, golf is more frustrating than the zoo. I think I'll just work, so I don't end up in my own clinic for treatment."

Leslie laughed and waved him off.

Windham got in the elevator and began his descent. He needed a moment to grab a paper or turn on the news. He wanted an update on Ray's wife. Her spiral had begun with nothing more than a herniated disc, and by the time she arrived at his door, she was on her third doctor. He treated her, refilled a prescription or two, and then quickly deduced her as retrievable and cut her off. She was smart and strong. He said he would lead her out of this. Then she had taken off, which usually happens because an ultimatum was delivered.

Windham never started any of his patients down this road. His daily dilemma was what to do with the folks that were already running down it full speed when they finally came to see him.

Then there was the boy.

The boy at least partnered with a legitimate distributor, though Dr. Windham wanted no knowledge of how that worked. The boy was his outlet for the hopeless, so they would stop showing up to the clinic. Instead of a script, Windham would write a phone number where they could get "help."

There might be a penance to pay for that. So be it.

***

It was 7:45 a.m. Wednesday morning, and Scott Windham had been up all night. He sat in his kitchen at the head of his rustic farmer's table obsessing over his people's missteps.

Tuesday had been one epiphany after another, and none of them were good. First Travis called him in a panic after barely evading Detective Howard Spruill. Oh, and by the way, he clobbered the drug cop over the head. Travis was now avoiding the light of day in Scott's horse barn-turned guest cottage.

Next was the call from Chris informing him that the business right down the road from Scott's own home was owned by Colonel Jim Dorn and not the Erwins, and Jim Dorn was now on the warpath.

The crème de la crème of this mess? Ray McCarthy had been standing at the end of his driveway yesterday, waving at him.

Scott had his tablet open to the news and was again watching Linnie Supall's interview with Ray.

"Whatever issue this person thought he had with my wonderful friend, he was not brave enough to confront Rob himself. I imagine that he is now cowering in some hole, and I have faith that detectives will soon flush him out."

"Bastard," said Scott. "Little bastard."

Yes, it had definitely been Ray at the end of his driveway.

Scott had evaded Spruill these last couple of years without too much effort, and now suddenly Spruill had a whiff of his ass, and there staring at him was one of the reasons. Both Ray and the Colonel were pissed, smart, and had time on their hands. Whether he wanted it or not, Spruill had help. One of these three had to go.

Scott wasn't going to go near a cop, and he was pretty sure it would be challenging to outflank the Colonel. If Rob's death hadn't taken the steam out of the Colonel's engine, then perhaps Ray's would. Maybe then Jim would start thinking about Rita and Jenna and whether or not this was worth all the trouble. Scott would see what Matt Roper found, and he would decide. He picked up his phone and dialed Travis, and Travis picked up immediately.

"Hey, get over to the main house. Matt's due here any minute. I'm in the kitchen." Scott hung up and pondered his options.

Ray lived on a quiet cul-de-sac that backed up to the woods, no family in the house. What if they caught Ray coming out the door on his way to the first service while the rest of Seven Lakes North was emptying toward the chapel? Travis could push him right back into the house.

Scott googled Ray's address and did a three-dimensional, panoramic view of the property. It was a small house with a front, side, and rear entrance, and a back porch. They could bring Ray right out the back door, drag him into the woods, and ultimately leave him in the considerable creek formed by the Lake Sequoia runoff. Scott looked up the properties adjacent to Ray's. The one to the right was vacant and for sale. The one to the left backed up to Sequoia Dam and was in foreclosure. That meant Ray had no immediate neighbors.

They would go in on the Harleys, same as they had for Rob. Both bikes had Vance and Hines Quiet Baffles attached to the exhaust pipes. This Scott had done merely to hear his music better, but it was also helpful in other situations. Travis would ride the Sportster. He would pilot the Low Rider. Scott wondered how loud Matt's bike was.

The answer came when Matt Roper walked into the kitchen unannounced.

"I'm here," said Matt.

"Jesus!" startled Scott. "I didn't hear you come in. Your bike's quiet. That's good. What do you have for me?"

Matt set his prize in front of Scott with a pronounced thump—a lamp base of ornately sculpted driftwood pieces that appeared naturally bound together.

"That's a very nice piece," said Scott.

"Wonderful," said Matt. "That's my last errand for a while. I'm headed to Raleigh."

"Hang tight a second."

Scott left the kitchen to go out to the garage, returning with a pair of pruning shears which he used to snip off the tips of the driftwood pieces. He then upended the lamp and slammed it on the table several times and then tossed the lamp to the floor.

Left behind on the table was a crumble of clay-like residue.

"What is that?" Matt asked.

"That, in and of itself, is a smokable morphine base, but what more enterprising individuals do is turn it into heroin. Unfortunately, I'm gonna need you for one more errand."

"I have an appointment in Raleigh, a possible job."

"That's fine. I just need you as back-up. You'll be in and out."

"I don't think you understand. I'm out now. I have an opportunity."

Scott tensed as Matt stepped closer and stared him down. He felt a new presence in the room. Scott looked over his left shoulder to see that Travis had entered the kitchen with an obvious hiccup to his stride, an injury with which Matt seemed preoccupied. When Matt returned his gaze to Scott, he had drawn his 45-caliber handgun and was making a pretense of checking the load.

Scott clicked off the safety.

"I don't think you understand, Matt. The last time we had to do this, it was messy, and it went on longer than it had to. If you'd have been there, we would have been in and out and without a scratch. This here…" Scott held up the handgun as if it were time for show and tell. "Is a last resort that leaves a trail. I let you out of the last gig because you were close with Rob. You are not close with this guy."

Matt looked at Scott and nodded. "Fine. I'm gone to Raleigh as soon as this is done. Where are we headed now?"

"All you need to know is that we're going down 73 toward West End. Travis will take the lead. I will bring up the rear."

"Let's roll then. Where's your pisser?"

Scott pointed with the gun to the door of a small washroom behind and to the left of Travis. Matt side-stepped Travis. Travis looked nervous. It was probably a rare thing for him to be in the presence of someone he knew he couldn't take.

"Make it quick." Scott filled the doorway to the washroom just as Matt exited.

"Give me your phone. I'm going to pull the battery out so cell towers can't ping your location until this is over."

Matt nodded and handed over the phone.

36
Reunion

"Whiteville?"

"Whiteville Ray. Again, I'm sorry."

"Don't be sorry Tom. You've had more success in a shorter period of time than all the law enforcement between here and Florida. Also, you've put her at ease. I know my wife. She has a temper, and she's fiercely independent. Now that she has a leg up on this problem of hers, she wants to finish it herself."

"I'd feel more comfortable if I could see this through personally," said Tom. "She's gone from eight to three pills a day. That's great progress, but it's also dangerous."

"I don't understand."

"Her body is adjusting to the new dosage. It'll cry out for more meds while not necessarily being able to handle the dosages of old."

"I have faith in her, Tom, but just in case, let's see if we can figure her intentions. She goes west, and she gets closer to home, which she is not ready to do. If she heads east, she'll hit Wilmington in about an hour. It's been a while, but we used to go to Wilmington all the time before Ava was born. Go down and poke around the shops, maybe grab some food at Riverboat Landing. Before I turn in, I'll have to you a list of every place we've ever stayed down there."

"You should give her a call, Ray, let her hear that you're concerned and not angry," said Tom.

"I will. I might give her a day's worth of space first."

"All right, kid. I'm heading east."

***

After reliving yesterday's phone call with Tom, I got out of bed and into the shower. I dressed in knee-length gym shorts and a faded Duke T-shirt just to put a wry smile on Arden's face. He'd always been a die-hard Tarheel, and I assumed that hadn't changed. It was about a quarter after eight Wednesday morning. This was going to be a weird day, but one way or another, resolution would be had.

If the anomaly accepted Arden into 1984, I had reason to believe it would let me drag Rob out of it. It was not a perfect plan, but it was the only plan I had left. I would recount that day at the gazebo with Arden, and I would prepare him for either becoming his twelve-year-old self or for witnessing my sudden disappearance, whereupon he should wait for me up on Cherokee Trail.

I sent Tom a list of every hotel and bed and breakfast in which Morgan and I had stayed. This I had done from both memory and via a search of confirmation emails from 2009 to 2011. I had no doubt that he would find them and then watch from afar. Regardless of how the rest of this day went, I had resolved to hit the road and rejoin my family once I knew for sure where they were. I'd leave Arden the keys to the house, ask him to linger a few days, and meet my daughter.

***

Howard Spruill had no trouble being up at the crack of dawn because he had never gone to bed. He was too busy looking for Colonel Jim Dorn, who was definitely not in the Philippines.

He was in Raleigh, North Carolina—or closer—and he had notified no one.

Patrolman McNair had returned to the barn with his sergeant and assisted Spruill with locking down the facility with little fanfare or traffic. The barn presented an opportunity that did not need to be broadcast.

Rita had reset the alarm and its passcode. Being the system's administrator, she was also able to make it so Jim Dorn no longer received access alerts. Then she turned the tablet over to Spruill. Spruill noticed the cameras in the trees. Rita had not known about the cameras and thus had no access to their footage, so Howard disabled them.

Killing the cameras would put Dorn on notice, but Spruill had a feeling Jim Dorn was already on notice. Spruill now knew what Jim Dorn had tumbled to already. Rob Erwin had probably been beaten to death because of Colonel Jim's retirement plan.

Spruill did not mention this to Rita. He didn't have to. He had told her that the furniture was stuffed with narcotic. The barn was now a whole new kind of crime scene.

"Jim couldn't have anything to do with that," Rita had said unsteadily.

Spruill simply looked at her and waited. Soon she began to tremble.

"Oh, god…Do you think? Is this why Rob..."

Spruill said nothing. Rita sat heavily on the front fender of the cruiser and began to cry, quietly. Spruill produced a handkerchief and handed it to her.

"It's too early to say anything for sure. Don't borrow trouble."

Spruill was pretty sure. Dorn had neither responded to the alarm nor had he returned Rita's calls even though it was the middle of the day in Cebu. He was laying low or in transit or both. Chances were he was watching them via the cameras.

Spruill asked Rita the airports and the airline Jim normally used to travel overseas, as well as his preferred cell phone carrier. Then he called Raleigh-Durham Airport to see if a Cathay Pacific Airlines flight from Cebu had landed in Raleigh in the last twenty-four hours. One had, yesterday morning, but the airline would not disclose its passenger information. Spruill decided to wake up a judge to get a warrant for Dorn's cell records, which was granted when Spruill said the following: "Felony cache of narcotics found on premises, owner of the facility also sought in connection to the death of architect."

It was drawn up, signed, scanned, and sent to Spruill inside the hour.

Rob Erwin was a popular guy.

Spruill, of course, did not suspect Dorn of being directly responsible for Rob's death, just indirectly. Concise, bold statements are what get a judge to grant your warrant in the wee hours of the morning.

From what Spruill knew from Rita, Dorn was tech savvy. That meant he would know how not to leave a trail. If the man was in the country to secretly check on his business venture, or worse, to deal out his own brand of justice, he would have to make at least one call to arrange some form of accommodation, even if it was from Cebu. No matter how tech-savvy, a man in his seventies prefers dealing with a live person. Spruill had never met anyone that age who did everything digitally.

His next call was to Verizon, and he waited until he got the highest-level supervisor on duty. It took about four transfers and said supervisor was in another time zone. Spruill asked for the man's email and then forwarded him the warrant.

There were two calls yesterday from Cary, North Carolina to a number based in Wilmington, North Carolina. Rita said those were to a man named Wyatt Halsey, Dorn's oldest living friend and business partner. Rita had his number. Spruill called it from Rita's phone and found it disconnected. There had been no more calls, not even a cell phone tower ping.

Gone dark, both of them, thought Spruill.

Spruill sent Rita home at about 6:30 a.m.

Spruill and the officers from Richmond County coordinated for an hour and a half, agreeing to keep the barn a secret and hashing out the beginnings of a sting operation. Spruill then considered his next immediate move.

He had no idea whether or not Halo Construction and its suspect holding company were involved in the area's drug problem, much less Rob Erwin's death, but Scott Windham's home was not that far from the barn.

***

The trio of motorcycles sprinted down the road at what felt like light speed to Matt Roper. Everything was happening too fast, and he hoped he had guessed the ultimate destination correctly. It made little sense, but Scott had said "guy," a guy with whom Matt was not necessarily close.

Matt had entered Scott's washroom with its small pedestal sink and free-standing cabinet over the toilet. A pair of silver knobs protruded from the cabinet at about chin level. Matt had withdrawn the business card and set it on the knobs. As the water flowed, Matt typed in the number with his thumb and then the message. He dropped the card in the toilet and flushed as he hit send and then deleted the message,

When the cyclists met the stoplight at West End, they hung a left toward Seven Lakes. They took a right on Seven Lakes Drive, but then made an almost immediate left on Trade Street and a right on Grant, cruising past the various small businesses that made up Seven Lakes Village. For a moment Matt thought he had made a mistake as they were nowhere near the residential parts of Seven Lakes. Travis eased off on the throttle of the Sportster and pulled beside Matt, letting Scott take the lead as they drove down the middle of the private side street. They continued on Grant Street past the Lake House Bar and Grill and Seven Lakes Marine, following it to where Grant Street dead-ended between a storage facility and an electrician's warehouse. Then Matt saw the shit-littered horse trail. Scott entered it without hesitation, easily absorbing the jostle of the slightly uneven terrain. Travis motioned Matt to follow Scott in. They enjoyed a brief canopy of tree cover before the bikes spit out of the woods and into a small cul-de-sac connected to Edgewater Drive. They followed Edgewater to Firetree Lane, and Matt knew he had guessed correctly.

***

At 8:15 a.m. Howard Spruill negotiated the long driveway of a home that seemed part antebellum and part dude ranch. Whatever it's architectural designation, it looked expensive. It was a lot of land for a guy who operated a business at a perpetual loss if what Ray said about Halo Construction was true.

Spruill rang the doorbell and banged on a mahogany door featuring a *W* carved in relief. No answer. His phone buzzed again. He had received a text message while driving, and he still hadn't opened it. He pulled out the phone. The number was not familiar, but the message was clear enough.

Ray's house now—Matt.

Spruill had not even reached the stoplight intersection of West End when the radio sprung to life.

"All units in the vicinity of West End and Seven Lakes, report of shots fired on Shadywood Court, Seven Lakes North…"

***

There's a reason I don't have frosted glass on my front door anymore, and that reason came just a little before 8:30 a.m. on Wednesday morning.

Truth is I was excited. There was a knock on the door. I had been rehearsing a smart-ass thing to say to Arden, and I imagined what he would look like after all these years. I figured that he'd be thicker and grayer, but that my childhood friend would still be there in essence—especially when he grinned.

He'd always been taller than Rob and I, and as I approached the door, his shadow filled the glass. I turned the bolt and opened the door.

"Well let's have a look at you old ma—"

My greeting was choked off when a catcher's mitt of a hand swallowed my face and pushed me back in the house and to the floor. I scrambled to my feet only to be met with a straight right hand to the face that sent me back down to the floor.

"Good morning Mr. McCarthy," said a Hulk-Hogan-sized individual. "Stay where you are."

Stay where I was? I had no choice. I couldn't get up. Everything had a halo around it, and I could barely form a thought. I pictured a referee issuing a ten-count. I resolved to get up at eight.

The behemoth walked straight through my open floor plan of a house to the sliding glass door by the dining area, his boots clumping across the glossy wood. I heard the latch, and then I heard the door slide open. I was only at the count of six when his hands were around my neck and pulling me to my feet.

He held his right hand at my neck and his left hand in the middle of my back, lifting me just short of off my feet and dragging me outside.

Then he threw me off my deck.

I hit the grass and rolled to the bottom of the yard. Nothing had broken, and my head actually began to clear, but I could not catch my breath. I watched Travis descend the short flight of steps to the yard. Suddenly the fleshy face of Scott Windham was looking down at me. He smelled of cologne and cigarettes.

"You've aged well my friend. This is an absolute shame, but you should have just minded your own business. I figured since you visited me I should visit you too, and I brought friends."

I struggled to my knees and then to my feet, and Scott let me.

"You...look...like shit," I stammered out, still trying to normalize my breath. "Is this...what you did to Rob?"

Scott nodded.

My giant attacker had paused in the middle of the yard and looked to his left. Matt Roper stood by my storage shed, cutting off my only other escape route. The giant seemed to defer to Matt, but Matt didn't move. I realized that Scott had no problem admitting to Rob because the same thing was about to happen to me.

Scott looked to Matt and seemed disappointed. Then he nodded to the big fella.

"Do it," said Scott.

Travis came toward me, and I noticed the limp in his left leg.

"I bet Rob did that."

He looked confused.

I took two quick steps toward Travis and roundhoused his left knee as hard as I could. He buckled, and I brought my own heavy right hand down on the corner of the behemoth's left eye. He was down, but not out.

I felt something crack across the back of my head, but the strike was a glancing blow thrown off balance. I spun around to throw the same kick at Scott's knee, but the left side of my skull was introduced to Scott's retractable baton.

Scott looked to Matt.

"What the hell are you good for?"

Matt approached. Travis stumbled to his feet. This was it.

In retrospect, it was a buzz…yes, the air buzzed like a sports car going by at a high rate of speed, just not as loud.

The air buzzed, and big fella screamed bloody murder. The tip of an arrow protruded from Travis's right side, skewering his love handle meat.

"Hit the deck! Hit the deck!" commanded Scott.

Roper went chest first to the ground as the air buzzed again and an arrow flew over Scott's head.

The giant crumpled to the ground and lay on his left side, hyperventilating.

Scott rose to a kneeling position, drew a handgun, and fired two shots toward what was the left of my house where the gravel drive pulled up to the side entrance.

Arden was here.

Another arrow let fly, and Scott ducked. Roper was on his feet and running. I got to my feet to meet him only to watch him veer toward Scott and tackle him to the ground. Scott held on to the gun.

"Run Ray!" screamed Matt. "It's your only chance."

I rose on rubbery legs and ran with an uneven stride. I had gotten around the side of the house Matt had been protecting when I heard the gun go off again. I looked at the driveway to find motorcycles and an SUV I didn't recognize.

"Arden!" I yelled. "Get deep in the woods and call 911!"

There was another gunshot, and then another—the sound of shattering glass.

I was picking up speed. I ran straight for the house in foreclosure, the one that backed right up to Sequoia Dam. I made it to the backyard and then through the spit of woods between it and the dam, bouncing off scrub oaks and tripping over underbrush. I heard a motorcycle fire up. And another gunshot.

The grassy hill of Sequoia dam is not just an incline; it's virtually an elevator shaft. A quarter of the way up I was on my hands and knees breathless and scrambling through the knee-high grass. I got within sight of the guardrail. I reached the guardrail. I was exhausted. I paused a moment. I looked down the length of Sequoia Dam to see one of the motorcycles turning from Cherokee Trail onto the dam.

Scott Windham was coming to kill me.

I looked right. I was probably 150 yards to what I hoped was the safety of 1984. I hopped the wire guardrail and ran.

The motorcycle sprinted across the dam. There was a gunshot that was not even close. I'd covered fifty yards.

Another gunshot rang out. I heard that bullet whiz by my right ear. There was another shot that went over my head. Scott had to be out of bullets.

Twenty-five yards away I could see the shimmer, feel vertigo. It was going to happen. I was going to make it. The motorcycle was bearing down on me.

Ten yards…five yards.

The motorcycle pulled up alongside me. Scott was smiling as we slipped into 1984 together.

37
There Can Be Only One

The heat-induced stillness of 2016 was supplanted by a slight breeze off Lake Sequoia in 1984. Scott Windham skidded his Moped to a halt. The sharp angular features of his face had returned, as had his auburn hair. He looked to be eighty pounds lighter. The gun was gone.

He looked confused.

I had turned to face him, backpedaling a few feet to put some space between us while keeping an eye on how he would reconcile the transformation.

"Hey, kid." Scott said. "Did you see where that guy in front of me went? What'd he run into somebody's yard? Where'd he go?"

"I saw him."

"Well then?"

"Tell me something, Scott. If you could go back to when you were a kid, what would you change?"

Scott regarded me anew. It was the tone of my voice and my demeanor.

"Who are you and how the hell do you know me?"

"Just answer the question, and I'll tell you."

"Sure kid. I'd change plenty. I'd probably go to college or something. Now answer my question."

"Scott, what if I told you that you have a chance to do that right now? To leave yourself a message—like to go to college and not be a murdering drug dealer?"

Scott absently applied the kickstand to his Moped and dismounted it, still not tumbling to the idea that he was no longer riding a Harley-Davidson low rider, and advanced toward me.

"I don't know who you are kid, but you're starting to piss me off with this Yoda routine you're serving up. Answer my question, or I am going to smack you into next week."

"It's me, Scott. It's Ray. You don't have a big enough hand to smack me into next week, because we are thirty-two years into the past."

Scott paused and looked me over.

"You do look like he did. You related? A nephew?"

"Take a look at your ride, Scott."

Windham cautiously looked over his shoulder and then looked back at me with mouth agape. I nodded.

"Go look at yourself in the rearview mirror."

Scott promptly turned and strode back toward the Moped, and I followed him.

"Do you remember that day at the pool where you got kicked out and then chased me on that stupid Moped?"

Scott studied himself in the rearview mirror of the Moped, his eyes wide and his hands coming up to his face. Then absently he said, "Yeah… yeah…you disappeared…hid in the woods…"

"I didn't hide in the woods. I ran back into 2016 just like I ran into 1984 just now. This is a time anomaly, and I don't know how long it will last."

Scott's gaze briefly drifted toward me and then back to the mirror.

"You're inhabiting your fifteen-year-old self, and I need you to focus."

I lifted my right hand and snapped my fingers a few times to get his attention. Then I stepped back. Scott, still looking confused, left the Moped and squared himself to me.

"Scott Windham, this is your life."

I stepped forward with my little adolescent left foot and then sharply planted my little adolescent right foot in Scott's crotch, a direct hit. He folded to the ground.

"Agggh! You goddamn little bastard!" Scott screamed as he rolled left and right on the Firetree Lane asphalt trying to mitigate the pain.

"Now that is not appropriate language for a man who builds churches. Hey, do you remember that day at the pool?"

"Yeah I remember now," Scott gasped.

His tone was changing. His anger was rising and giving him focus. I was going to have to bring this to a close now. I mounted him and drove my right hand into his face and then my left.

"I didn't hide in the woods. I ran right back into 2016. I've been visiting this place for a week trying to undo what you did to Rob, you murdering piece of shit."

I drove another straight right hand into Scott's face, but young Ray did not have the heavy hands of adult Ray, and I was not making much progress in incapacitating Scott. I clutched his shirt with my left hand, pulled him toward me, and hit him again.

"You'll be happy to learn that I haven't achieved my objective, so all I have left is to kick the shit out of you and drag you back across that dam to the cops."

I let loose another right hand, and Scott caught it with his left. His right hand came up and grabbed me by the throat. He was bruised and bloodied but still perfectly functional. He squeezed as he sat up. Then he threw me off to the side, planted a hand on the asphalt, and slowly rose to his feet.

Scott was three years older than I, and in 1984 that meant he was three years taller and three years stronger.

I was in trouble.

Scott stepped to me quickly and kicked me in the guts. I rolled into a fetal position, gasping.

"What's going to happen, Ray, is that both you and I are going to disappear. You are going to disappear into Lake Sequoia, and I am gonna get the do-over to end all do-overs. I am gonna stay right here and relive the best years of my life, with a few changes."

I wasn't sure how that was going to work for him, but I didn't care. Everything would change if I died in 1984. Maybe Rob would never move back to North Carolina only to die in the same lake thirty-two years later. There would be no Morgan, no Ava, but I'd die knowing that they existed.

Scott commenced picking me off the street by the throat, squeezing tight. I looked at him, bug-eyed, and fought for breath.

"Goodbye, Ray, and thank you."

Across the street, a front door flew open and a man in his early sixties stumbled out to the landing in a Pinehurst T-shirt and denim shorts, glasses slightly askew.

"What the hell are you two kids doing in the middle of the street?"

Scott let me go and turned to him. I started to gather myself a bit. I remained in the fetal position playing possum. I was limited by what young Ray could do physically, but adult Ray was still inside, and adult Ray had studied martial arts with his pal Rob. Sometimes a smaller body can work for you.

"It's OK!" Scott called out to the old man. "We just took a spill on the Moped. We're OK."

"Your little friend does not look OK. I'm calling security."

The man turned back into his house, and Scott turned back to me and kicked me in the gut once more for good measure, but I had braced myself for that. I acted the part though and gasped out loud.

"I'm gonna have to make this quick Ray. I'm gonna end you and then hide you."

He reached down to pick me up by the throat again, and I let him. He put his left hand on my back much the same way Travis had, and I could tell he intended to choke-slam me to the asphalt like a professional wrestler. Then he'd probably drag me half-conscious to the lake and drown me in the shallow water.

He lifted me high in the air, and I kept my eyes closed while fumbling for a grip on his forearm. I swung my legs up and locked my ankles around Scott's shoulder, his right arm falling neatly between my knees as I unfurled my torso toward the ground. I secured my forearms across his wrist and pointed his thumb to the sky.

Scott remained standing and howled while I briefly swayed like a pendulum upside down from his hyper-extended arm. The swaying stopped, and the armbar was fully locked in. Scott panicked and tried to shake me off, which only made his arm feel like it was coming out of the socket. I was not sure how long young Ray could hold this.

Inevitably Scott sank to the ground to relieve some of the pressure. My grip slipped, and I made no effort to keep the armbar secure. Scott's right arm was now jelly. I sprang to my feet, and roundhouse kicked Scott in the head.

Young Ray had legs that were adult strong.

I adjusted position and kicked him again. His face exploded in blood as his nose broke. Again, I kicked him, and Scott fell back to the asphalt unconscious, and I bent over to catch my breath.

Now what?

I left Scott for a moment and jogged back to the slight rise to the dam and saw the shimmer. I held my breath as I passed through it.

I emerged on the other side and immediately looked toward Sequoia Point wherein 2016 there should be a marina and a beach.

There were no such things. I was still in 1984.

I was gonna have to go three miles around the lake to get back home. And, unless I wanted to kill him or leave him here to cause God knew what kind of trouble for me in the future, I would have to take Scott Windham with me.

I jogged back toward the Moped. It had the long banana-like seat with upright chrome backing to which a passenger might hang on. It would keep Scott from falling off the back if I could drag him onto the seat. I went to Scott, who was moaning back to life on the asphalt, and I kicked him again.

I gathered him by the armpits and slowly dragged him over. I flipped him over, bent down, and hugged him around the waist and heaved forward. I got his chest on the seat. I heaved again and got his belly on the seat and let him hang limply across the Moped, his feet slightly touched the asphalt, but on the other side his dangling hands missed the one exhaust pipe, so that was good. Actually, I didn't give a shit.

I fired the engine and slumped the Moped forward off the kickstand. I gave it a little throttle, and we moved forward. I kept my legs extended toward the ground, and my feet padded forward across the asphalt in time with our forward progression. I drove a half mile before I attempted to pick up my feet and give it full throttle.

When I did go for full throttle, we warbled a bit. I kept us upright across Lake Echo dam. I leaned forward and put my feet to the asphalt again when we climbed the slight hill toward Overlook Drive, stepping in time with half-throttle speed to keep our balance up the hill.

The rubber tips of Scott's sneakers intermittently bounced off the roadway.

I crested the hill and looked down toward Longleaf Dam to see if Rob was indeed fishing in that lake. It was early afternoon in 1984. It would be close.

There was no sign of him.

I rolled to a stop where the U-shaped Overlook Drive intersects Firetree Lane for the second time. Scott slumped off the Moped seat to the ground, coming to an awkward rest against the dam's wire guardrail. He rubbed his face.

"What happened," Scott moaned.

"You lost."

"What are we doing?"

"We're waiting for Rob."

"There is no Rob. Leave me here."

I marched over to Scott and kicked him in the face again. Out he went.

I walked to the intersection of Firetree and Overlook and paused at the edge by the street sign. An unholy sun beat down on my neck, and yet I was cool. I reached up with my right arm and watched the hairs on it rise in unison. An almost imperceptible hum rang through the air.

Less than 100 yards down this stretch of road was my best friend's home. If he had lived in the first house on the water I could have seen him casting into Sequoia and waved to him, but he lived on 104 Overlook—not 102—and 106 Overlook was an empty lot that would eventually become his home in 2010.

I squared myself to the intersection and ignored the shimmer. I closed my eyes and stepped forward and was thrown to the pavement. The watery reflection of my sprawled adolescent body slowly stilled itself.

I sat up, gravel and dirt sticking to my sweaty palms and calves, and watched myself come apart. It started with a whimper that became a cough. Tears spilled, and the cough became a sob. I bent over and dry-retched into the pavement, crying not like a forty-four-year-old, but like a twelve-year-old boy who had lost everything. The anomaly would not let me approach Rob's house. I had blown it. My time here was done.

"I'm sorry…I'm sorry." I fought for my breath, but I could not catch it.

A white Ford pick-up truck with *Security* stenciled across its door snuck up on us from the direction whence we had come.

"Fellas," said a white-haired man with a gray mustache, "I got a call that said two boys wrecked a Moped, but they said it was down by Sequoia Point. Are you OK boy?"

I gathered myself to a standing position and dusted off my knees.

"Yes. Yes, sir," I said, still catching my breath. "We did, but we got it started again, and we were just taking a break. We're fine."

"You don't look fine, and your friend looks horrible."

"I just need to get…"

From the opposite direction, a familiar Oldsmobile station wagon approached. I watched the electric passenger-side window go down and a man lean over the bench seat to have a look at us. The wagon passed, turned around in a driveway off Firetree, and then parked itself behind the security truck.

Colonel Ed Erwin stepped out of the wagon in a white Panama shirt, khaki shorts, and slip-on loafers. A gray-white fringe of hair still framed his mostly bald head. He sported the deep tan of a golfer. He stopped short, put his hands on his hips, and regarded me with a smile.

"What the hell did you get yourself into Ray?"

I quickly composed myself. A million possibilities were running through my mind.

"We had an accident."

"I'll say you had an accident," interjected the security guard. "These bikes ain't built for two, and one of ya better be at least sixteen years old to be operatin' this thing around here."

Colonel Ed wandered over to Scott and examined his nose. Then he looked over at me. A moment later, Ed was in my face assessing my damage. I smelled cigar smoke as he lifted my chin and examined my neck.

The security guard returned to the truck and answered his CB radio.

Ed took a knee in front of me and looked me in the eyes.

"Ray, tell me now, did you beat the hell out of this prick?"

I nodded.

Ed suppressed a grin and stood up and walked to the security truck, muttering to himself. "Bet the little shit leaves 'em alone now. Sir," Ed called out to the security guard as he approached the door. "I know these boys. The Moped belongs to the older one. His dad's a doctor. I'll take the both of them home, and I will come back and collect the bike."

"That works for me," said the security man. "Some fool ran out of gas in the middle of Lake Sequoia. Guess I'm a mobile service station for boats now."

Ed laughed as he patted him on the back.

"Come on, Ray. Help me get Scotty here in the back seat."

I sat in the passenger seat and began answering questions.

"You're lucky. I was checking the mailbox one last time before we head to the beach house. I'm pretty sure that guy would have held you two at the guard house while he called the cops. Where do the Windhams live?"

"Corner of Firetree and Cherokee Trail," I lied.

We passed the pool and the mailboxes and headed down the stretch of Firetree Lane where Scott had tried to chase me down a few days before. I didn't have much time. Adults were involved now, and adults are not easily convinced of fanciful things. I mean, what was I going to ask of this man? Was I going to ask him to leave Scott and to bring Rob to me so we could go for a walk?

"Tell me what happened. I'm going to have to tell Dr. Windham something when he comes to collect that Moped out of my garage."

"He followed me. He started a fight the other day that I avoided, but he tracked me down by Sequoia Point as the man said. We fought. I won. I almost didn't win."

"I can tell by the look of your neck. Did you drive halfway around the lake with him unconscious across the back of that thing?"

"I tried. It's probably best you tell Dr. Windham that you just found the Moped and remembered that his son drove—drives—one. Maybe if we cover for him with his dad, Scott won't come after us for a while. Colonel, when you get near Cherokee, can you pull to the side of the road?"

"Sure, Ray."

Ed looked at me with concern as I continued my impromptu speech.

"I want to talk about Rob. Scott will come for Rob as he did me, but it might not be for some time. He will corner Rob with the assistance of a friend, a big one. I want you to promise me something."

"OK, said Ed. "I'm listening." His voice was soft and without the air of a parent indulging a child. He acknowledged that the situation was serious—if only to me. It was something I always liked about Ed. He was a natural parent who never had need of appearing parental.

"If they corner him near a body of water, tell him to just swim. Tell him to jump in and just swim. Rob is fast as hell in the water. It will save him for sure. Tell him that every day for as long as he's your boy. Scott wanted to hurt me…bad, and he will want to hurt Rob bad. No amount of talking to Scott's parents will stop that. Rob has to stop it himself."

Ed nodded and I promptly hopped out. I shut my door and then opened the rear one to gather Scott out of the back seat.

"Let me help you, Ray."

"No Colonel. I got this. It was good to see you again. You were one of my most favorite people. Please remember what I said to tell Rob. Tell him today, and tell him every day. Make it a thing. Promise me."

"I promise."

"Good. Now watch this shit."

I pulled Scott from the back seat of the Oldsmobile and threw his arm around my shoulder.

"Walk. I know you're at least somewhat lucid," I told Scott.

Scott and I stumbled toward the shimmer that only he and I could see.

***

Colonel Ed Erwin watched Ray half carry Scott Windham toward the intersection of Firetree and Cherokee Trail and tried to quickly process what just happened. It had felt like he was speaking to someone else, and not just because he had never heard Ray swear before. He thought maybe it was one of those coming-of-age moments for Ray—defeating the bully and whatnot—and that was why his tone was so…adult, but it was more than that. It was unsettling.

Yes, it was unsettling, especially the part where Ray referred to him in the past tense.

Then Ray and Scott disappeared.

Ed fired up the Oldsmobile and drove forward, taking a right on Cherokee…nothing. He drove across the dam…nothing.

Ed kept his promise, even though Ray never explained how he had just vanished, nor did he ever explain why they had stopped nowhere near the Windham home. Ray just always smiled and looked at Ed like he was nuts.

Ed didn't just repeat to Rob what Ray had said. For years he was fond of telling the whole story of Ray and Scott and the Moped until it became a family parable, one with a central metaphor for defying the odds.

"And remember what your bully-beatin' buddy says my boy," Ed would grin.

"I know Dad…Just swim."

38
Mr. and Mrs. McCarthy

"Good god almighty Ray! Good god almighty!"

Arden Miller was running across the dam toward me. Scott Windham slumped his fatness to the ground and buried his face in his hands.

Arden sported a full beard. He was lean with a shag of brown hair streaked with gray as he ran toward me in jeans and a fitted T-shirt. It appeared he had very much embraced running as he shot across the dam like a gazelle regardless of the Timberland boots on his feet.

He came to a breathless stop before me and grinned.

He still looked like Arden.

"I thought you were dead. What the hell is this all about? Your detective buddy is scouring the north side for you and… Is that who I think it is?" Arden asked.

"This is Scott Windham, and he killed our friend."

Scott moaned to life.

"You can't prove that in the least. You can't even prove what happened today."

"Shut up boy," said Arden. "I'll slap you to sleep and then slap you for sleeping…been wantin' to do that for decades."

"He's not entirely wrong Arden. He emptied the gun at me, and the gun is gone. He probably tossed it in the lake."

"I beg to differ. That blonde fella he gut-shot is alive and very much aware of who shot him. The detective brought EMS with him, probably saved that man's life. Oh, and that Yeti of a man that I drilled? He's singin' like a canary to any uniform who'll listen. They'll find the gun, and…wait…what'd you say again about Rob?"

An information download commenced in my mind just as it had done last time I returned from 1984.

Rob Erwin was alive.

"Damn Ray, Rob's in bad shape but don't bury him yet. You're supposed to be the optimistic one."

"They…found him on the island…not tied to the boat…" I said hesitantly.

"Yeah man. He swam for the island with a busted wrist, a busted kneecap, and with a cracked skull. Are you OK? It looks like both you and shit stain here need to see EMS."

"I'm good enou—"

A black SUV roared down the street toward us and then screeched to a halt.

Jim Dorn got out of the driver's side wearing desert fatigue pants and a white T-shirt.

"Greetings Ray, you got any holes in you young man?"

The door of the SUV remained open. There was a police scanner abuzz on the dashboard and a man who looked to be about Jim's age staring straight forward. Arden and I looked at each other, confused, and then finally I spoke.

"No, sir. What are you doing here Jim?"

"You know I intended on looking into this mess myself. And I believe I've identified the cause of it. Is that pile of humanity next to you Scott Windham?"

I nodded.

"Did he try to kill you?"

I nodded again.

"Did you break his nose?"

"Yes."

"Good man. I'll take it from here."

"What do you mean you'll take it from here?"

Colonel Jim stepped closer to me, shot a quick glance at Arden, and then lowered his voice.

"I mean Rob is in a coma at Duke Medical Center and will most likely die. I'll not lie. I am partly responsible for this. Rita I'm sure will be more than happy to explain that, as will Detective Spruill. The least I can do is save the taxpayers a buck and give Rob the justice he deserves."

Scott Windham rose to his unsteady feet.

"Just what the hell is that supposed to mean?" Scott asked.

Jim opened the back-seat door on the driver's side and then called to the man in the car.

"Get ready old friend."

The man in the passenger seat hopped out and opened the back-seat door on his side. Jim turned from the SUV, stepped past me, and delivered a ruthless left hook to Scott's head. Scott folded, and the Colonel caught him by the armpits and then dragged him to the back-seat door. His friend had already scrambled across the back to help settle Scott into a seat and buckle him in.

"I'll put him out chemically. I brought the wheelchair," said Jim's assistant.

Jim then turned back to me and put his hands on my shoulders.

"Ray, I'm sorry. I may speak with you again, but I'll probably never see you again. When you get the whole story, know that I had the best of intentions. I wanted us all to live well. I wanted both Jenna and Ava never to have student loans. I…I'm, sorry son. I have to go."

Jim turned and then disappeared behind the tinted windows of his SUV and drove off.

"What just happened?"

"I'm not sure Arden, but I know my detective friend is not going to like it." Arden and I began walking back to my house.

"Thanks for saving me. You gave me just enough time to run. What did you bring that stuff for anyway?"

"I bought it when I landed. I wasn't sure of the rules about planes and weapons. It's a lot like my rig back home. I thought I'd leave it here and come back for hunting season. I thought maybe you and I could shoot at a plastic deer for old time's sake."

I stopped and looked at him. It took him two or three steps before he realized I was just standing. He turned and grinned.

"OK, all that stuff is true, and I thought you'd get yourself in trouble, and I don't use guns. You don't leave anything alone."

"It's damn good to see you, Arden."

We rounded the corner and began to descend into the Shadywood cul-de-sac, both of us with damp shirts and necks and arms glistening. My face had started to swell. I could feel it and see it—the flesh under my right eye had crept into my sightline. I made a mental note to swallow a fist full of ibuprofen. The adrenaline drained from me, and I felt whipped. My ribs hurt and I cared not for the fate of Scott Windham. I cared not for the hell I was going to catch from Spruill. I cared about one thing.

Rob Erwin was clinging to life in the hospital.

I felt the beating sun abate. I looked up and saw cloud cover that suggested a shower. In the distance, the sky still shone clear. Arden and I made it to the end of my driveway when Spruill screeched to halt behind us and succinctly removed himself from the driver's side and grabbed me.

He examined me much the same way Colonel Ed had.

"You look like shit, but there appears to be no permanent damage. Where is Scott Windham? Did you kill him?"

"No, but when he ran out of bullets, I did beat the hell out of him. I'm pretty sure he tossed the gun in the lake near Sequoia Point. Arden found the two of us stumbling back on to Cherokee Trail."

Spruill looked to Arden, who nodded.

"I was bringing him to you when Jim Dorn showed up in a black SUV. He grabbed Scott and threw him in the car after decking him."

"He did what? Damn it! Make and model now!"

"I saw the bowtie, so it was a Chevy…four doors, big, probably a Suburban."

"Where was he headed?"

"I have no idea! Oh. Call Rita now and put it on speaker." Spruill obeyed. It rang only twice.

"Hello, detective. I haven't moved…"

"Rita. It's Ray. Jim Dorn is in the States, and he was just here. There was another man with him about his age. They took the man that kill… hurt Rob. Where is he going?"

"Well, it seems he's a drug dealer, so I'm guessing out of town if not out of the country."

"He's a what?"

"Rita this is Spruill. Jim obviously has an exit strategy. Can you explain to me his resources?"

"He has a plane. I would guess the man with Jim was his friend and assistant Wyatt Halsey. Wyatt probably flew up from Wilmington to meet Jim here."

Spruill ducked back.

"Dispatch, copy, this is Spruill."

"Go, detective."

"I want all units on the lookout for a black Chevy Suburban headed for Moore County airport carrying a trio of men armed and dangerous. Driver is Jim Dorn wanted for felony drug possession with intent to distribute. Passengers are Scott Windham, wanted for attempted murder, and Wyatt Halsey, assistant to Mr. Dorn. They are headed for a private plane belonging to Dorn. Call the airport too. I want that plane held up."

While Spruill spoke to dispatch, something began to dawn on me. I was thinking of what Rob had said—why he could not come to my race. Then I was thinking about why Colonel Ed was driving from the opposite side of Longleaf Dam when he saw Scott and me.

"You're lucky Ray. I was checking the mailbox one last time before we head to the beach house."

"Rita! Don't get off the phone!"

"Ray? Is that you again?"

"Yes. Didn't you sell your place at Carolina Beach last year?"

"No, I put the cottage on the market last year, and on the market it has sat for a year. The Realtor told me it was twenty-five years overdue for a facelift and that's why I was not getting any bites. Rob had no time to do the updates, so I hired somebody down there. Renovations begin next week—new kitchen, adding another bathroom…"

"Rita! Tell me the address because I don't remember. Then I'm coming by for the keys."

"It's 1714 Carolina Beach Avenue North. You don't need to come by here; the key is hidden inside a ceramic frog by the AC unit. Always has been. What is this about?"

"I'll explain later. I gotta go." I looked up at Arden.

"I know where my family is."

Arden nodded, held up an index finger, and ran to a silver Jeep Cherokee. He popped open the back hatch and tossed his bag on my lawn.

Then he rummaged about the passenger side and came back with a T-shirt and shorts folded on top of running shoes. Under his arm was a water bottle.

"Strip off that shirt of yours. It's got blood on it."

I did, and he wet it down with the water bottle and motioned for me to take it.

"There's blood on your face too. Take care of that and then put this on."

I wiped my face and neck and pulled on Arden's Montana Grizzlies T-shirt. Then Arden tossed me his keys.

"Where they at Ray?"

"Wilmington. They were slowly working their way home, but Morgan got cold feet."

"Take my rental and give me your keys. It will be easier for me to get in and out of the gate using your truck with the grid sticker. I'll hold down the fort here."

Spruill re-entered the conversation.

"Go. Get them. Come back. No exceptions, and call me when you are on your way back."

Spruill pulled out his wallet and fished inside.

"Take this too. I went to school down there. I have a pair of buddies I'm still in touch with. One runs a gym. One is a police officer. Here is Officer Smith's card. You have any questions on how to proceed with your wife, call him."

"Go get your girls, Ray," said Arden.

Wearing a T-shirt a size too large and sporting scuffed legs clad in grass-stained gym shorts, I climbed into the Jeep and left with a heart full of hope.

***

Found them at 1714 Carolina Beach Ave. N.

Yellow house on white stilts.

Have a look and call me.

I'm on my way.

I had texted Tom when I stopped for gas in Laurinburg. About thirty minutes later my phone lit up.

"It's her car in the driveway. How'd you figure that out?"

"It's Mrs. Erwin's beach house. The Erwins rarely used it anymore. For a while, they rented it out, but it was up for sale a year ago. I thought they had sold it; otherwise I would have figured it out sooner."

"I guess there's not much need for a beach house when you live on a lake," said Tom.

"I think neither Rita nor Rob were too fond of going after Rob's dad died."

"I understand. What's the call here, young man? I do have a suggestion."

"OK shoot."

"I'm going to sit out here about a block down from the house. This is a one-way street, so if she leaves, she'll have to drive right past me. She's probably pissed about the tracker, so me knockin' on the door is not gonna do you any favors."

"What's your advice?" I asked.

"Walk around back and see if you find them on the deck. Just walk right up to them. No calls, no knocks. If you have to, wait until someone comes out. If no one comes out, try the door. Hug whoever sees you first, even if it's Morgan, and if it is your wife, say nothing more than 'let's go home.'"

It sounded like a fine plan to me mostly because I had no plan.

"All right, Tom. I'll call you when the dust settles."

"I'll be here. If it goes well I may show up in Pinehurst in a couple of days and visit the reunited McCarthys."

"I would very much like that Mr. Cianci."

"Ciao."

It was when I crossed the Cape Fear Bridge and got a view of the USS North Carolina that a breathless nervousness came over me. My window was down. I had driven three hours in windblown solitude. I could smell the sea. I closed the window and let the paranoid thoughts come for processing.

What if Morgan wants nothing to do with me? What if they had gotten used to being on their own? How much had Ava changed? What had I missed? Would she recognize me?

Of course, she'd recognize me.

That was the only insecurity I could put to bed. The assault continued until I pulled right into the driveway and into one of the three carports formed by the piling foundation. There was nowhere else to park. I looked at myself in the mirror: a fully-evolved black eye, some small cuts, handprints on my neck. I smoothed my hair and got out of the Jeep and walked to the side of the house and negotiated tufts and tangles of marram grass.

I passed the AC unit and the ceramic frog. The sky was an impossible blue.

I saw her.

Between the deck stairs and a wall of boulders that separated the house from the beach proper she sat in a toddler tankini, her blonde ringlets adrift with the slight wind. She was digging in the sand and singing, asking the wind if she knew the muffin man. I took a few steps and knelt, waiting for her to look up, and she did. It was almost a whisper.

"Daddy?"

"Yeah, honey. It's me."

"Daddy!" She bolted into my arms. The smell of her, the feel of her, flooded me, and we both began to laugh-cry as we tumbled back into the sand. We rocked side to side in a pile on the sand for what seemed like a wonderful eternity. It was Ava who finally spoke.

"Daddy, what happened to your face?"

"I had an accident."

"With your face?"

"Yes."

"Mommy is in the house. Does she know you're here?"

"Not yet baby. It's OK. I'll go find her."

"She had to potty. She's been in there a lotta minutes now. It was a poo, like a big one."

I smirked. Ava had not changed, and she was probably right. Morgan suffered from opioid-induced constipation.

"Let me go find her, baby. Then we're going home."

"Let me get my toys!"

Ava scrambled about the patch of sand that served as a yard picking up various pails and pieces of plastic.

I walked up the back steps of the stick-built, tin-roof home circa the late '70s. I tried the back door adorned with a gooseneck lamp and found it open. The inside smelled of age and perhaps tobacco. Pictures of Rob and Rita adorned the walls. A leather recliner indented with the ghost of Colonel Ed Erwin sat facing the ocean.

I passed through the great room to the small hallway that leads to the bathroom. The door was closed and artificial light spilled from its gaps. The old floor creaked under my heavy footfalls.

I tapped on the wood with a single finger.

"Morgan, I love you. Let's go home."

I heard something clap to the floor.

"It's OK honey. Open the door."

I waited for a beat and tried the door, which was not locked.

Morgan's blonde hair was swept back off her shoulders in the careless tresses she always wore at the beach. She sat there on the small toilet staring forward. I knelt in front of her. Her face was beautifully sun-kissed, and it highlighted the blueness of her eyes, which were vacant.

I held her face in my hands. No breath escaped her lips. I felt her neck.

She was gone.

I started to breathe heavy and almost hyperventilate. I sat down on the floor.

"We don't deserve this," I said out loud.

I thought of her in the red dress the night we met. I thought of her dressed in white standing before the altar. It thought of her blonde hair plastered to her face as she brought Ava into the world.

Dear god what about Ava?

I looked down at the floor and saw what had fallen. A PEZ dispenser had slipped out of Morgan's hand. I waited a moment and gathered myself. I put Morgan's face in my hands, and I kissed her as my tears fell.

I stood her up and leaned her against me as I pulled up her underwear and shorts and buttoned them. I gathered her in my arms and carried her to the nearest bedroom and laid her down. I found an afghan and covered her up to her chest and arranged her hair on the pillow.

I went to the other bedroom and found Ava's clothes. I quickly threw things in the pair of duffle bags on the dresser I found shopping list paper and a pen magnetized to the fridge. I took it and sketched out a note. Then I went outside to find Ava right where I had left her.

"Let's go, Daddy. Where's Mommy?"

"She needs a nap buddy. She's sleepin'."

Silence.

"We're gonna hit the road, Ava. Mommy will be along later. She has to drive her car. I have to drive mine. I borrowed a new car. Wanna see it?"

"Yes! Why's Mommy so tired? Is it 'cause we went out in the middle of the night?"

"You went out in the middle of the night?"

"Yes, in the car. Mommy needed stuff for the morning. She didn't feel well."

My heart sank. Tom had been right. All Morgan had left was whatever meds Tom had given her yesterday morning. So, she went looking for more. She held out until morning, but by then the withdrawal was so bad she probably took a little extra.

"Ava, come inside."

I grabbed the note I wrote off the counter, and Ava and I walked hand-in-hand down the hallway.

"Mommy's asleep, so we're going to kiss her goodbye and leave a note that says we started home. Be very quiet."

I pushed open the door to the bedroom, and Ava quietly approached Morgan. She stood on her toes to whisper in her ear.

"Feel better Mommy, and don't wait too long to come home. I will miss you."

With that Ava kissed Morgan on the cheek and the corners of my eyes began to leak. I quickly wiped my face with my hands, pretending to rub the sleep from my eyes. I knelt to face Ava.

"OK now go get your bags. I left them in your room. I laid out some clothes too. I'll help you in a minute."

Ava smiled and ran out.

I kissed Morgan on the forehead one more time, and then I pulled the afghan up over her head and left the room.

Once Ava was in the car, I called Tom. Then I got in the back seat of the Jeep with Ava.

"I have a surprise for you. A friend of yours is going to take you to breakfast, and I will meet you there in a few minutes."

"What are you gonna do?"

"I am going to pack up Mommy's stuff for her so she doesn't have to do it."

"Well, that's nice, but who's your friend?"

Tom's Lincoln pulled up behind us. I looked at Ava.

"How about you see for yourself."

She hopped out as Tom walked around the front of the Lincoln with outstretched arms. Ava ran to him.

"Tom! My goodness, we can't eat meatballs in the morning! Or do you have burritos?"

"Hello, dah-lin...I was thinkin' about pancakes at the Hang Ten Grill. Whadda you think?"

"I think that is a good idea. Can Daddy join us?"

"As soon as he finishes what he's gotta do, sure. Hop in the front seat, and I'll buckle you in."

Ava's eyes got wide.

"The front seat? Oh my goodness."

"Your old pal Tom doesn't have a car seat, and this is a short trip. Don't tell anybody."

Ava placed a hand over her mouth and quickly scrambled into the car when Tom opened the door. He closed it and walked closer to me.

"I'm sorry, Ray."

Tom Cianci carried himself similarly to that of Colonel Jim but with less rigidity. He was a distinguished looking gentleman who seemed to deal with life as it came to him. That was the difference between Tom and Jim—Jim tried to control how life should be. Tom looked sad and resigned. He looked like a man who had become accustomed to loss, but who had not suffered a loss for some time.

"It's no one's fault. It was one of many possibilities. I don't know what else to say."

Tom put a hand on my shoulder.

"I'll take her to eat and then to the park near the restaurant. Handle your business. I'm gonna stick around awhile in the Pinehurst area... play some golf with Baumann. You should call him."

"Tom, Colonel Jim..."

"He wired me money this morning."

"Good. It looks like he may be into something dirty. Take the money and run."

"This does not surprise me. I will advise the good father. Neither one of us will run, but neither one of us likes answering a lot of questions either. I'll see you in a few."

Tom pulled out of the driveway as Ava exuberantly waved from the passenger seat. I reached for my wallet and pulled out the business card Howard Spruill had given me.

39
Strategic Avoidance

"Cessna N974MH you are clear to taxi to runway five."

"Roger that, tower."

Wyatt Halsey saw the three sheriff's department vehicles with lights ablaze pull into the circular drive of Moore County Airport. He tapped Jim Dorn on the shoulder and pointed. Jim looked with disinterest.

"It's too late. They don't even know who they're looking for, and when we land, the Brits are not going to care. We'll have to be careful in Canada though."

***

Howard Spruill had been on the phone with the airport manager all the way down Doubs Chapel Road.

"There is no plane at Moore County Airport registered to a Wyatt Halsey or a Jim Dorn, detective."

"I do not care. I have a trio of suspects—two in their seventies and one in his late forties."

"There is a Jim Doolittle who filed a flight plan to the Providenciales of Turks and Caicos."

"Who is he traveling with?"

"A Victor Charles, a resident of the Providenciales."

"Stop that plane."

"If you want it stopped," said the manager, "you'll have to stop it and take the responsibility. You have no formal charges, and you have names and passengers that don't match any manifest. I can't help you."

"How did they pay for the fuel? What was the name on the credit card?"

"That will take a moment to check."

"So check!"

Spruill ran through the small terminal to the plane parking slots. He hung a right and ran towards runway five. The Cessna was already in a takeoff sprint down the tarmac. Spruill jogged to a halt and was catching his breath when the manager came back on the phone.

"The fuel was paid for with a credit card issued to Abian Industries."

Spruill hung up the phone and opened the Google application on his phone. Perhaps Providenciales International Airport would help or at least tell him if a Victor Charles had documented any additional travel plans.

***

While he was still in range of a tower, Jim Dorn took a breath and then pulled out his phone and dialed.

"Hello dear."

"Oh, Jim, what in god's name have you done?" asked Rita.

"Nothing of which I am proud."

"Drug dealing Jim? For god's sake, you're seventy-four years old."

"I am not a drug dealer Rita. I import a plant product, and these hicks do what they will with it, but that is neither here nor there. I'm sorry. I will tell you what I told Raymond. I wanted us to live well. I wanted the kids never to have a student loan. If something were to happen, I thought it would happen to me. Never did I imagine that my business dealings would hurt my family."

"How could you not? You are family. If something happens to you, it hurts us all. This hurts us."

"It has been my great honor to be part of your family. I hope you can forgive me, for all of it. Ed was and is my greatest friend. He was my conscience too, and more than likely he would have steered me elsewhere. He usually did. I'll not see you again dear, but I will speak to you. Goodbye. Love to you, Rob, Jenna…even Candace."

***

Corporal Smith of the Wilmington Police Department was not entirely surprised to get my call as Howard Spruill had left him a voicemail.

He coordinated with the Carolina Beach police and got the county coroner out to the house. He even gave me the contact information for a company who would transport Morgan to Boles Funeral Home in Seven Lakes. I would have to return to the beach and collect the car.

I explained to him what I believed to have happened and that I had moved Morgan to the bedroom. All in all, it was a relatively painless experience. I answered a few questions, and then the professionals took over as I sat in a cocoon of numbness on the back deck staring at the Carolina Beach fishing pier.

Nothing seemed real as I methodically moved about in a fog and matter-of-factly tended to details. I retrieved the car seat from Morgan's Toyota, packed up most of her personal effects, and put the house keys back in the ceramic frog. I found Ava and Tom in the park, and Ava grilled me about Uncle Rob because Mommy had told her that he'd been hurt real bad. That gave me an idea.

Ava chatted with me for about five or six miles before she nodded off. First, I called Rita, who cried and said she had spoken briefly to Jim. I asked her for directions and told her to call the hospital and clear myself and Arden to visit Rob. Then I called Arden and told him to get in the truck.

I headed to Durham. I was not in a hurry to walk through my front door with only two out of three McCarthys. Also, there was the police tape and the blood-stained backyard. I wasn't even sure if I was allowed to go back to my house. I had enough to explain to Ava as it was.

Next, I called Spruill as I had promised to do. He thanked me for my call, offered his condolences, asked if Corporal Smith had been of service, and then he promptly tore me a new one because Jim Dorn had gotten airborne as the police descended on Moore County airport, and presumably he had taken Scott Windham with him.

I half listened to Spruill as he spoke on subjects ranging from Travis screaming like a girl as they pulled Arden's arrow out of him, to grief counseling. My mind did what many grief-stricken minds do: indulged absurd thoughts, like the fact that my wife had gone out like The King and in the same year as Prince.

The rest of the drive I hummed the melody to "Purple Rain."

***

Scott Windham rustled to life in a cramped, darkened space. He felt around, heard the hum of an engine, and banged on the wall to his right.

"Hey. Let me the hell out of here!"

Scott's left ear crackled. He reached up and felt a radio earpiece shoved inside.

"Mr. Windham, can you hear me? Knock once or yell."

Scott cautiously knocked.

"Good. I want you to know that Rob Erwin is officially my godson, but as his father was a brother to me, I also often refer to Rob as my nephew. I want you to know that there was no reason to hurt him. First of all, I consider that kind of collateral attack cowardly and unacceptable. Secondly, I was closing up shop, retiring. I want you to think of that especially."

Scott heard a mechanical whine and then a click as Colonel Jim Dorn depressed the release button to the luggage hatch.

"I want you to think of that all the way down."

Wyatt Halsey rolled the plane left, and Scott Windham tumbled out of the Cessna TTX's luggage compartment and plummeted soundlessly toward the Atlantic.

40
Duke

Coincidentally Duke Medical Center is on Erwin Drive. However, the intensive care unit is on 40 Duke Medical Circle. I hoped Arden had figured this all out. I stopped in the lobby and got Ava a sandwich out of a vending machine that took debit cards. I reached up to swipe the card to find my hand was shaking. I was also sweating. The soreness in my ribs had hit its peak.

Somewhere near Raleigh, Ava sprang to life and demanded that we stop and pee immediately, so I found a Walmart. Ava peed and then she helped me find a pair of khaki-colored cargo shorts, some loafers, and a blue button-down cabana shirt. I got another look at my face in the changing room. The swelling under my eye had gone down a bit. My gray-brown hair looked like that of a homeless person. I bought a khaki newsboy cap and stuck it on my head.

We approached the ICU receptionist. Due to the circumstances surrounding Rob's injuries, only family was allowed up to see him. This I had figured, which was why I had called Rita.

"Ray to see my brother Rob Erwin."

"It seems all of Mr. Erwin's siblings are here today."

"Is my brother Arden here?"

"Yes, and your sister."

What that meant I hadn't a clue. Ava and I got in the elevator.

"Uncle Rob is hurt real bad like Mommy said. He can't talk, but he can hear you. Be good."

Ava nodded.

The door pinged open on the third floor to a quiet, foreboding hum broken by the occasional beeping machine. The overall feeling was one of quiet badness. This was a place where people tried to undo horrible things. The nurses wore poker faces that broke into quick, obligatory smiles at the sight of Ava and then morphed back into an armored state.

We stepped toward the nurse's station and a woman who looked not much older than Jenna Erwin pointed to the room directly across the hall. We stepped inside.

Rob Erwin looked like a pasty shell of himself with grotesque bruising about his forehead that resembled marble-colored fungus. I instantly regretted bringing Ava as she hugged my leg in a death grip. The rhythmic sound of the ventilator dominated the room. Arden was standing to our left against the wall, staring at Rob impassively. Finally, he looked at us.

"I've seen worse."

Then I realized that I had too. At least Rob was not face-down in the lake. I took Ava from the room and asked the nurse for a chair.

"Ava honey, Uncle Rob is getting better, I promise, but you can sit here if you want."

The chair came, and she hopped in it. I gave her the sandwich and walked back in the room to the other side of the bed, knelt, and took Rob's hand.

"Good to see you old friend. I have much to tell. You won't believe who's here."

"Neither will you," said Arden, and I looked to him confused.

I glanced over my shoulder to the wall where the TV was mounted. To the left of it was another door and I heard water running that suddenly quit. The door opened, and a woman stepped out dabbing at her eyes with a towel—green, spectacular eyes. I stood up.

"Ray?" she asked.

I nodded breathlessly, and then Olivia Allen stepped forward and embraced me. We both quietly cried. Then she dropped the towel and cupped my face in her hands.

"You look one step away from needing a room of your own."

"I had a rough day."

"I filled her in on most of it. The parts I know," said Arden. "You'll have to explain what happened in between."

"I'm not sure I even remember everything that happened."

Ava poked her head into the room. Olivia looked at me with surprise.

"She's beautiful Ray."

Olivia knelt and regarded Ava.

"Who might you be?"

"I'm Ava Elizabeth McCarthy, and I'm here to see my Uncle Rob who had an accident. My daddy had an accident too, with his face, but he's OK. He surprised me today at the beach."

Arden snorted.

Olivia laughed and then looked to me.

"Your daddy has always been full of surprises."

41
Home

Victor Charles and James Doolittle landed in Turks with an open luggage hatch. An hour later they boarded an Air Canada flight to Toronto where they caught a Cathay Pacific flight to Hong Kong and then Hanoi, Vietnam.

Vietnam, where there was no extradition. That was where Jim Dorn was going to call home in his golden years. Howard Spruill had relayed this to Rita, who relayed it to me.

Scott Windham was not on any of those flights.

No shit. I'm pretty sure he was on the first one though. I didn't care. The British at Provo and the Canadians at YYZ didn't care either, but Spruill did. He cared a lot.

Summer had come to an end, and Ava and I were coping as best we could. Morgan's funeral was as big as Rob's—except I was the only one who knew Rob ever had a funeral because Rob's still in the hospital. Ava and I went running every day. She played with her Leap tablet in the relative comfort of the Bob Jogging Stroller. We stayed in 2016.

The anomaly had disappeared.

Ava and I had no intention of leaving Seven Lakes. There was something about the place, a decency. It's an island removed from most of the horrors one sees every day on the news or a TV show hosted by John Walsh. Kids still rode bikes with wild abandon, walked down the street with fishing poles and without a care, and they played in the front yard with marginal supervision.

I think that was why the anomaly happened. I think the enchantment of this place saw an atrocity for which it would not stand, and it selected someone to try to set things right.

It remained to be seen if I had set things right.

Mostly Ava and I moved from day to day in disbelief. Both of us expected Morgan to walk in the door at any moment, home at last from the beach.

I told Ava that Mommy never woke from her nap and that she had been sick. Ava suspected the medicine. The toxicology report said Ava's instincts were correct. As a result, Ava refused to take medication, not even a gummy vitamin. I was not allowed to go to the Carolina Beach ever again. There's nowhere to stay anyway. The Erwin cottage was under contract.

I sat on my living room couch as I wrote this, my feet propped on the ottoman and Ava snoozing beside me wrapped in her *Frozen* blanket and nuzzling Bunga, a character from Disney's *The Lion Guard* whom I keep referring to as Bungahole.

During her naps, I worked on the book. I'd put a pretty good dent in it, and I'd been judicious in sending my publisher updates. Their feedback had been positive. Being that this novel was such a departure from uplifting themes I had indulged in before, they suggested I published this one under a pseudonym. That way, if it bombed, I could pretend some other guy was responsible for the shitty story you just read. I don't mind telling you that if you'd made it this far.

I came up with something plain but Irish. Then I went to work on an item that had eluded me the longest: the novel's opening line. Oddly enough it just sort of spilled out onto the page:

I'd decided there was nothing creepier than the ringing phone of a deceased individual. It meant someone didn't know.

Epilogue

(Ray's Diary Sept 2016—Jan 2017)

September 2016

Dear Rob—

So, Ava and I have been in therapy for a month—we have sessions together and separately. Ava sleeps in bed with me every night. She has nightmares, and sometimes they are out loud. She talks to Morgan in her sleep. Sometimes she cries in her sleep. One of the things the therapist said I should do is keep a diary. I'm not sure how dedicated I will be to that. I decided that I would write an occasional letter to you. Then you can see what you missed.

I bet you can guess that no one ever saw Scott Windham again. Spruill is still pissed at me as if I were responsible. They did find Scott's gun in the lake. I guess he tossed it before we crossed over. The court will most likely convict him in absentia.

Spruill did stand up for your buddy Matt, though. Matt's down in Wilmington now refereeing MMA fights—quite a comeback from almost bleeding out in my back yard. I visited him in the hospital after they took Scott's bullet out of him, and we talk on the phone from time to time.

Ava Facetimes with Tom Cianci on a regular basis. Tom sent her homemade spaghetti and meatballs packed in dry ice. When the FedEx guy dropped it off, and Ava saw her name on the package, she squealed. When we opened it, and she realized it was spaghetti from Tom, she lost her mind. You'd have thought Christmas had come.

Jenna, of course, sees you every day. College agrees with her.

Your mom is OK. She refuses to talk about Jim. She's a local celebrity now. I'll explain some other time.

Candace and Rita are actually getting along. I'm not sure what happened. Perhaps they realized they need each other. Not sure what you want to do about Candace, but you might want to reevaluate. I think she has changed quite a bit.

October 2016

Dear Rob—

I exchanged Facebook messages with Olivia today. She's going to visit in December. That would be an excellent time for you to wake the hell up if you still have not. Olivia's parents gave up the house in Seven Lakes and moved to Belle Meade. I've been there. It's like a college campus for old folks. I want to live there.

Arden will visit next month. He's considering a move back here to Seven Lakes. Could you imagine the three of us together again after all these years? Problem is Arden does not know what he'd do with himself—professionally I mean. I told him to work in a training capacity for the military.

Oh, I had your boat winterized. Rita, Jenna, Ava, and I took it out for one last spin. People honked and waved when they saw your mom out there.

Howard Spruill had a huge write-up in The Pilot and was all over the news at the end of June. He and Rita went on with the sale of the furniture stock. Spruill coordinated with law enforcement from eight different counties, tracked all the buyers, and orchestrated the largest drug bust in North Carolina history. He gave a lot of credit to Rita for setting it all up. She went from unwitting accomplice to clandestine badass overnight.

November 2016

Dear Rob –

I talk with Olivia a lot. Maybe the holidays being so close have something to do with that. She mentioned for the first time that she's divorced, but I'd already figured that out.

Arden is here! He's out hunting as I write this. We are going to a Duke football game with Jenna this weekend, and then we are coming to see you at the medical center.

December 2016

Dear Rob—

Jesus Christ, enough with the coma. We have shit to do you and me, and I need your advice.

That movie has been out on DVD since September, but we found a dollar theater in Jamestown that was still showing it. Yes, I drove all the way to Guilford County.

We watched the opening scene. Some curator gets attacked in a historically haunted mansion, the Ghostbusters theme music kicks in, and then Olivia's hand crept into mine. We held hands the whole movie.

January 2017

Dear Rob—

Happy New Year buddy. I have a feeling this is my last entry, and I'm writing it in your hospital room. I have not slept. I spent New Year's Eve with you. At 12 a.m. I squeezed your hand.

At 12:01 a.m., you squeezed my hand back.

At 7 a.m. you moved your right arm. The nurses have been aflutter. You have like seven doctors, and they have all been in and out of here a dozen times at least.

You are going to have one righteous hospital bill, old friend.

Thank God.

Thank you, God.

Ray

Acknowledgments

Forty-nine thousand, seven hundred sixty-eight words into this novel, on April 15, 2017, my closest friend passed away suddenly. Though he knew I was writing a novel, I kept the plot a secret because he was going to be the first reviewer of the completed work.

I can tell you that the passing of Joe Alexander affected me a great deal, and it made the completion of this tale more difficult, but the story remained the same. Joe and I have been inseparable since high school. He left behind his wife, Heather, and a little girl named Maya.

The setting of this novel, as well as many of the places referenced, are real. Most all of the characters are complete works of fiction; I just borrowed the names of real people I know, some of whom are still in my life.

I indeed knew a Rob Erwin in the 1980s, and he is still very much alive and living in Virginia. I think the last time I laid eyes on him was sometime in the late 1990s. I tracked him down just before the completion of this book. Jo Erwin, Rob's mom, was a wonderful woman who passed away from cancer in 1987. His father remarried years later, and he is still living in Seven Lakes. Rob and I finally spoke in January of 2018, and I learned he is married with three children.

Matt Roper is one of the myriads of kids Rob, and I knew in the '80s, but I have no real knowledge of him at all. It was just helpful to use names from that period.

I knew someone by the name of Arden Miller in the 1980s, and I recently found him married with children and living in South Carolina. He is a big fan of his fictional namesake.

There are a few people who make cameos in this tale as themselves. Art

Dykeman passed away on my daughter's second birthday in 2014. The irony is that he and his wife Anne lived two doors down from me in the '80s, but I never actually met them until the year 2000. Art was a retired marine and a phenomenal woodworking craftsman. He did, in fact, tool around in a golf cart. Anne Dykeman passed away shortly before this book went to print.

Rick Rhyne was killed in the line of duty in 2011. The terms "sheriff's deputy" or "police officer" do not do him justice. "Community protector" is probably a more accurate description.

Former Spectrum News reporter Linnie Supall, and Pinehurst attorney Buck Adams are casually mentioned as well.

Christi Ebel is happily married with two children and living in the mountains. Her daughter looks almost exactly like she did as a kid.

Tom Cianci was a real man whom my family adored. Though I have fictionalized his past in this novel, there are some who would say I was not far from the truth.

Pete and Barbara Murphy were indeed the only people we initially knew in Seven Lakes. They had lived in the Orange County area of New York same as we did. Pete passed away in December of 2017.

The Red Rose restaurant was a real place in the Carroll Gardens section of Brooklyn.

Antonio and Santo Romano didn't have any mafia ties. They just created a beautiful family restaurant to which my Aunt Mary often brought me. It closed in September of 2017 when the Romanos announced their retirement.

I took a few artistic liberties. One of them was the poster featuring the Duke Blue Devil basketball team. The 1984-85 "Right Stuff" poster would not yet have been released in June of '84. It is a real thing, though, and someday I'll have Jay Bilas sign it. Also, some will notice that the layout and appearance of Sacred Heart Church are different—all of their stained-glass windows depict saints, and none of them portray Jesus catching a beating. Also, I have taken fictional liberties with the layout of Samarcand Training Facility.

I have no idea what the actual dimensions of the Ellerbe Fellowship Baptist Church are, and I don't know who built it, but I'm pretty sure a fictional drug lord did not construct it.

I know that there have never been places to rent above the Garden Bar in Bigfork, Montana and that there is no gated community in Cary called Carolina Vistas.

I must thank Don Tickle of Southern Pines for briefing me on the furniture business and the logistics of importation. He also gave me a tutorial on the Philippines. If I got anything wrong, it is most assuredly my fault and not his.

About the Author

Sean Patrick Smith lives in Moore County, North Carolina with his daughter, Reilly, and four cats: Moo, Kissie, Roxy Music, and Tom.

He is a former newspaper and magazine writer and a former high school English teacher. He has coordinated the services of the developmentally disabled for over a decade in Greensboro. Sean and his daughter frequent Cary, North Carolina to see his significant other, Lauren.

Three Miles of Eden is his first novel.

seanpatricksmith.com
twitter.com/SeanPatrickSmi1
facebook.com/sean.p.smith.12